"WELL, JACK, SEE ANYTHING YOU LIKE?"

And with that she kicked aside one of the dining room chairs, and positioned herself on the edge of the table, letting the strap of her dress slip just enough to reveal an enticing glimpse of her breast.

He moved to her, wondering for a moment what he was doing. But he knew the answer. She was everything Melinda was not. An anonymous, careless, emotionless fling. And even if it would only last a minute, it would be one minute less that he would be aching for the woman he had loved and lost.

"Listen," he said, still needing to be fair. "I'm not . . ."

She covered his mouth with her hand, interrupting.

"Neither am I."

He pushed her back against the eighteenth-century mahogany table, and without comment, accepted her for the gourmet offering that she was. . . .

Books by Leah Laiman

The Bridesmaid
Maid of Honor
For Richer, for Poorer
For Better, for Worse
To Love and to Cherish

Published by POCKET BOOKS

THE BRIDESMAID

Another Summer of Love

LEAH LAIMAN

POCKET BOOKS
New York London Toronto Sydney Tokyo Singapore

An *Original* Publication of POCKET BOOKS

POCKET BOOKS, a division of Simon & Schuster Inc.
1230 Avenue of the Americas, New York, NY 10020

ISBN: 0-671-53405-X

First Pocket Books printing August 1995

10 9 8 7 6 5 4 3 2 1

POCKET and colophon are registered trademarks of Simon & Schuster Inc.

Cover art by Punz Wolff

Printed in the U.S.A.

THE BRIDES-MAID

1

"Are we rolling?" asked Barbara Walters, looking into the red eye of the camera. "Are we? What's happening, guys?"

Her smile never faltered, but a hint of irritation was discernible in her voice. "I'm sorry, Mrs. Roca, we seem to be experiencing a little confusion. I'm sure they'll have it straightened out in a minute. Thank you for being so patient."

Melinda Myles smiled and said, "Not at all."

She had been married for two years, but hearing someone call her Mrs. Roca—especially the way Barbara Walters pronounced it, not quite Woca the way she was mercilessly mimicked, but not with the rolling *r*'s that the San Domenicans used either—was still strange to her ear.

Melinda stayed where she had been positioned beneath the flowering arbor in the garden of the presidential palace, as Walters left to consult with her crew. The two women were a contrast in styles with Barbara in a blue Chanel suite, blond hair perfectly coiffed, makeup expertly if generously applied, and Melinda in a simple white lace dress, mane of chestnut hair pulled casually off her face, hazel eyes and perfect cheekbones unenhanced.

Clear blue skies and a brilliant afternoon sun warmed the air, which was redolent with the smell of jasmine. Although the pink palace was still pockmarked by the bullets of the revolution, its terraces and balustrades, embellished with wrought-iron lattice work, still made an imposing backdrop.

"It'll just be another minute," Barbara called apologetically.

"That's fine," Melinda said graciously. "You forget I was once in show business myself. I know all about waiting."

The crew laughed, grateful that the wife of the president of San Domenico was so cooperative. Seeing her so poised and reserved, the picture of respectful propriety, it was hard to imagine her as the impetuous movie star she had once been. Even Melinda, her Academy Award sitting neglected on a mantle in her palace bedroom, had almost forgotten what that life had been like.

"We're ready now," said Barbara as she joined Melinda and squared her shoulders to the camera, looking like the world-class journalist that she was.

"Five, four, three, two . . . ," came the drone, and

then a finger pointed in their direction, and they proceeded to walk slowly, as though on a casual tour of the gardens.

"The island nation of San Domenico," Barbara Walters began, looking into the camera, "is often called a natural paradise, and with its lush jungle vegetation pressed between white sand beaches, it would be hard to dispute that claim. Adding to its allure is the glamour of its reigning couple: the mesmerizing president, Diego Roca, and his beautiful wife, the former Academy Award–winning movie star, Melinda Myles, with whom we are talking this gorgeous afternoon. Thank you, Mrs. Roca, for speaking with us."

"You're very welcome, Barbara." Melinda laughed. "And I'm sure my husband will be intrigued to hear himself described as mesmerizing."

"Well, he is, don't you think?" asked Barbara conspiratorially.

"Of course *I* do," Melinda shared in the moment of bonhomie. "But I'm not sure he considers that his most salient attribute."

"Still, yours is a rather fairy-tale-like story. A beautiful actress from Hollywood gets caught in a revolution and ends up marrying the handsome rebel leader who deposes both a tyrannical dictator and the military junta, becoming the first democratically elected president of San Domenico."

Melinda smiled indulgently. "When you put it that way, it does sound rather like a fairy tale. But the true story, like all realities, is much tougher and less picturesque. Many lives were lost in the revolution, and the country's recovery from years of exploitation and deprivation has not been an easy one, as you know. My husband and I are both committed to making San Domenico as appealing for its quality of life as the quality of its flora and fauna. But there are many hardships to be faced along the way."

"I'd like to talk about that, with both you and the president, who will be joining us later in the program. But, for now, while we are alone, Mrs. Roca, I'd like to touch on your own remarkable personal story. You began as a small-town American girl, had a meteoric rise to stardom in Hollywood, which, forgive me for adding, did have an added element of scandal, and then gave it all up to become first lady of an emerging nation. How have you dealt with these enormous changes in your life?"

"First, let me say that my life in Hollywood, which I must admit was not always exemplary, was the easiest link to sever. I did enjoy working as an actress. But as I learned very quickly, the values promoted by that system were ultimately not fulfilling for me. I am still a small-town American girl, and my family in Oakdale, Illinois, is very important to me. But seeing the courage of the people of San Domenico, joining them in their fight for freedom, changed my priorities forever."

"And would you say falling in love with Diego Roca, the dashing rebel leader, exerted a powerful influence as well?"

"Barbara, you are determined to turn this into a romantic adventure," Melinda said and laughed good-naturedly.

"Well, it is very romantic," asserted Walters with a smile. Then turning full into the camera she added, "We'll get the president's perspective on this when we return."

The camera was turned off and for a moment, there was a visible reduction in tension. Then, Melinda heard a hum, and the air seemed to charge with electric current. Without even turning her head, she knew that her husband was approaching. Walters jumped up to greet him.

"Mr. President. Thank you for giving us your time."

Diego Roca took Barbara Walters hand in his and held it there. His dark eyes, flecked with fires of gold, seemed to search hers.

"Barbara, I hope you are not going to embarrass me by making me sound like the hero in a soap opera," he said with evident humor.

Melinda had to smile as she saw Barbara Walters melt. She wasn't surprised. Diego had always had the ability to capture attention. Mellowed in the two years they had been together by both his political and personal security, he had learned to capture hearts as well.

"Well, Mr. President. You and your wife make a striking couple, and there's no denying the circumstances of your meeting are the stuff of many a fantasy. Are you willing to talk about it on the air?"

"I most certainly am, providing we can also talk about some of the substantive issues that concern my country." Still holding Barbara Walters's hand, he glanced over her shoulder at his wife and saw an almost imperceptible nod. When the request had come for an interview, they had both been hesitant. Melinda had experienced the power of the media firsthand, and Diego, having evolved from a skilled warrior into a consummate politician, knew the advantage of being able to control the spin on the situation. The opportunity to publicize the plight of San Domenico, caught in a vise of rising inflation and declining tourism, was too good to pass up. So they had agreed to let Barbara Walters into their home and their lives. But not without a clear understanding that they had an agenda beyond titillating the insatiable curiosity of the American public for the private thoughts of people with a modicum of celebrity.

The cameras were rolling again. "We are so pleased to have you join us, Mr. President," Barbara Walters intoned unctuously. "Your wife is trying to demythologize your union, but it's hard for us in America to see your situation as anything but a dream come true."

"You are right, Barbara. My wife is modest. But, in fact, she is not only my personal dream come true, but San Domenico's as well. Her obvious beauty is only surpassed by her compassion and kindness. Your countrymen think of her as a movie star, but mine know her as a champion of their cause. We could not have won the revolution without her courage, and I could not govern without her encouragement. If I am the arm of the people, she is the heart. And not a day goes by that I don't thank God that she is beside me."

There was an almost reverential hush as Diego stopped talking and looked at his wife. They did not touch; they did not need to. The connection between them was so strong and so visceral it seemed almost visible.

When Barbara spoke, there were tears in her eyes. "That was a very beautiful speech, Mr. President. And I'm sure there isn't a woman in the world who doesn't wish you had been speaking about her."

They laughed and Diego said, "Now, Barbara, you promised not to embarrass me."

"I'm sorry, Mr. President. I'm a journalist, and I have to speak the truth. Does it ever worry you, Mrs. Roca, that your husband has become the matinee idol of the diplomatic world?"

"You heard him," said Melinda affably. "Would you worry?"

"I guess not," chuckled Barbara as the camera zoomed in on Melinda and Diego, sharing a smile. "At least not about his being a good husband."

"He is also a good president," said Melinda quickly, sensing, before anyone else, a change in the tone of the conversation. Her media responses were still honed enough to recognize the sound of impending danger.

"We would like to believe that," said Barbara with an abundance of sincerity. "But there have been rumblings."

Melinda looked at Diego. It was immediately clear to her that he was not worried. He had been expecting this, and he was prepared.

"There are always rumblings, Barbara. That is the nature of democracy. People are allowed to speak their minds, and it is impossible to have one hundred percent agreement."

"With all due respect, Mr. President, it is said that

the freedom promised by the revolution has not come to pass. They say your government is restrictive and not truly democratic."

"Well, the fact that you have heard these things and that people are allowed to say them should tell you something, Barbara. As for the promises of the revolution, unlike American politicians, I did not campaign on promises. Yes, we had hopes and still do. But under the dictator Jorge Alvarro and then the military leader Raul Guzman, San Domenico was pushed into third-world status. Bringing a nation back from the brink of ruin is no easy task and requires many sacrifices. Unfortunately, not all people are willing to relinquish their individual comforts for the sake of the community. So, there are, as you say, rumblings."

He looked to Melinda, and she knew it was her turn to speak. "Let me add, Barbara," she moved in smoothly, "these people are in the minority. The vast majority of the people in San Domenico understand that change takes time and are willing to do whatever is necessary to see it happen. Believe me, no one wants to go back to the way it was."

Diego smiled at her. She'd done well. Impulsively but not unaware of the effect, she leaned lovingly against him and was rewarded with a grin from the cameraman, who, relishing the moment, motioned furiously for them to move to the right and stay in the shot. With the instinct of the actress she was, Melinda stepped to the right, blocking Diego for an instant until he could position himself beside her again.

It came in that instant: a pop, barely discernible above the whir of the camera. Melinda felt a sting.

There was another pop, and someone shouted, "He's got a gun!"

Then, burly men, security guards, were pushing them to the ground, their own guns drawn, and the screaming began in earnest.

Melinda wondered why they were looking at her instead of at the disheveled man who was being tackled by the guards. She followed their eyes and saw a crimson stain spreading over the white lace front of her dress, like a valentine gone wild.

Only when she felt Diego's arms close around her and heard him crooning, "Melinda, *mi amor, mi amor,*" did she understand that she had been shot.

"Oh, my God," she heard Barbara Walters say, "are we still rolling?"

And then she passed out.

"This is it?" asked Sam, disappointed, as they approached the nondescript, government-issue quarters of the State Department in the Foggy Bottom district not far from the Lincoln Memorial.

In the two years since they'd been living in Washington fulfilling a contract to supply vehicles for the military, Andrew Symington, heir to the D'Uberville Motor Company fortune, and his wife, the beautiful Samantha Myles Symington, had been invited to a number of receptions and galas. Even Sam's notorious sexual harassment suit against the once up-and-coming Senator Amos Kilmont hadn't dimmed their social lustre. But no event had piqued Sam's interest quite as much as this formal dinner for five hundred given by the secretary of state to celebrate a new

Franco-American cultural exchange. Now, after being directed to the elevators by a stony-faced receptionist in the severe Twenty-third Street lobby, Sam wondered if perhaps she had been anticipating too much.

"Do you think I'm overdressed?" she worried aloud.

Drew eyed his wife. She was wearing a deep ruby red strapless gown, its shimmering folds ending in a train that swept behind her. Her copper curls, reflecting fiery highlights from her dress, had been swept up, emphasizing her long neck and the expanse of perfect honey-toned skin exposed by her daring décolletage.

"You look perfect," Drew said simply, but his voice had the hush of reverence reserved for the sight of miracles and objects of sublime beauty.

A moment later, the elevator doors opened on to a crystal-chandeliered corridor with marbled pilasters, and all doubt was gone.

"I didn't expect this," whispered Sam as they made their way through the entrance hall that looked like the drawing room of an eighteenth-century house.

A little awed, they proceeded down a hallway framed by Palladian windows and lined with American Chippendale and Queen Anne furniture. Following a gathering crowd, they moved into the John Quincy Adams State Drawing Room, where a reception line stood to welcome the dinner guests. A trio of crystal chandeliers illuminated the yellow-and-red-damask-covered eighteenth-century furniture, fine paintings, and precious Oriental rugs as they passed through the line and into the Thomas Jefferson State Reception Room with its celadon walls and restrained neoclassical motif. At last, they came to the Benjamin

Franklin State Dining Room, where large round tables elegantly laid out to accommodate the five hundred expected guests filled the space under the seal of the United States carved into the ceiling. Eight chandeliers threw brilliant sparks on the walls bordered by faux marble columns, topped with gilt Corinthian capitals.

"Here comes Jack," Sam said, pointing at the handsome blond lawyer in the elegant tuxedo striding across the room.

They watched as he made his way toward them, stopping every few steps to bestow a dazzling smile, shake an outstretched hand. Sam smiled, remembering how not so long ago, he'd been a ponytailed stranger working on the assembly line beside her. Only her need had made him finally acknowledge the law degree that he'd kept secret for fear of getting sucked into a lifestyle he couldn't and wouldn't tolerate. They'd left the line together and worked their separate ways up, Sam to designing her beloved cars under the auspices of a husband she adored, Jack to his position as a union advocate, even though it meant giving up the love of Melinda, Sam's sister. Then, two years ago, again responding to an appeal by Sam, he had made his appearance in Washington, representing her in her case against Senator Kilmont and ultimately discovering the evidence that forced Kilmont to concede defeat. Sam had expected him to return home to Oakdale and the auto union after that, but he'd been offered a job at the State Department, and the challenge of a new adventure had been too compelling to refuse. In the two years since, he had risen rapidly both professionally and socially, as nothing quite caught the eye of Washington's aristocracy as a handsome, eligible, well-connected bachelor.

"Aren't you two the glam couple?" Jack greeted them.

"What's up, Bader?" Drew smiled as Jack hugged Sam and she kissed the air beside his cheek.

"Funny you should ask," Jack said, striking a deliberately casual note.

But it was no use. They knew their old friend too well not to recognize the timbre of alarm, no matter how faint.

"What?" was all Sam said quietly, clutching at her husband's arm and Jack knew what she was asking. Since Melinda had married Diego Roca and become first lady of San Domenico, they had relied on Jack's connections with the State Department to give them advance notice of any rumblings, favorable or not, in the small island domain.

Jack took a breath. "Okay," he began, "let me start by telling you right off everything is fine."

"Why shouldn't it be?" Sam said peremptorily, preferring to hear the real news instead of the reassurances.

"Barbara Walters went down to do an interview with Melinda and Roca in San Domenico."

"I know that," Sam interrupted, impatient.

Jack saw it would be best just to tell her the whole story and be done with it. "During the interview there was an assassination attempt. Some nut with a gun and a silencer, so he got to shoot a couple of times before they dropped him. No one was killed. But Melinda was wounded. But she's all right."

The blood drained from Sam's face.

"She's all right," Jack repeated forcefully. "She got hit in the chest, but the bullet missed the heart and any major arteries. They operated on her immediately, took it out, and she's recovering."

"When did all this happen?" Drew asked while Sam caught her breath.

"A couple of hours ago. Because I left the office early to dress for this stupid shindig, I wasn't there when the information came in, and it took the guy who was covering a while to figure out where to direct it. I just found out myself on the way over here. I tried to call you at home, but you'd already left. It'll be on the news tonight."

Drew looked at his wife. They had heard the phone ringing as they left the Georgetown house, but because she'd been so excited about the evening ahead, they'd decided to let Mrs. Halsey, the middle-aged baby-sitter they had been using since Natalie's unpleasant departure, answer.

In spite of all Jack's assurances, Sam's eyes were filled with tears.

Again, he tried to reassure her. "Soon as I heard about it, I went to my office and called our rep down there. All the reports are positive. She's in stable condition."

"But you're always saying that it's getting harder to get verified reports from San Domenico," Sam pointed out.

"Well, as a matter of fact, I figured you might worry about that. So I got an aide to stay on the horn and try to make contact with Diego Roca himself on your behalf. I told him to come and get you here when he gets through."

"Oh, Jack." Sam threw her arms around him, grateful for his foresight and thoughtfulness. Suddenly, she stepped back, worried again. "How's he going to find me? Maybe I should go to the office now and wait there."

Jack laughed. "First of all, I just told him to look for the gorgeous redhead. Second, it's just been two years since your face was splashed all over the front page. People in Washington forget but not that fast. Third, I gave him the seating plan, so he knows where your table is. And finally, there's no telling how long it's going to take, so you might as well eat. Or at least drink. They're pouring some exceptional wines tonight, and it wouldn't hurt to get a little snookered, if you know what I mean."

"Thank you, Jack," said Drew fervently, speaking for both of them.

"I've got to mingle," he said. "It's my job. But I'll keep checking in with you. And don't worry," he added, looking at Sam's still-stricken face. "Melinda's all right. We'd know it if she wasn't, wouldn't we?"

Sam rewarded him with the first smile since she'd heard the news. She and her sister had a visceral bond that extended over time and space. If something were really wrong with Melinda, Sam was sure she'd feel it in her heart. After all, they were the Myles Militia.

"You're right," she told Jack, meaning it. "Go circulate. We'll find you when we get the word."

Feeling more unsettled than he knew he should, Jack took his leave and moved through the crowd. He grabbed an unidentifiable cocktail from a passing tray, downed it, and took another. He hadn't eaten all day, and the drink was stronger than he had expected, which was just as well, since he felt he could use a little of the numbing he'd recommended to Sam.

It had been four years since he and Melinda Myles had parted ways, as certain of their love for each other as they were of their inability to live together. It was ironic that Jack's refusal to leave the simplicity of life in Oakdale and Melinda's determination to taste the glamour of Hollywood had driven them apart. And here was Jack, wandering through the elegant corridors of the Washington elite, while Melinda languished in the spare conditions of an emerging nation. Still, being the wife of Diego Roca was not without its own high profile, and for all Jack's advancement in the State Department, it was still an elementary existence he craved.

"Which means," he said to himself, hardly aware that he was speaking out loud, "you're an idiot for still thinking about her. Get over it!"

"Talking to the most interesting person you could find?"

"What?" Embarrassed, he whirled around to see who had caught him.

Almost as tall as he was and sliver thin, she was what had once been described as a long drink of water. Barely combed, her hair was the white blond of movie stars in the thirties, but it hung straight and long, like platinum strands brushing her pale white shoulders. She was dressed in a slip of a dress, cut on the bias, clinging to the contours of her body, an intriguing juxtaposition of angles and curves. The dress, too, was white, and for one irrational moment, Jack was reminded of the childhood pleasure of licking icicles.

"I have to admit," she said, "the crowd is more boring than usual."

"Present company excluded, I assume," he said, playing along.

"That remains to be seen," she answered. "Let's get out of here."

She reached for his hand and swayed a little, and he saw then that she was a bit drunk. He moved to steady her, wavering somewhat himself, and realized with a laugh, so was he.

"Where are we going?" he asked.

"Does it matter?"

He looked at the swell of her ample breasts rising above the scoop of her neckline, then raised his eyes to her face. Her mouth was full and turned up at the edges in an ironic smile that didn't quite eliminate the sensual pout. Her slate gray eyes seemed to mock him or herself, he wasn't sure. He was sure that she was beautiful, and the involuntary rise of sensation he was beginning to feel told him she was desirable as well.

"No," he answered, letting himself be led. "I guess not."

"Then shut up and come with me."

She started pulling him through the large reception room, moving swiftly. He followed, keeping his eyes averted from the people they passed, feeling an urgent need right now to avoid contact with anyone except the mysterious stranger who was taking him away.

"Jack!" someone called. He tried to ignore it.

"Jack!" again, and he recognized Sam's voice. He stopped short. She looked at him, her lopsided grin revealing perfect white teeth.

"So you're Jack," she said, and it sounded almost like a taunt.

Before he could respond, Sam was at his arm. She was too overwrought to even notice he was not alone.

"Your assistant found me. As soon as he puts me on the phone, they're going to connect me to Diego Roca. Are you coming?"

Automatically, he went to follow, turning momentarily to the woman beside him to proffer his apologies. She was watching him with downcast eyes, a seductive smile playing on her lips. She was exquisite. He heard his own words come back to him like instant replay. *Get over it!*

"Listen," he said to Sam. "You're his sister-in-law. I'm just . . . just . . ." He didn't even know what word to put on it.

"Okay," said Sam, understanding. "I'll let you know. I'm going to take it in your office, okay?"

"Of course," he said and watched as she hurried off. For a moment, he wanted to run after her. Then he forced himself to take hold of the blunt reality. Melinda was going to be fine. He didn't need her husband to tell him that. *Get over it,* he repeated to himself like a litany.

"Well?" she said. He wondered at her uncanny ability to make everything she said sound like both an insult and an invitation.

He grabbed another drink off a tray and threw it back, relishing the fire as it went through his body and rekindled his desire.

"Let's go," he said and blindly trailed as she pushed through a door and out of the light and the din.

"What have we here?" she breathed excitedly as their eyes adjusted to the gloom.

"The James Madison Dining Room."

"Aren't you knowledgeable?" she said, and he wondered why he found her derisive tone so enticing.

"I work for State," he said, instantly regretting that he had given her so much information.

"Well, Jack, who works for State, see anything you'd like to dine on?"

And with that she kicked aside one of the sixteen Sheraton chairs and positioned herself on the edge of the table, letting the strap of her dress slip just enough to reveal one round and rosy nipple.

He moved to her, wondering for a moment what he was doing. But he knew the answer. She was everything Melinda was not. An anonymous, careless, emotionless fling. And even if it would only last a minute, it would be one minute less that he would be aching for the woman he had loved and lost.

"Listen," he said, still needing to be fair, "I'm not . . ."

She covered his mouth with her hand, interrupting. "Neither am I."

She opened her purse and extracted a condom, handing it to him without a word. He pushed her back against the eighteenth-century mahogany table and, without comment or criticism, accepted her for the gourmet offering that she was.

"Sarah," Forrest Symington spoke tersely to his daughter. "Ian Taylor is your brother. You'd better stop trying to have children and get a divorce."

Sarah looked at her father. Ever since she was a

child, she had heard stories about his legendary cruelty. While turning her mother's inheritance into a huge automotive empire, he had gained a reputation for ruthlessness that was unsurpassed. Not that Mathilde D'Uberville had ever seemed to care, but he had been unfaithful to her almost from the beginning of their thirty-year marriage. But, until now, he'd never turned his venom against her.

"Daddy, why are you saying that? You know it's not true." She was hurt, but she wasn't going to let him get to her.

"It is true. I had an affair with his mother. That's why she gave him up for adoption. Didn't want poor, dumb Harvey Myles raising my little bastard." He chuckled maliciously.

"That was a mistake, Daddy. They took tests. Ian is not your son. He's Harvey's son. Diane just didn't realize it."

He gave her a pitying look, as though thinking it must be intolerable to be so stupid. "Grow up, Sarah. Do you think Diane Myles would have given him away if he was really Harvey's son? Those tests were faked."

He was being ridiculous. "Why? Who would do something like that."

"I would," he answered matter-of-factly. "Otherwise, I would have been opening myself up to a lawsuit."

She felt herself getting queasy. "Come on, Dad. You would never have let me marry my brother just so you didn't have to pay child support." But she was afraid it was exactly the kind of thing her father would do.

Forrest just shrugged. "I work hard for my money.

It's what sent you to finishing school and to Europe. It bought us this estate. I'm not about to give it away."

"Stop it," she shouted. "I don't believe you." But the problem was that she did.

"I slept with his sister, too, you know. Melinda. She was a hot one," he added, smiling to himself as if at the memory.

Sarah began to cry. "I can't give up Ian. He's my whole life."

"Well, you're going to have to. What you two are doing is against the law."

"No. There's got to be a mistake. Where's Mom? She'll tell them."

"There's no mistake. Your mother's got nothing to say about it. Anyway, she's in Europe. She doesn't care about you any more than she cares about me."

"I can't live without Ian," Sarah sobbed.

"Well, that's it, then, isn't it?"

Her father was looking at her strangely. For a minute, she didn't understand, and then it became crystal clear. They were on the grounds of Belvedere, beyond the cultivated lawns and into the wild acreage that had been preserved for hunting, a sport Forrest Symington relished. They were standing on the edge of a ravine, on top of a sheer cliff that fell into a rocky riverbed. Her beloved Ian was in the mansion far away. Her father was right. There was only one thing to do.

Suddenly, she was utterly calm. "I hate you, Father," she said without emotion. And then she stepped over the edge and fell, screaming Ian's name.

"I'm here. I'm right here, sweetheart," soothed Ian as he shook his wife awake.

"Oh, my God," she said, clinging to her husband. "I was dreaming."

"That's what you were supposed to do, isn't it?" he asked gently.

She nodded. "I just didn't expect such vivid results." She had been to see Dr. Tibor Horvath, a psychotherapist who specialized in hypnosis, that afternoon. She had told him immediately that she didn't really believe in what he did.

He had not seemed the least disturbed, just gently curious, when he asked, "Then why have you come?"

He was older than she had expected, silver haired, and serious. She realized as she looked at him that what she had envisioned was a man who looked like Houdini with a pencil-thin moustache and a watch that swung back and forth on a gold chain.

"Well, it's silly really," she had said, a little uncomfortable. "My husband, Ian, and I have been trying to get pregnant for the past couple of years. We've had all the tests and everything, but nothing seems to be the matter. My doctor suggested maybe it could be psychological."

"And he recommended you try hypnosis?"

"She. Yes. Do I have to believe in it for it to work?"

He smiled again. "Not at all. Let's try a little test. Lay your arm flat on my desk."

Sarah did as she was told.

"Now you don't have to do anything to help me. Just don't try to fight me. Close your eyes, keep your mind open, and listen."

Sarah sighed. She knew this wasn't going to work. She had been prepared to go straight to in vitro, but Ian had urged her to at least try this. If it didn't work, they could always turn to surgery. Her eyes were closed and even as she tried to brush the extraneous thoughts from her mind, she could hear Dr. Horvath's voice telling her in a quiet drone that there was a helium balloon attached to her wrist and it was making her arm go higher and higher. She felt ridiculous. She was wasting both their time. She opened her eyes.

"Look, I'm sorry, but I'm just not . . ." She stopped in midsentence, her mouth agape. Her arm was halfway over her head. "Oh," she said in shock, "I didn't even realize . . ."

"The power of suggestion is very strong and not very complicated," he told her, not unkindly. "Would you like to try lying down and just seeing what happens?"

She was suddenly nervous. She had no idea she was so susceptible. "What if . . . ?" She wasn't exactly sure what she wanted to ask. *What if I lose control? What if I go under and never come back? What if you take advantage of me while I'm insensible?* Although the last seemed rather unlikely.

He seemed to understand. "All I'm going to do is put you in a perfectly relaxed state. You will be completely conscious, completely in control. You could stand up and walk out of here if you wanted. What I want is to offer you a posthypnotic suggestion that you vent out in your dreams reasons why you may not want to get pregnant. How does that sound?"

"Fine," she said, still unsure, but decidedly relieved.

She lay back on the dark leather recliner and closed her eyes. His voice was rich, soothing.

"You are feeling tired, letting go," he told her. "You are moving far away, very, very far . . ."

She smiled a little. At least the litany was exactly what she had expected. And she *was* feeling tired.

"You are going into a deep sleep. Deeper than any sleep you have ever known." He raised her hand and dropped it. It fell heavily. "Good," he said. "Now I'm going to count to ten. At each count, I want you to take a deep breath and, as you let it out, say the words *far away.*"

He placed his fingers gently on her eyelids and began his count. "One . . ."

Sarah took a deep breath. "Far away," she said, feeling rather silly.

She felt his fingers pressing into her lids. She saw purple dots. "Two . . ." he said.

She breathed in. This time, when she said, "Far away," it came out as a quiet sigh.

By the time they reached ten and he had removed his fingers from her eyes, she knew she was in a hypnotic state.

"Now I want you to feel good about yourself," the doctor told her. "Better than you've ever felt. You have confidence and you know that whatever you do is going to work out right . . ."

He had gone on in that vein for about five or ten minutes, speaking in general terms, before getting to the point.

"Tonight, when you go to sleep, you will dream. And in your dreams, you will vent out if and why you are preventing yourself from getting pregnant. When I count to five, you will be awake and you will feel extremely refreshed, not tired, but full of energy and ready to tackle the rest of the day. One, two, three, four, five."

Sarah opened her eyes. She sat up a little uncertainly, trying to ascertain what, if any, effect the hypnosis had had. She had to admit she felt more relaxed than she had in a while, but still, she didn't quite trust the process.

Now, as she recounted her dream to Ian, she had to accede that the treatment was far more effective than she could ever have believed.

"That is a very weird dream," Ian acknowledged when she had told him all the details she could remember.

"But kind of telling, don't you think?" she asked, pulling his arms a little tighter around her as they leaned against the headboard of the antique four-poster in the east-wing bedroom of Belvedere that they had been occupying ever since Drew and Sam had moved to Washington. Even with a hyperefficient male nurse named Buddy taking full-time and exclusive care of Forrest Symington since his debilitating accident, it had been decided that a member of the family ought to remain in close proximity at all times.

"What do you think it means?" Ian asked his wife, still stroking her brow and planting little absent-minded kisses on the top of her head as they talked.

"Well, some of it is pretty obvious. I mean, I know you're not my brother. We've got all the proof. But I guess the heart still fears what the mind accepts. Maybe that's why I'm afraid to get pregnant."

"Well, we're just going to have to find a way to get over that."

"And in a funny way, I think it's my father, too."

"What? You think he's going to suddenly get unparalyzed and try to screw things up?"

"No, not really. I know that can't happen. But there's just something about his presence that is so oppressive."

"We can move out of here, Sarah. I mean I can't afford a mansion. But if you'd be content with a little house . . ."

"Oh, Ian. With you, I'd be happy in a tent. But we can't go. Not yet. Maybe when Sam and Drew come back. Or when . . ." She stopped herself from saying it. "I can't leave him alone."

"Not that he would know or care," Ian said a little derisively.

"It doesn't matter. *I* know."

"Okay," he whispered, not wanting her to get upset. "Then, if we can't move, we're just going to have to reprogram you."

"What do you mean?" she asked warily.

"Well, to overcome fears or phobias, the patient is gradually introduced to the things that are feared and shown that they are innocuous."

"And how do you propose to do that?" she asked, smiling, seeing that he was teasing her.

"Let's start with the basics. Are you afraid of this?" He kissed her gently on the lips.

"Mmmm," she responded. "No, I don't think so."

"Good. Now how about this?" His kiss became more passionate, insistent.

She put her arms around him. "I think I can live with that."

"This is going to be more challenging," he cautioned as he slipped his hand down the front of her nightgown.

"You'll have to work on that part some more, Doctor." She sighed as he began to caress her breast.

"A man's got to do what a man's got to do," he intoned, making her giggle as he pulled her nightgown over her head and moved himself between her legs.

There was a knock on the door. They looked at each other.

"This isn't part of the treatment, is it?" she whispered.

"It wasn't in the training program." He gave her back her nightgown.

"Who is it?" she called, holding it in front of her, not willing to give up their game if they didn't have to.

"Sorry to bother you, Sarah. It's your dad."

Quickly she dropped the nightgown over her head and grabbed a robe as Ian went to open the door.

"What's the matter, Buddy?" Ian asked the large man who stood shaking in the corridor. "Has something happened to Mr. Symington?"

"Yes, sir, I'm afraid it has. I think it was a stroke."

"I'll call an ambulance," Sarah volunteered hastily, picking up the phone.

"I don't think that's necessary," Buddy said quickly before she could dial.

"If he's had a stroke," Sarah said anxiously, "he ought to be in the hospital."

"I'm sorry, Sarah. It's too late," said Buddy quietly, his eyes filling. "Your father has passed away."

"Daddy's dead?" asked Sarah, her voice tinged

with disbelief. Ian put his arms around her in anticipation of the tears that would inevitably follow. But Sarah couldn't cry yet. The sadness had still to work its way through the guilt. All she could think, as she laid her head on her husband's shoulder, was: be careful what you wish for . . .

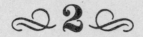

2

On her husband's death, as specified in a prenuptial agreement widely regarded as one of the first of its kind, Mathilde D'Uberville Symington inherited the car company that her family's fortune had helped to found.

"Je ne le veux pas," she told her children when they had gathered after the appropriately grand funeral in which there had been many eulogies but few tears.

"What do you mean you don't want it?" her son protested. "You don't have to do anything. There's a board—"

"No!" she scolded. "Zat ees not zee point," she went on in the heavy French accent she had willfully maintained for the past forty years. "I hate cars. I don't want eet."

Sarah and Drew looked at their mother and at each

other. Mathilde hadn't even driven a car since she'd accidentally killed a young bride in France many years ago and let Drew take the blame for it. Her loathing for the business world in which their father had flourished was well known in the family. Since Forrest had had his incapacitating accident several years ago, not only had she shown no interest in the family corporation, she'd had very little desire to remain in America. They understood that, for her, Forrest had been more a shackle than a husband, keeping her away from her own people and places where she felt truly at home. There was a brashness to the auto industry that she found distasteful, and now that her low-born, self-aggrandizing husband was gone, she didn't have to pretend to an ecumenical appreciation for all levels of society. She was born an aristocrat, and she wished to live the rest of her life as one. Even though the D'Uberville Motor Company was a multibillion-dollar operation in a thriving national industry, it was still just a dirty car company to her.

"Well, what do you want to do, *Maman?*" Sarah asked before Drew could make any more objections.

"I want to geev eet to you. To you and Drew."

"Maman, I'll still handle things for you if that's what you're worried about," Drew tried again. Both he and his sister had been well provided for through various trusts and bequests. He had no need to take what was rightfully his mother's, and he knew Sarah would feel the same way.

"Listen to me, *mon cher."* Mathilde was insistent. "I am not worried. I don't want it. I already 'ave zee papers. *Mes enfants,* you two own DMC. 'Ow you run eet ees now your business. You can handle zees, no?"

"Of course we can," Drew said, "But—"

"Zen zere ees no but. *C'est finis.*"

Then, Mathilde informed her children that she would stay for a week of mourning, but after that, she'd be returning to her family's chateau in Annecy. She hoped they would come and visit and, at the very least, bring Moira and any subsequent grandchildren to see her every summer. But more or less, she was through with Woodland Cliffs. In the thirty years that she had spent there, having and raising a family with Forrest Symington, she'd grown attached to nothing outside of that family. And conversely, the moment she had returned to France, it was as though she'd never been away. Once Sarah and Drew understood that, they stopped arguing with her about her plans.

It wasn't much of a decision for Sam and Drew. The renovation of the DMC plant in Washington was complete, and the operations were running smoothly enough not to need Drew's constant presence. Belvedere had always been home to Drew, and without the repressive atmosphere prescribed by the presence of the elder Symingtons, even Sam agreed it would be a wonderful place to live. She liked her brother and sister-in-law, and the mansion was certainly expansive enough to accommodate the two families without their ever getting in each other's way. The staff was large and loving, and the grounds would be paradise to growing children.

After the initial flurry of activity in Washington, Sam's professional life had been virtually curtailed. Even though she had won her case against Senator

Amos Kilmont, whistle-blowing was still not an honorable exercise in the nation's capital. Except for a couple of requests to speak for women's groups, there had been no further interest in her or her expertise from either government or industry. And after her cataclysmic experience with their young au pair, who happened to be Kilmont's niece and who had developed a dangerous obsession with Drew, Sam had decided it would not be a bad idea for her to stay home with Moira for a while. But now, Moira was ready for school and the company of other children, and Sam was just as ready for work and the company of adults.

"When we go back," Sam asked Drew, because it was already assumed that it was only when, never if, "can I start working on the VT-12 again?"

Drew looked at his wife. She had made the question sound casual, but he knew how much the new racing car she had been designing before coming to Washington had meant to her. Between the move to D.C. and Drew's fear of her injuring herself during a test run, she had had to abandon the project, and he knew it still rankled.

Drew hesitated. As a businessman, he knew it was a sound investment and there was no reason not to go forward. But he still had vivid memories of the terror that gripped his throat when, standing with their baby daughter in his arms, he had watched her plow into a wall. When she had emerged from the wreckage unhurt, he had sworn to never let her put herself in such danger again. Even now, he knew he could stop her. The question was, did he have a right to?

"It's not that I don't believe in you," he began

carefully, "but I couldn't bear for anything to happen to you. What about Moira?"

He didn't have to say anymore. Sam took his hands in her own and kissed them. She understood and accepted his misgivings, realizing that had the situation been reversed, she would probably feel as he did. But she was also aware that no man would give up the work of his life because his wife was afraid.

"I love you, Drew. And I love Moira more than anything. I wouldn't willfully put myself in danger. You have to trust that I know what I'm doing when I'm on a track."

"You can't know everything. Experienced drivers have fatal accidents all the time."

"Accidents happen. To everyone. There's nothing you can do about that."

"You don't have to court them."

"We can't protect each other from fate, Drew. Ivory towers don't work. Like I said, I love you and Moira. But I was making cars before I met you, and it's as much a part of me as being a wife and mother. I think you know that."

"Fine," he began. "But can't you do it without—" He stopped himself. He already knew the answer.

"I can only do it the way I need to do it. The best way possible. The right way. It's how I do everything and it's how you work, too. Don't ask me to do something you would never ask of yourself."

For a long time, Drew didn't speak. Sam knew that she had won. She felt relief but no joy. Because even though her husband had no argument to offer, he was still upset, and there was nothing she could do about it without relinquishing an essential part of herself.

The Georgetown house was quiet. Flattened cartons were stacked in the middle of the kitchen floor, waiting to be packed. Moira was out in the park with Mrs. Halsey.

"Do you remember what we did when we first rented the house?" Sam asked Drew.

"You mean the 'christening'?" he asked, trying not to smile.

"Every room," she reminded him, glad to see she was getting to him.

"What are you suggesting?" he asked, although he knew perfectly well what she had in mind.

"Well, we will be leaving soon. Never to return."

"We hope."

"We hope," she agreed fervently. Neither one of them would miss Washington. For all its vigor as the seat of power, they had found the city and the majority of its inhabitants to be clever but petty, people with deep thoughts but shallow purposes. Yet, as well as their hardships, they had had some spectacular moments in this house. "Do you think it would be appropriate to, shall we say, unchristen it?"

"Is that like taking back a kiss?"

"I guess so." She laughed.

She was sitting in a kitchen chair, and he came to her, kneeling before her and putting his head in her lap. She could feel his breath, warming her through her clothes.

"I take this back," he said slyly as he slipped his hand under her skirt and began to caress her thigh. She sighed and opened her legs a little wider.

"And this," he added, letting his fingers slip inside, into the moist invitation of her spreading desire.

She felt herself slipping off the chair, and he laughed and caught her and somehow managed to remove her clothes as well as his own before sitting down himself and lowering her on top. Gently, he moved her up and down, letting her balance herself on the tip of his anchor before sliding down to nestle in his lap again. He put her nipples in his mouth, first one, then the other, teasing them with his tongue, while she kissed the top of his head and her fingers, grazed down his back. Suddenly, he stopped and lifted her off.

"What?" she asked, baffled. She could see that his desire had not abated any more than hers.

"I want to watch you."

He stood, and without a word, she straddled the chair. Slowly, she let her fingers run over her body, savoring the touch of her own hand. Her nipples were already hard, but she squeezed them between thumb and forefinger, listening to her husband's breath coming faster and deeper. She let first one hand, then the other stray down the flatness of her belly to the copper mound and the space that he had occupied moments before. Pressing into herself, she began to move, grinding into herself with increasing urgency. He dropped to his knees, watching for the moment when she would release herself. And when it came, he pushed into her, replacing her hand with his own desire, feeling wave upon wave of her ecstasy close around him and bring him to a bliss of his own.

Later, in the shower, after the process had been repeated with variations in both living room and bedroom, they talked about the practicalities of their new life.

"The company is half Sarah's, too. Even though she hasn't had experience, she has as much right to it as I do. I'd like to encourage her to do more than be a silent partner," Drew said as he ran the soap down his wife's back, hesitating longer than necessary in certain strategic areas.

"Stop, Drew," Sam warned. "We should be dressed when Halsey gets back with Moira."

"You're absolutely right," he agreed, kissing her soapy shoulder before playfully pushing her out of the way so he could rinse off.

"What about public relations? Do you think that might be an area for her?" he gurgled as the water coursed down his face.

"Why don't you ask her?" Sam said, managing to divert a stream of water in her own direction.

"Good idea. And Ian, too." He turned the water off and held out a towel for her. Sam stepped out of the shower after him.

"Ian, too." She smiled, pleased that her husband was as concerned about her brother as he was about his own sister.

Sarah and Ian had no reservations about sharing a home. They had always expected Sam and Drew to come back to Belvedere with Moira. The west wing had remained intact, kept up and cared for until their return. But it had never occurred to them that they might become an active part of DMC.

"I didn't really expect this," Sarah said to Drew when the welcome homes had been extended and the talk turned to business.

"You have a right to it."

"Well, I have a right to half our shares. But you always worked with Dad. I've never had anything to do with it."

"Did you want to?"

"Hah," she scoffed. "As if I had a choice."

"You do now."

"Okay then. Damn right. Yeah. I want to. I'm done being a useless social butterfly."

Her brother hugged her. "Damn right," he echoed laughing. "But I never thought you were useless," he added judiciously.

"Drew?" she said quietly, extricating herself from his embrace.

"What, Sarah?"

"What can I do?"

"We'll find something, honey. We'll find something. We're going to make this into a real family business."

They walked, arms looped around each other, silent for a while. They had left their respective spouses back at the mansion and decided to revisit some of their favorite childhood haunts on the estate grounds. Sarah realized that they were heading toward the ravine that had figured so prominently in her dream.

"Drew?" she broke the silence.

"What?"

"Do you ever think about Dad?"

"Not if I can help it."

"Do you hate him?"

Drew thought about it for a moment. Everything he had, he had because of his father. But everything he was, he was in spite of him. There was never any doubt as to which was more important.

"Yeah, I guess I do. He was our father, but he was a pig."

Sarah was quiet for a minute. "I don't know how I feel about him."

"It doesn't really matter. He's dead."

"It matters to me. I've been going to a shrink, a hypnotist, because I'm having trouble getting pregnant and the doctors think it might be psychological. It's making me have all kinds of dreams. And he's usually in them."

"What does he do?"

"Different things. All of them menacing."

Drew shrugged; he wasn't surprised. "He's dead, Sarah," he said again. "Let him go."

"I wish I could." She felt a constriction in her throat just talking about him. "Let's go back," she said. It was a warm day and the sun was shining brightly, but she felt a sudden chill.

Sarah let Drew tell Ian they wanted him to be in the business as well. His first reaction was to laugh.

"You guys are great."

"This isn't a joke," Drew said, but Ian's good humor was so infectious he couldn't help smiling.

"I'm going to be part of it. Why shouldn't you be?" added Sam.

"Because you're a car designer and I'm a math teacher."

"Well, I'm not anything," said Sarah, "and it's not stopping me."

"Sweetheart, you own the company," Ian said without rancor, "which means you are anything you want to be."

"Well, there's an opening in the finance division, and you're going to get trained, and we're not taking no for an answer," Drew said adamantly. "And the pay's better than you get for teaching."

Ian thought for a moment. "Does anybody talk back?"

"Not to the boss's husband," quipped Sarah gruffly.

"Then you've got yourself a deal."

It was going to be a family affair. Siblings married to siblings, sharing a house and a business. There was excess enough to satisfy them all. And there was enthusiasm enough to keep everyone happy. Still, as they clinked their glasses in a champagne toast, they all knew that what they had designed was a blueprint for either a dynasty or a disaster.

It was the song of a nightingale that woke Melinda. The doors to the balcony had been left open, and she could see the bird, perched on the balustrade, warbling at the moon. There was a soft breeze that carried his song to her and, with it, the scent of the garden. She sat up and listened, alert and smiling. It had been four days since she had been truly awake, having allowed her body to command the inertia needed to heal. She was pleased to find herself hungry and free of pain for the first time since the surgery that had removed the bullet from her chest, where it had lodged perilously close to her heart. A small clock on the night table told her it was almost midnight. Diego was not beside her.

A small gold cord hung from the ceiling and dangled within reach of the bed. During the extravagant reign of Jorge Alvarro, it had been used to summon servants to fulfill the whims of the dictator. In the two years since she and Diego had occupied the bedroom, it had never been used. Not really expecting a response, she pulled it.

"Where is the president?" she asked the palace guard who appeared almost instantaneously.

"In the president's office, Señora Roca."

"Is he in conference?"

"No. I believe he is alone. There was a meeting. But the others left several hours ago. Do you want me to send for him?"

Melinda considered it. She had emerged from her anesthetized state several times in the past few days to find him leaning over her, face grave. She had tried to acknowledge his presence, ease his concern, but could only mumble a few words of comfort before falling back into her drugged sleep. There had been some tension between them before the fateful interview with Barbara Walters, when they had discussed how to deal with her inevitably challenging questions. But she had no way of knowing what had happened after the incident, what crises might have ensued, and where Diego now stood in relation to herself and the people.

She felt disoriented, out of touch, unsure of the day of the week, let alone the state of affairs. She wanted some hint of what to expect from her husband. And she was still hungry.

"Do you think it would be possible to send down to the kitchen for something for me to eat. Nothing special. Just if there is some soup or something."

"Of course, madam." He smiled, indicating his own relief at her recovery.

She understood and warmly smiled back. "And could you also send up a newspaper. I've been so out of touch the past few days, I'd like to catch up."

The guard looked at her uncomfortably.

"Is there something wrong?" she asked, knowing there was.

"Uh . . . , Señora Roca . . . , you see . . . there is no newspaper."

"It doesn't have to be the latest edition," she said, relieved it was nothing more. "Just whatever is lying around."

"But . . . uh . . . there is nothing . . ."

San Domenico was a small island. Since the revolution, with all the adherent difficulties in starting new businesses and keeping old ones going, only one national newspaper was still printing. But it was well staffed and served its constituents daily. It seemed impossible that it would suddenly cease functioning.

"Why? What has happened?" she asked anticipating but dreading the reply.

"By order of *el presidente,* the press has been closed."

She was careful not to let her face show her emotion. "Thank you," she told the guard. "You can go."

"Your food, madam?"

"I'm sorry, I'm not as hungry as I thought. I'll wait until morning. Thank you," she said again, hurrying his departure.

The minute he had closed the door behind him, she pulled aside the sheet and stood up. A robe had been laid on a chair beside the bed in anticipation of her eventual recovery. She pulled off the short cotton hospital gown she had been wearing and slipped on the robe, moving a little gingerly so as not to disturb her bandage. The night was warm, and the feel of cool marble on her feet was a relief. Leaving her feet bare, she made her way not to the imposing gilded double doors at the front of the bedroom, but to a small wooden door hidden in the paneling at the back. It creaked open onto a long corridor that bypassed the main hallways of the presidential palace and led directly to the president's office. In the old days, it had been used by Jorge Alvarro to sneak women into his private quarters. For Diego and Melinda, it had become one of the internal arteries that connected them and even, on occasion, enabled them to have their own clandestine assignations, moments stolen from cabinet meetings and official appearances to indulge in the ecstasy they still felt in each other's arms. Now, Melinda pushed through the hidden passageway into the president's office with something other than passion on her mind.

Sensing another presence, Diego looked up and saw Melinda. In her diaphanous white robe, framed by the dim light of the corridor, she looked like a dark-haired angel. For a moment, joy filled him to see her recovered enough to be standing in his office. He stood, ready to run and embrace her, but he saw her face was dour, and it occurred to him that she had been watching him for some time. He had hoped in the wake of their near disaster, all their differences would be forgotten. He suspected that they were not. He sat down again, forcing the elation back inside him.

"You shouldn't be here," he said, uncertain of her purpose in coming and unwilling to risk a rebuff.

She couldn't tell if he was being solicitous of her health or protective of his turf. "What are you doing?" she asked him.

"Working," he answered shortly. "You should be in bed."

She knew he had deliberately chosen to misunderstand her question.

"You've closed down the newspaper."

He said nothing, choosing instead to busy himself with the papers on his desk.

She began again. "You can't just—"

Now, he looked up and with a wave of his hand, silenced her. "Don't tell me," he intoned icily, "what I can and cannot do."

She met his eyes. There was no anger in her voice, only sadness. "And are you to be my dictator, too? Am I to be silenced like the opposition?"

"Is that what you think I am? A dictator?"

She saw she had hurt him, and though it had not been her intention, she was pleased to see her words still affected him. It gave her hope. "Oh, Diego. I know you're trying your best to keep control of the situation and it's hard. But this revolution was fought for the sake of freedom. People died for it. What right do you have to take it away again?"

He was angry now. "I *have* the right," he said, his eyes blazing. "You could have been killed . . ."

"Is that what this is about? Punishment because some crazy guy shoots at you and accidentally gets your wife? Because if you're doing this for me, it's not what I want."

Diego shook his head. She was a noble person, his wife. But she was naive. And she had an unfortunate tendency to personalize all actions. As though what was good or necessary for the country had to reflect what was good or necessary for her.

"Try to understand, Melinda. To tolerate an assassination attempt is to show weakness. To show weakness is to relinquish leadership. To relinquish leadership is to acknowledge instability. To acknowledge instability is to undermine the government. And if the government is undermined, then there is no democracy."

"I don't accept that. Kennedy was killed by an assassin. There have been attempts on every president since then. They don't close down the newspapers after every incident."

"San Domenico is not the United States. America is admirable, but it took hundreds of years to evolve. We've just begun, and we are still vulnerable."

"You mean you are."

She was personalizing again. "Fine. Yes, I am. And if I fall, what will happen? Oh, we have elected officials, but what experience do they have with government or democracy? They take orders from whoever gives them. They need to learn. Isn't it better they learn from me than from some military demagogue who steps in to fill the vacuum?"

"You don't know that would happen."

"You don't know that it wouldn't."

She was silent for a moment. "Couldn't we just increase security?"

"My darling, I wish it were that easy. But you know as well as I do that wouldn't help. As long as people are encouraged to express their disapproval, someone's going to have his hand on the trigger. They don't know any other way here. I have to show them. But first, to protect us both, I have to crush the opposition before it crushes us."

She didn't know what to say. Ever since he had become president, she had noticed little erosions of freedom that disturbed her greatly. As much as he gave her credit in his interviews for helping him govern, he tried to keep her from involving herself in his daily decisions. She generally learned about them through press reports, which were often unfavorable. When she questioned him about it, as today, he always had answers that were hard for her to dispute. How could she argue that she knew better than he what was needed to raise San Domenico out of its depression. No matter how much she committed herself to her new country, she would always be an American, born privileged by the very fact that she was able to bring herself to fame and fortune. Still, she was disturbed by the Draconian measures she saw her husband taking in the name of saving his country, and even though she could not best him in an argument, she knew that he was wrong.

Defeated and disappointed, she turned away, heading for the door. He watched her for a moment, silhouetted against the light, saw the soft folds of her silk robe caught between her legs. They had not been together since she had been shot. But clearly, she was recovered. He stood, pushing his papers away and walked quickly to stop her.

She felt his hand on her shoulder. As much as she disapproved of his actions, his touch on her body was still electric. She wanted to keep moving, as though to deny him would strike a blow for democracy. But the heat of his desire encircled her and held her captive. For a moment, she fought her own craving. But then he turned her to face him, and politics were forgotten. There was no diplomacy in his eyes, only love and a hunger she knew matched her own.

She closed her eyes as his hands moved gently over her body. There was still a bandage below her shoulder, where the bullet had struck her, and he traced its contours, careful not to hurt her, before moving down to her breasts. She caught her breath as his lips followed his fingers, teasing, exploring, revisiting the terrain of her body, no less desirable for its familiarity. She bent over him, letting her hands go inside his shirt, feeling the hardness of his body, the sinewy muscles of his back.

He stood and pulled her to him, and she gasped involuntarily. Quickly, he let her go.

"Did I hurt you?"

"Only when you press against it," she said, indicating her wound.

Carefully, he turned her, so that her back was to him and her injury out of reach. He leaned her over the table, where just that morning he had sat with his advisors and signed the edict to which she objected so strongly. But as he entered her from behind, neither one of them was thinking of the assault on democracy. And as she clutched the table and felt herself closing around him, holding his passion within her body, there was no disagreement. For now, love still conquered all.

3

The last thing Jack Bader felt like doing was partying, but he knew he had no choice. He'd been working with Griffin Sloane ever since he'd arrived at the State Department two years ago, and even though they weren't exactly confidantes, they did consider themselves friends. In Washington, where just showing up, whether at a charity event or on the Senate floor, fulfilled most requirements, Jack's absence from Griffin's engagement party would not only be noted as unfortunate, but would be amplified to insult.

"Hey, Bader," he heard Griffin calling him from the fifty-foot marble bar of the glamorous River Club, "glad you could come."

"Me, too," lied Jack as he made his way past the tables and across the sunken circular dance floor. A band had replaced the usual Friday night pianist for the occasion, and he dodged a few couples swaying desultorily to the music.

"You're finally going to get a chance to meet Daisy," Griffin oozed, accepting Jack's congratulations with an exchange of handshakes and back pats. "She's off with her father doing the usual diplomatic thing, but she'll be back in a minute. I would have introduced you a long time ago, the night of the French cultural exchange party, but you were Mr. Now-you-see-him-now-you-don't."

"I was . . . uh . . . mingling," Jack responded. There was no way he was going to tell Griffin Sloane what he had really been doing that night. They had shared a few personal experiences over sandwiches working late in the office. Jack had mentioned he'd once dated Melinda Myles, and Griffin had waxed poetic about his fiancée, the daughter of a second-level diplomat posted at the American Embassy in Paris. But his brief encounter with the anonymous blonde, as preposterous as it was, seemed both too unimportant and too implausible to bear the prurient scrutiny of a working buddy, especially a straight-arrow Republican like Griffin Sloane. Jack could just imagine Griffin detailing the escapade for his prim little Daisy, milking it for every titillating image to heat up their own prosaic sex life.

In the few months since it had happened, Jack had often thought about the incident himself. He had no way of contacting her, didn't even know her name. When he had turned discreetly away after their encounter in the James Madison Dining Room to give her a chance to dress and compose herself, she had taken the opportunity to disappear. He had thought of looking for her at the reception and then thought better of it. It seemed it was one of those situations best left unexamined, unrepeated. Instead, he had gone to his office where Sam and Drew had given him an unsurprising but positive report on Melinda, then slipped out and gone home. Since then, torn between hope and horror, he looked for her at every official event, disappointed and delighted when she never appeared.

"Well, Bader"—they were joined by Mort Freeman, one of their colleagues at State—"it looks like your friend is turning into another Fidel Castro."

"What?" asked Jack, genuinely confused. Mort was known as the guy around the office who liked to bait people. He was a brilliant theoretician, but no one took him too seriously.

"Roca. He's shut down the press and thrown the publisher, who incidentally fought alongside him in the illustrious revolution, into prison. So much for democracy."

"He's not my friend," Jack said stiffly, unwilling to let Mort see that, this time, he'd succeeded in getting to him. "I met the guy once."

"But you know his wife."

"Knew."

"In the biblical sense, I take it. Does she dig the domination scene, too? I mean you'd be surprised how much of the world's politics is governed by the bedroom proclivities of its leaders."

"Shut up, Mort," said Griffin, and for a minute, Jack was touched that his friend felt he needed defending. "Here comes Daisy," Griffin went on, "and she doesn't need to hear you talk that kind of trash."

Jack smiled. He should have known better than to expect sensitivity in the place of politics as usual. But it didn't matter. He'd take any distraction to change the subject. Even if it meant making small talk with a simpering society girl.

"Honey, this is Jack," he heard Griffin say as he turned to the bar and motioned for a refill. This would require fortification.

"So you're Jack from State," she said.

Jack stopped. He'd heard those exact words before. He knew the voice. He couldn't look. He couldn't not look. He picked up his drink carefully. His hands were shaking, and he was afraid he might drop it. Slowly, he turned.

"Jack, this is the famous Daisy Howard," Griffin said, beaming.

She looked different tonight. Her tousled hair had been tamed into a sleek pageboy, one creamy wave dipping over her forehead to obscure a mocking eye. She was wearing a short-sleeved, fuzzy, angora sweater with tiny sparkling buttons and a long bouffant taffeta skirt in matching pale pink that seemed to absorb the pink neon glow from the coved ceiling. Instead of an icicle, tonight she reminded him of cotton candy. But she still looked like something he wanted to put in his mouth.

"We meet at last," he managed to say, aware that what sounded appropriate to Griffin must sound insipid to her.

"I love that song," she said, not skipping a beat. Jack couldn't even tell what the band was playing. "Want to dance?"

He turned to Griffin, hoping for a refusal or at least a reality check.

"Go ahead," Griffin smiled, clapping him on the back. "You're the one guy I know I can trust with her."

No help there, Jack thought as he followed Daisy to the dance floor. He put his arm around her, trying to keep a seemly distance. The little hairs on her sweater stood on end. He knew it was just static electricity, but it felt like they were reaching for him like thousands of slender tentacles. She moved closer, and for one bizarre moment, he thought she might kiss him. He was shocked and thrilled. Then he realized she only wanted to whisper in his ear.

"Don't tell," she said.

He hadn't thought of saying anything. Now, it occurred to him that maybe he should. "Griffin's my friend."

"What does that mean? He's my fiancé."

"Maybe he has a right to know."

"What? That the woman he's engaged to got drunk one night and fucked a stranger at a diplomatic reception? Do you think that's the kind of knowledge he'd appreciate?"

Jack didn't say anything. He knew she was right. No one liked the messenger with bad news.

"Do you make a habit of it?" he asked.

"Getting drunk? Or fucking strangers?"

"Either. Both."

"Do you want to know to assess the harm to Griffin or to your own ego?"

"Either. Both."

"No."

He pulled away to look at her. For the first time since they had spoken, there was no irony in her voice. Other couples whirled around them, and he realized they had stopped dancing. He tightened his grip around her waist and propelled their bodies into motion again. They danced in silence. He could hear the music now. They were playing "Stardust."

"Don't you want to know why I did it?"

Jack did want to know. But he wasn't going to ask. "You were drunk."

"Yes," she said, "I was. But I knew what I was doing."

"We were both drunk, and I guess, we both knew what we were doing. It doesn't matter." There was no point in pretending she had acted alone.

"It matters to me. I'm not going to marry Griffin."

"Hey, I'm not going to say anything if that's what you're worried about." It had been one of the most remarkable twenty minutes of his life. He was glad that she was willing to admit it meant something to her as well. The least he could do was let her off the hook. "What happened, happened. You can forget about it."

She cocked an eyebrow at him. "Can *you?*"

He had to smile. "Well, maybe keep it as a secret and treasured memory. But it shouldn't get in the way of whatever's between you and Griffin."

"It sort of does."

He wasn't sure he wanted to hear this. But Daisy was going on. "Griffin's a great guy. He's kind, sweet, loving."

"Then maybe you should marry him. One fall from grace doesn't disqualify you."

She smiled, appreciating his generosity of spirit. He noticed the sneer was gone. He hadn't thought it would be possible for her to become more beautiful, but she did.

"I know. It's not guilt. It's greed. Griffin is what he is, and he can only give what he can give. And I thought maybe that would be enough for me. But I needed to know for sure. You helped me figure it out. I want more."

"So I was part of the random sampling. Thanks." He knew he sounded petulant, but he didn't care. He'd gone over the event enough times in his mind to want it to be more than an experiment for a restless libido.

"Don't be bitter." The irony was back in her voice. He found it irritating. And enticing.

"So what are we doing celebrating your engagement?"

"The invitations had already gone out. There's a lot of confusion and embarrassment canceling a party this size. My father's in the State Department. So is Griffin. I just thought they could both save more face if I went through with it. In a couple of weeks, I'll break it to him that I make a better bridesmaid than a bride. By then, nobody will even be thinking about us, then we can make a rueful announcement."

"Daisy Howard, diplomat's daughter."

She pulled away from him and shrugged, assuming he was being derisive. In fact, he had only wanted to say her name.

"Hey," she said with full-scale scorn, "it wasn't the worst thing that ever happened to you."

"No," he agreed, "it wasn't." He was tempted to offer an explanation for his own behavior, an apology for using her to prove something to himself, just as she had used him. But she was already gone, and it didn't seem to matter much. Still, he could not deny the hint of regret as he watched her go, a pink cloud floating away and forever out of reach.

He made his way back to the bar alone. Mort Freeman was there, waiting to pounce.

"So, tell me, buddy. What's your take on San Domenico? Got any inside info?"

"Why? You looking for new boots to lick?"

"Very funny. I've got to do a position paper. Truth is, it doesn't look so good. We're doling out aid, and Amnesty International is piling up complaints."

"Sorry, Mort. I really don't know. I'm not in touch. The last time I was down there was for the wedding. Roca was a big hero."

"Well, the worm turns. How come we always end up backing the wrong guy?"

"Maybe because there are no right guys," said Jack, "us included."

"What made you so cynical?" asked Mort, only half joking. "You used to be the people's choice."

"No, just naive. Washington has a way of teaching you everybody's got an agenda. And it ain't about the public weal."

"Okay. But you've got a personal contact. Maybe if you could find out a little something from Mrs. *El Presidente,* you could pass it on? I'm coaching my kid's soccer team. I don't want to have to go down there and miss half the season."

Jack laughed. "No promises, but I'll see if I can get in touch with her and let you know."

"Thanks, you're a pal."

"No problem," Jack said, failing to add he had his own agenda, too. He hadn't talked to Melinda for two years. Maybe all he needed was an excuse.

Jack had gone through diplomatic channels. Melinda looked at the date of the fax from her old friend requesting contact with her and saw it was a month old. She realized that had she not been sneaking through the files in her husband's office, looking for an order of detention that he had denied issuing, she would not have known of Jack's efforts to reach her. Every day, Diego was becoming more secretive. Every day, he was hiding more from her. Every day, he was answering her increasing questions with bigger lies.

She heard voices and footsteps approaching in the corridor, quickly put the papers back where she found them, and settled herself, smiling, into the worn sofa reserved for guests.

Diego stopped short when he saw her. "What are you doing here?" he asked.

She didn't react to the suspicion in his voice. "Waiting for you, my love," she responded sweetly.

"Are you feeling all right?" She could hear the

genuine concern in his voice. Although she had reason to question his politics, she never doubted his love for her.

"Much better," she said. She'd been having spells of nausea and dizziness, which she attributed to the medication she'd been taking since she'd been hit in the assassination attempt. But her wound had healed, and she'd stopped the medication and she did, indeed, feel better. "I thought since I was feeling so good today, if you didn't have a meeting, maybe we could have lunch together." In fact, she had known he had a meeting in the large reception room of the presidential palace and had not expected him to return to his own office until much later.

"I am sorry," he said, coming to her, putting his arm around her. "I am in the middle of a conference. I only came to get something." She wanted to fling her arms around him and hold him, beg him to stay with her, to stay the person he had always been with her. She only nodded sorrowfully.

There was a discreet cough from one of his advisors, waiting timorously at the door. She could hardly tell them apart. They were a band of sycophants handpicked from the ranks by Diego to replace the old friends who had a habit of telling him what they really thought. As the situation in San Domenico had worsened, Diego had stopped wanting to hear it. Now, he listened only to himself and to the people who agreed with him.

"If *El Presidente* would like," came the toadying suggestion, "we can postpone the meeting for a few hours. No one will mind taking a lunch break."

Diego looked at his watch. "We'll reconvene at four," he said, dismissing them. He turned his full attention to Melinda. His eyes were gentle and full of concern. He looked like the old Diego. Her Diego.

"Why?" she asked him before she could stop herself. "Why have you thrown away everything we were fighting for?" He made an abrupt turn away from her, and she could have kicked herself. She had not intended to confront him. She knew it would only arouse his indignation.

But to her surprise, when he spoke, he sounded more sad than angry. "I wish I could make you understand. I haven't thrown anything away. I'm doing what has to be done to put the country back on its feet. If I don't maintain control, there is chaos. And if there is chaos, San Domenico has no future. Once the economy is moving forward, there will be time for democracy. We can't afford to have it now."

"We can't afford not to have it."

"Melinda, you are a spoiled American. You think that because you dream a dream, it can happen just like that."

"No. I know you have to work to achieve it."

"That's what I'm doing."

"How? By throwing all your old friends in prison? What about their dreams?"

She saw his face harden. "My friends do not try to undermine me. And anyone who dreams of doing so is a traitor." He looked at her, the concern in his eyes masked by a curtain of steel. For the first time, she felt a veiled threat directed against her. It shocked and frightened her.

"Are you trying to tell me something, Diego?"

"Only to be careful, *mi amor*. This is a crucial time in San Domenican history. I can let nothing stand in my way." It was both warning and entreaty. He loved her and wanted her by his side. But he would not allow her to challenge him.

Stunned, she said nothing, and he took her silence for submission. "Nothing has changed," he said reassuringly as his lips grazed her cheek.

Everything has changed, she thought as nausea suddenly gripped her, and she turned her face away. "I'm sorry, I guess I'm not feeling as well as I thought."

"I'll send for the doctor," he said, full of concern again as he looked at her pale face. "You go lie down."

"Maybe I'd better," she agreed, glad to have an excuse to leave him without admitting that she feared it was his presence that was making her ill.

She placed the call from her bedroom, knowing it meant that Diego would learn of it, but she did not have the strength to leave the presidential palace and explain to someone, who would probably just report back to her husband anyway, that she needed an unsecured telephone.

She was grateful for the human response on the other end of the line. Uncertain as she was about what she was going to do, voice mail would have undone her.

Thirty seconds after she gave her name to his secretary, Jack Bader was on the phone. "Melinda? Is it really you?"

He sounded wonderful. She wished he could see her smiling. "It's really me."

There was a momentary stillness. She thought perhaps there was interference on the line.

Then he said, "Are you all right?" And she heard in his voice that the stop had come from his heart and not the wires.

"I'm fine. I've got the flu, but otherwise, I'm fine."

"There have been some rumblings from down there. We've heard . . . I don't know . . . not good things." He knew he sounded ridiculous, but he didn't know what else to say. It would be indelicate to make accusations about a political leader, especially to his wife. Especially when he had no idea how she felt about it all. Although he could guess.

"The things you've heard are all true," she said, and he saw he had guessed right. "Oh, Jack, I wasn't going to get into all of this. I was just going to say hello, hear your voice. But I have to tell someone. I'm not fine. It's getting awful here. I don't know what's happened to Diego."

"The same thing that happens to every other revolutionary who gains power. They're good in the mountains and the jungle, but something happens when you put them in the seat of power," he said without stopping to think whether he was going too far.

"Well, it's happened. And I don't know what to do about it."

"That's kind of how we feel in the State Department."

"But you don't have to live with it," she said softly, and something he heard in her voice made him afraid for her.

"Melinda, is he . . . Are you . . . ?" He didn't even know how to phrase it. But she understood.

"Not yet. Diego loves me. He wouldn't hurt me. But he won't let me get in his way."

"Fine. Then stay out of it. Don't get involved, Melinda. It's true what they say about power corrupting. It's dangerous."

"Do you think I should just keep my mouth shut and let everyone think I go along with this?"

"It doesn't matter what everyone thinks."

"It does to me. I can't do it. It's not a choice."

"Then come home," he said. And with those three words, she saw an alternative she'd refused to recognize before.

"How?" she asked softly, already knowing and fearing it was possible.

Jack reminded himself this was about a developing political situation, not about getting an old flame back. But he was still more excited than he had any right to be.

"We'll find a way." He was thinking fast, off the top of his head. "We can make it an official visit. The State Department can invite you on a goodwill tour. We'll get the Lincoln Center Film Society to give you an award or something. It can be done. Then, you'll just stay."

"He's my husband."

"He's a megalomaniac dictator, who's getting more tyrannical by the minute. If he can be abusive to everyone else, it's just a matter of time before he gets abusive with you. Don't wait for it to happen, and it's too late to get out."

She hesitated. "I don't know."

"Just let me look into it. Let me set some wheels in motion." He realized he had selfish motives for saying what he did, but he also knew that what he said was true. So did she.

"Okay."

"Thank you, Jesus," he breathed fervently, and she laughed.

"Thank *you,* Jack. You're always there for me."

"And always will be."

When she hung up the phone, her heart felt light for the first time in weeks. She didn't feel sick at all. But the doctor had already been called, and not wanting to arouse suspicion, she gamely submitted to his examination.

He took her temperature and her pulse, looked into her eyes and down her throat. He felt her glands and pressed his hands to her abdomen. Finally, he put his assorted instruments back into his bag.

"Señora Roca," he said respectfully, "when was the last time you had your period?"

She was a little taken aback by the question. "I don't really know. I'm fairly regular and I don't have pain, so I'm afraid I've never bothered to keep track. Why do you ask?"

"Because I don't think you are suffering from the flu, madam."

A little knot of dread formed in the pit of her stomach. A wave of nausea hit her again, and she had to lean back against the pillows.

"It is possible?" he asked when she said nothing.

It was more than possible she knew, although she

could not speak. She was amazed she hadn't realized it before. She normally took precautions. But that day in Diego's office, three months ago, when she had come to confront him about closing down the newspaper, she had not been prepared. And since then, the months had come and gone without her thinking about it.

Her face told the doctor all he needed to know. "I will bring a test, just to be sure. But I know my business," he smiled benignly. "You are pregnant."

She knew he was still talking to her, giving her instructions, making arrangements. And she nodded and smiled, responded when necessary with appropriate words. Finally, when he was ready to leave, she made her plea.

"Don't say anything," she begged, and from the look of his face, she knew she needed an excuse. "We should be certain everything is all right before we get *El Presidente*'s hopes up. And if it is, I'd like to tell him myself. You know, in a special way."

The doctor patted her arm, understanding. The wives of the wealthy were always romantic about the first child. Only the poor and the tired had no illusions.

"I will be back tomorrow," he said. "Rest. Everything will be fine. *El Presidente* will be happy," he added as he left her. She smiled and nodded in agreement. When the door closed behind him, she burst into tears.

Drew had wanted to make a ceremony of it, and Ian and Sarah had agreed. For Sam, it would have been enough just to press the button on the control panel and watch the assembly line for the D'Uberville VT-12 start to roll for the first time. There would be time to celebrate when the first car was driven away. But outvoted as she was, she knew the gracious thing would be to comply.

She sat on the small dais with her husband, brother, and sister-in-law, surrounded by designers and foremen, all people who had made the car of her dreams possible. Facing them were the union laborers who would be working the line, and behind the workers, a couple of camera crews. Since the Symingtons and the Taylors had joined forces to keep DMC running, they'd been making good copy. It had more to do with the romantic notion of a wealthy brother and sister married to a blue-collar sister and brother than with the work they were doing, but none of them minded. The publicity was good, and in a competitive marketplace they were going to need all the help they could get to launch a high-end car like the D'Uberville VT-12.

Lunch had been served to the workers and invited guests in the simple but appealing dining room built for the new plant, and now everyone had gathered on the edge of the work floor to hear a few speeches and watch Sam push some buttons to get the machinery started. All of them were aware that it was more a photo opportunity than the actual operation, which would begin in full force in a few days, but as the new director of publicity, Sarah had decreed its importance, and there was no reason to doubt that she was right.

"Don't go to sleep," joked Sarah as she stood to make the opening remarks. "I'm going to keep it short."

Sam smiled at her sister-in-law. Both she and Drew had wanted to include Sarah and Ian in the process of running DMC, but neither one of them could have anticipated how strongly Sarah would take to it. While Ian, with his innate fiscal sense, had quickly found a niche in the financial department, Sarah had positively blossomed in the area of public relations. Drew was amazed to see his once retiring sister leading tours, conducting interviews, supervising advertising, and generally prodding DMC into a higher, more profitable profile. Once stymied by first a domineering father and then an abusive husband, Sarah had, at last, found her own voice.

Fortunately, even though she was no longer too shy to be heard, she also knew when to stop talking, and today, true to her word, her remarks were brief.

"Friends, family, and fellow workers. Today, five years before the millennium, DMC takes us into the twenty-first century. We may not know where we're going in the future, but we know how we're going to get there. In a D'Uberville VT-12. As you well know, the car was designed by our resident automotive genius, my sister-in-law, Samantha Myles Symington. And here, to introduce her to you, is my brother and partner, Andrew Symington."

There was applause and Drew stepped up to the podium. As Drew began his comments with a joke that brought waves of appreciative laughter from his audience, Sarah fidgeted in her seat.

"This is embarrassing," she whispered to Ian, "but I have to go to the bathroom."

"Just go. No one will notice."

"Even if they do, I don't really have a choice. I'll be back in a minute."

Stepping behind the chairs, she moved quickly and quietly in the shadows at the back of the dais until she came to the steps that led down to the factory floor. Then, hurrying so as not to be too conspicuously absent for too long, she headed toward the rest rooms in the rear, behind the belts, the wheels, and widgets that constituted the actual machinery of the line.

Still in a light mood, Drew ended his comments with a rousing introduction of his wife that brought wild applause from the assembled group. Feeling the burden of her popularity, Sam stepped to the control panel, realizing how much she represented to how many people. For the press she was the great female hope, a photogenic woman who was succeeding in a traditionally male bastion. But for the people, she was the future. She would bring them work and the chance to step out of the cycle of unemployment and poverty. They would build her cars and, in so doing, build aspirations and ambitions of their own.

Proudly and profoundly moved, Sam slowly brought her hand to the green start button and pushed. There was a rumbling as the apparatus churned into motion. The conveyor belt started to roll. The applause grew louder. And then, suddenly, drowning out the cheers and the gears, there was an explosion from behind the dais, loud enough to shock them into silence as everything came to a sickening halt.

For an instant no one spoke, allowing the horror to register. Sam stood with her mouth agape, her mind already tracking and dismissing possible explanations for what went wrong.

And then, Ian screamed, "Sarah. My God, Sarah went back there."

He jumped up, sending his chair flying backward as he ran off the dais, Drew following close behind. Sam froze as pandemonium broke out. People were running around her onto the factory floor toward the explosion. A steady murmur grew into a rumble, interspersed with shouting. She could not make out the words over the beating of her heart and the screaming in her head.

If anything happened to Sarah . . . She could not even finish the thought.

She had no idea how much time had passed, she assumed only seconds, before the words broke through. The cameras were on her and the reporters were pressing around her.

"Mrs. Symington . . ."

"Sam . . ."

"What happened?"

"What went wrong?"

"I don't know," was all she could say, still stunned.

"What does this mean for the future of the VT-12?"

Sam looked at her interrogator incredulously, then realized they didn't know. Only the family and the few people gathered around the dais had been able to discern Ian's anguished cry. She didn't know what to say.

"The car doesn't matter. My sister-in-law . . . ," she began and then she stopped in midsentence.

"What?" they were asking confused.

But Sam was already moving away from them, running toward Ian and Drew, who were coming toward her, Sarah between them, all of them whole and unharmed.

"Oh, God, Sarah," she said as the four of them met in the middle of the room and hugged. "I was so scared."

"Me, too," Sarah laughed ruefully. "I was on the pot when I heard it. You know the expression 'scared the shit out of me'?"

They all laughed and hugged again. By now, the press had caught up and were demanding to know what was going on.

Drew took over. "We don't know. There was an explosion in the motor that drives the conveyor belts. There's a lot of twisted metal, and pieces of machinery were thrown in all directions. Fortunately, no one was in the vicinity and there were no injuries. When we are able to assess the cause of the explosion and the extent of the damage, we will make a statement."

There were more shouted questions, but Drew raised his hand in protest. "I'm sorry. As you can see, this has been quite a shock to the family. We'll get back to you when we know more." And huddled together, like a phalanx of four, they pushed their way out of the factory.

Filled with relief that Sarah was unhurt, the crushing disappointment of the failure of her work didn't hit Sam until they were back at Belvedere. The police and fire department had anticipated it would take them a few days to conduct their investigation, and then the painstaking process of reexamination would begin in earnest. She had no idea what had happened or how to fix it, whether the problem lay in the design of the robotics on the assembly line or in some specification she herself had laid out. As they sat in the salon, with Ian assessing the financial damage, Sarah remarking on the publicity setback, and Drew wondering about the effect on other cars in the DMC lineup, no one blamed Samantha. Still, she blamed herself.

Expecting no conclusive news for several days, they were surprised when barely an hour later, Chief Joseph Mulcahey of the Oakdale Fire Department was ushered into the room.

Sam and Drew greeted him warmly, remembering his kindness to them after a factory fire years ago, and introduced him to Ian and Sarah.

"I'm sorry to be meeting you folks again under similar circumstances," he said solicitously.

"You're telling me," answered Drew. "The fates seem to want to line our path with obstacles."

Chief Mulcahey shook his head. "I'm afraid the fates have nothing to do with it. You got sabotaged again."

"What?!" The four of them were on their feet.

"Who would do that?" cried Sarah.

"I was hoping you could tell me," Mulcahey responded.

Sam looked at Drew. She knew they were thinking the same thing. Forrest Symington was dead. He could not come back from the grave to ruin them as he had once tried to do. This time, they had no clues.

"Are you sure about this?" asked Ian.

Mulcahey nodded. "Whoever it was used the simplest device possible. Plastique with a timer slapped right onto the machine. There're bits of it all over. Someone put it there. But we can't tell when, and we don't know who."

Drew turned to his sister, hopeful. "Sarah, you went back there just before it happened. Did you see anyone?"

Sarah thought for a minute. "To tell you the truth, I was so dazed by the explosion, I literally can't remember a thing from the time I got off the dais to the time you came back and found me."

"Well, you folks put your heads together and see what you can come up with. Explosive experts are still on the site, and the police are going to want you to come down tomorrow and make some statements. Meanwhile, you better all be careful. Someone's out to get you."

That night, no one was hungry and dinner went untouched. Too confused and shell-shocked to discuss it any longer, Sam and Drew went up to the west wing to relieve Mrs. Halsey. They'd brought the baby-sitter with them from Washington to help Moira make the transition. She'd become just plain Halsey and a member of the family by now, but they still enjoyed putting their daughter to bed themselves.

"What about you, honey? Are you tired?" Ian asked his wife.

"Exhausted," she acknowledged as she let him lead

her to their east-wing bedroom. The day had worn them all down.

But an hour later, after Ian had long since fallen into a deep sleep, Sarah lay with her eyes wide open. The window was open, and a soft breeze made the curtains billow around the frames. Still, she felt as though she could not breathe. Slipping silently out of bed, she threw off her nightgown and wriggled into a T-shirt and a pair of jeans. She hesitated a moment to make sure her husband was still asleep before gently closing the door behind her. Then taking the stairs two at a time, she ran out the door.

Looking back at the house from the circular drive in front, she saw that it was dark. Only the exterior lights left on all night to illuminate the majestic columns and porticos of the mansion were beaming. Her car, a small D'Uberville sedan, was parked in the drive where she had left it. Usually, Robert washed it and put it away for her at the end of each day as part of his butler's duties. But in the bedlam of the after noon, she had forgotten to give him the keys. Now, as she got in, careful not to slam the door behind her, she was glad she didn't have to use the garage opener and risk waking up the staff or, even worse, her family with the motorized sound of the rising doors.

She drove quickly, not certain where she was going, and found herself leaving the tree-lined boulevards of Woodland Cliffs for the starker streets of Oakdale. She drove for a while, thinking she might be lost, then suddenly realizing she knew what she was looking for as she passed a sign flashing its identity in the shape of a red neon bottle. She crunched into reverse and came to a stop in front of the bar.

Inside, there was a desultory crowd, mostly men, mostly gathered around a pool table in the back. She sauntered to the bar and perched on a stool.

"Hey, how're ya doin'?" the bartender greeted her, putting a short glass in front of her and filling it with a shot of standard whiskey. She downed it neat and plunked her glass on the bar for another. He filled it again, smiling.

"Tough day, huh?"

"Tough life." She laughed.

She hadn't noticed the man at the other end of the bar, but now he made his way to her and, without invitation, took the stool next to hers.

"Don't I know you?" he asked, a hopeful grin on his unshaven face.

She looked at him and took another swallow.

"I doubt it," she said. "I don't even know myself," and then she laughed so long and hard at her own joke that he thought she must be crazy and moved back to where he had come from.

In the morning, when Ian woke up, his wife lay beside him, her breath soft and measured. He kissed her gently on the cheek and she stirred.

"It's after eight," he said. "Do you want to get up for breakfast?"

"I hardly got any sleep last night," she mumbled. "I had weird dreams. I think I'm just going to stay in bed."

"All right, sweetheart." And then, unable to resist, he kissed her again and said, "I love you, Sarah."

"Sunny," she seemed to say through her slumbering haze.

"What?" Ian asked, unable to discern her sleepy muttering.

But she was dead asleep and did not answer.

4

Melinda was still in bed when Diego came with flowers, a huge bouquet of anthurium, orchids, and birds-of-paradise, trailing vines of sweet-smelling jasmine. She understood immediately why he was there.

"He wasn't supposed to tell you," she said. "I told him I wanted to tell you myself."

Diego was beaming. "Don't blame the doctor. I was worried about you. I wouldn't let him go until he gave me a prognosis. I think he was afraid I'd put him in jail." He laughed but stopped when he saw that his wife didn't consider his last remark funny.

"Ah, Melinda." He leaned over her on the bed, resting his head on her belly. Even when she was angry, she could not resist his touch. Of their own accord, her fingers moved tenderly through his hair.

She closed her eyes and fervently wished for things to be the way they once were.

It wasn't the first time he'd read her mind. "Listen to me, *mi amor.* We have to move forward. You weren't here before. You don't know what terrible times the people had. For their sake, for the sake of their children, for *our* child, we can't go back."

"I know that, Diego. But it seems you've forgotten your own principles."

"I haven't, believe me. But I'm like a doctor treating the sick. The patient has pneumonia. It is getting worse. He insists he only has a small cold and can do whatever he likes. If I don't force him to stay home and take his medicine, the patient will die. When the patient is well, then . . ." He shrugged. "Whatever he wants. Until then, freedom makes no sense. It is no more than a sentence of death. I want more than that for our country. For our baby."

Melinda heard the plea for understanding in his voice. She could see he was completely sincere in what he said. She had always trusted him, his instincts, and his honor. Why should she doubt him now? She looked at him. His eyes were tender. She could feel the warmth of his hands as they gently pressed her abdomen.

"My son," he said quietly as she guided his hand to a spot below her right rib. They stayed that way for a moment, not speaking, Diego's head on her breast, his hand on her belly, her hand on his.

"Or daughter," amended Melinda, a touch of warning in her voice.

"Do you think I would mind?" he crowed. "A daughter, a son, it doesn't matter. It will be our child.

Half you, half me. Boy or girl, there will be love. Boy or girl, there will be opportunity. Isn't that what's important? Don't we still agree on that?"

"Of course."

"Then let's forget politics between us. Let's be mother and father. Husband and wife."

Melinda sighed. She still had faith in his essential goodness, even though his tactics frightened her. He was kissing her neck. She couldn't think when he kissed her.

"Diego," she whispered, tears in her eyes. "You were such a hero. Not just to me. To everyone. Don't betray that."

He stopped kissing her and pulled away. "I'm not a hero," he said vehemently. "I am just a man. Whatever else people imagined I cannot change. Like any other man, I can only do what I think is right." His eyes sought hers, and she saw that he was suffering as much as she was. "Don't punish me for not being what I never claimed to be."

"I? How could I punish you?"

"By taking away your love. I know things were simpler in the jungle. There was one enemy and one way to fight him. Now, the enemy is intangible. It's not a man, but an attitude I have to fight. I admit not everyone agrees with what I'm doing. Not even you. Does that make me less of a person? Do you need me to be a hero to love me? Because if you do, I am lost. I cannot be more than I am. And without you, I am nothing."

Melinda touched her husband's cheek. He was so beautiful, so gentle, it was hard to remember that, lately, she had known him to be cruel. And even though his words, so full of passion and ardor, confused her, they still gave her hope. He took her hand and put it to his lips, the pain gone from his face. For now, he knew that he had won.

It had taken Jack several weeks to get everything in order. He had realized immediately that getting Melinda into the country would mean more than booking her a ticket on the next flight out. Diego Roca was developing a reputation as a ruthless autocrat and would not take kindly to the notion that an American had helped his wife escape his clutches. If things weren't handled with subtlety, there was no question an international incident would occur. Everything had to appear spontaneous, without ulterior motive. She had to be invited to the States for a legitimate reason, and then her choice to stay would have to be only her own. At least, as an American national, she had every right to remain.

In the end, it was the Academy of Motion Picture Arts and Sciences that came through for him. The Academy Award presentations were only a month away. Jack made them realize how prestigious it would be for Melinda Myles to present the Jean Hirschorn Humanitarian Award. It was the perfect rationale—not just an occasion for selfish glory, but an appearance to applaud service to humankind. It would be hard for even Diego to turn down the opportunity for such good press when he needed it most.

Jack was surprised by how long it took her to come to the phone. He nervously waited, wondering if perhaps something had happened to her, if the proposed rescue had come too late. He kicked himself for insisting on fine-tuning the details before calling her. As it happened, he was right to worry.

"Jack," she said when she finally answered. "It's so good of you to call." Her voice was warm but distant. He wondered if it was safe for him to speak. He doubted it.

"I've been working on what we talked about, Mrs. Roca," he said carefully.

She understood his caution and followed suit. "I knew you would. And I thank you. But it appears I won't be needing your assistance after all."

"But it's all arranged," he said, trying not to let the dismay ring in his voice. "In one month, the Academy Awards wants you to present—"

She stopped him, interrupting. "In one month, I won't be able to travel."

"Why?" he asked, and she could hear the alarm. Obviously he thought she was being detained against her will, and she hastened to assure him that was not the case.

"Because, Jack," she said softly, "I'm pregnant."

He sat down; his knees were shaking. He had expected all sorts of difficulties, but not this. Somehow, with all the provisions he had had to make, he had thought of what he was doing as negotiations for the return of a prisoner of war. He had conveniently forgotten that her captor was her husband.

"Oh, no," was all he could say.

"No," she responded, "don't be upset. I'm happy about this, really."

"What about Roca?"

"He's happy, too. He's in a difficult position, and

maybe I made things harder with my naive demands. But I think things are going to be different."

"Because you're pregnant?" he asked incredulously.

"Well, yes," she said, a little uncertain.

"You think a baby is going to bring back the democratic process?"

When he put it that way, she knew it sounded stupid. But, in fact, she did feel that her being pregnant had made Diego open to listening to her. She felt herself resenting Jack's scornful tone.

"Diego knows my concerns and is sympathetic to them," she announced with a little more hauteur than she had intended. She softened. "Becoming a parent changes the way you feel about a lot of things, Jack. I can't explain it. It just does."

He froze at her condescension, at the insinuation that he just wouldn't understand about family since he had no part in it.

"In that case," he said stiffly, "I take it you'd like me to inform the Academy that you won't be able to participate?"

"I'm sorry. I know you must have worked hard to make it happen."

"Don't worry about it. It's all part of the diplomatic process. That's what you do when you work for the State Department."

"Please don't be angry."

"Of course not." He forced himself to smile, as if his expression could transmute into his voice. He was furious. "Circumstances being what they are, I certainly understand your decision."

"Thank you, Jack," she said, although she could

hear he didn't understand at all. There was a hint of desperation in her voice as she added, "I need to believe that I'm doing the right thing. For me and my baby."

"Well, you know how to reach me if . . ." He let his voice trail off. "And Melinda . . ."

"Yes?" she asked, hoping for a word of compassion, conciliation.

"Congratulations." He hung up the phone before she could respond. He knew it wasn't State Department policy to end a conversation with the wife of the leader of another country, especially one with which relations were so tenuous. But the combination of love, anger, jealousy, disappointment, and yearning that raged within him made it impossible for him to exchange any more small talk.

He tried to make himself calm down. He didn't know what he had expected. He hadn't articulated his dreams, even to himself, but he knew that he had been hoping for the impossible. What could she have done? Come to America, move into his small Washington apartment with him, forget she was married to the president of San Domenico? Whatever he had imagined, the reality was that she was pregnant by Diego Roca, not by him. He could not fault her for trying to maintain a relationship with the father of her unborn child. And yet, he did.

Still angry, he strode across the hall to Griffin Sloane's office. Even though Jack didn't like to introduce his personal life in the office, since it was State Department business, Griffin had been privy to his stratagem for getting Melinda home. Now, he wanted to blow off steam, share a few disparaging words with someone who could empathize. But Griffin was not in his office and his secretary, heading out for lunch, said he'd been called to a meeting with the Senate Foreign Relations Committee. Not completely aware of what he was doing, Jack watched the secretary get into the elevator, then casually strolled over to her desk and started rifling her Rolodex. It only took him a moment to find Daisy Howard. Hastily, he jotted her address on a piece of paper. And then, after returning to his own office just long enough to switch on his voice mail, he announced that he was leaving for the day.

"Is Miss Howard expecting you?" the doorman at the luxury apartment building on Connecticut Avenue asked him.

Jack hesitated. He knew he had no business being there. He wondered if perhaps she would refuse to see him.

"Sir?" the doorman asked again.

"Uh, yes, she is," Jack lied foolishly. "Jack Bader. I'm her lawyer," he explained, offering too much information as all his guilty clients were wont to do.

The doorman put the phone to his ear. "Mr. Jack Bader to see you, Miss Howard. He said you were expecting him."

There was an inordinately long pause as the doorman listened. Jack waited to be turned away. It served him right. He should have called. Actually, he shouldn't even have come.

"Go right up, sir. Eighteen A. First elevator on the right."

Jack moved quickly. He wouldn't leave her time to change her mind. Or his. The elevator door opened on a long carpeted corridor. He walked quickly all the way down the hall until he found A. He pressed the bell and heard the chimes ring inside.

"It's open."

He pushed his way in. The apartment was bright and modern, with shiny hardwood floors and spare, classic furniture. He was surprised. Somehow, he had expected something blue and smokey, like a boite in a basement in Paris, a scene set for the second-rate film noir he felt himself to be living. Instead, all the furniture was white and Italian, except for a black leather Eames chair, clearly an original, that was positioned by a bay window that looked out over Dupont Circle.

"So, Jack from State," she said from behind him in that voice that always seemed to hit him in the gut. He whirled. She was wearing a Japanese kimono, black with white dragons and drying her hair, which hung in wet silvery waves over her face.

"I'm sorry," he stammered, realizing he'd gotten her out of the shower. "I was . . . uh . . . just passing by and I . . . uh . . ."

She grinned, and he knew he sounded like a fool. What could he say? He had no idea why he had come. He was angry at himself for being there, angry at her for making him want to stay.

"I was in the shower," she said huskily. It was just a statement of fact, but it sounded like a taunt.

"So I see." He looked at his watch. It was almost two. "Is this the crack of dawn for you?"

She raised an eyebrow. If he was trying to get a rise out of her, that was as far as she would go.

"Actually," she informed him, "the crack of dawn is the crack of dawn for me."

"Personal trainer kept you busy all this time?" he guessed. Nature alone could not make so perfect a form as the one he glimpsed enveloped in her tightly wound kimono.

She shook her head, spraying water like a dog. He took a step back, aware it had been directed at him.

"Soup kitchen," was all she said and started to head to the back of the apartment, dismissing him.

"What?"

"I work in a soup kitchen twice a week from six to noon. I'm righteous enough to go but not to dispense with an hour-long shower every time I get home. My virtue, as you well know, has its limitations."

He thought he detected a note of bitterness. He felt like a heel. Quickly, he stepped in front of her and blocked her path of escape.

"Can I start again?" he asked humbly.

"Do you want a cup of coffee?"

"Very much."

He followed her to the small but complete kitchen on the other side of the living room. Coffee was already brewing, and she poured a mug for each of them.

"I don't know why I came," he admitted.

"I do," she said softly. There was no archness in her tone. It was just a statement of fact. He realized he knew, too; he just wasn't ready to say. She was braver than he was, more honest.

"Did you . . . ?" he asked.

"Yes. Didn't Griffin tell you?"

"No."

"It's embarrassing for him, I guess. That's why I didn't want to make a big announcement before the party. This way, people will just forget about it, and then when they say, 'Hey, weren't you supposed to be getting married?' He can just say, 'Oh, that! No, that was over a long time ago. She was a bitch.' And then they can say, 'Well, you're better off without her then.' And that will be that."

"Is he heartbroken?"

"Griffin?" she laughed as though it were absurd to even imagine the possibility.

"I would be," he said softly.

She saw that he meant it and was touched. "That's why . . . after you . . . I couldn't stay with Griffin."

She had thrown aside the towel, and her hair had dried naturally in soft waves around her face like a downy halo. She looked scrubbed and innocent, all traces of the sleek femme fatale washed away. But she was just as beautiful and even more alluring. His hand reached out and traced a silky curl to her cheek, then moved down her cheek to rest in the hollow of her throat, then down again to linger in the curve of her breast. She sighed deeply but did not move. He rose then and came to her, letting his lips trace the route his hand had drawn. Her robe fell open and he saw what he had only felt in the darkness of their first driven encounter. The sharp angle of her hip bones separated by the soft curve of pearly flesh, leading to the small triangular rise of golden curls, darker than the white blond hair of her head, bespeaking the treasure within. He let his hand drop down and maneuver between her guardian thighs, neither giving nor resisting, until he found the prize he sought, warm and moist, ready for discovery.

"Do you have a bed?" he whispered.

"Do we need one?" she asked, and he heard the mocking tone that had identified her from the moment they met.

Again, it enticed and irritated him. He wanted to surrender to it and conquer it at the same time. "We've already done it on a table. Now, I want to make love to you in bed."

He picked her up and carried her down the hall from which she'd come to greet him. He was surprised at how light she was in spite of her height. The bedroom door was open, the bed unmade.

"I was late this morning . . . ," she began by way of apology. He would have laughed to realize that in all that she'd revealed to him since they met, only a messy apartment embarrassed her. But he was already kicking aside the white Battenburg lace-covered quilt and laying her down on the plain white sheet.

"Don't move," he instructed her as he gently removed her kimono, then quickly stripped off his own clothes.

Fully naked together for the first time, they allowed their eyes, their hands, their mouths, to explore each other's bodies. Then, letting the length of him cover her, with his lips upon her lips, he gently entered her, moving them together, conjoined in flesh and spirit, until they exploded in a fusion of heat and desire that reverberated in both body and soul.

Afterward, she lay in the crook of his arm, his fingers entwined in the silky white gold of her hair.

"We still don't know very much about each other," Jack mused, teasing her with the truth.

"Really? I think we know all we need to know. At the very least, we know more than most."

He knew she was right. But still, there was something about the wry, brittle surface of this woman that made him want to crack it open and expose the sweet, delicate core within. He was intoxicated with what he saw, but he was prepared to love what she might reveal.

"I'm interested in the stuff that *doesn't* matter," he countered. "Like did you have a dog when you were growing up? And do you remember your first kiss ever?"

She laughed, "Actually, I do. Bahati Buyoya. I was nine years old. My father was posted in Burundi. And his father was a chief of the Tutsi tribe. We found each other very exotic."

He smiled. "Unconventional even then."

"What about you?" she teased in turn. "Do you have a past?"

"Yes."

"Do you want to share it with me?"

"Right now, Daisy Howard, I want to share everything in my life with you, past, present, and future," he said without thinking and was surprised to realize that, for the moment, he meant it.

She rewarded him with a dazzling smile, and an even more breathtaking kiss. After that, they didn't talk again for quite a while.

* * *

Ian heard about it first. The letters had been sent out on DMC Financial stationery, and irate stockholders had begun to call his office the next day. He had dismissed the first caller as a crackpot, calmly insisting that under no circumstances would DMC send a letter to shareholders admitting to misrepresenting the company's financial status because nothing was further from the truth. But when the second, third, and fourth calls turned into a barrage, all complaining about the same supposed letter, Ian realized he had a "situation" on his hands. Rather than admit bafflement to nervous investors, he deftly sidestepped their inquiries, assuring them that a mistake had been made and that everything was under control. Then, he stopped taking calls.

He asked his secretary to find a way to get hold of this letter without admitting that his department had no idea of what was going on and then rushed to see his brother-in-law.

"Drew, did you send out some kind of mea culpa letter from my office?" he asked, bursting into the office without waiting to be announced.

"What are you talking about?" Drew asked evenly, not at all dismayed by Ian's lack of ceremony. Unlike his father, Drew was dismissive of formality and had fostered an open-door policy for everyone, not just family members.

"Apparently, someone sent a letter to the stockholders telling them that DMC is in serious financial trouble and is misrepresenting their status."

"What?! Who the hell did that?"

"That's what I'd like to know."

"Do you have the letter?"

"My secretary is tracking one down for me now. But I was quoted portions of it. It's not good. And it's definitely not true."

"Shit. More sabotage."

"It's internal, isn't it?" asked Ian, knowing the answer.

"Has to be," brooded Drew. "That's how they got past security to blow up Sam's line. That's how they got a mailing out to DMC shareholders."

"This is scary."

"You're telling me. We've got to find out who's doing it and who they're doing it for and destroy them before they destroy us."

Security was beefed up and new passwords installed on the computers, but if the enemy was within, he wasn't going to be easily exposed.

Sarah put out a press release, trying to countermand the effects of the letter, insisting that DMC was as sound as it ever was. But a certain amount of damage had been done. The shot, once fired, could not be put back in the gun. Then they gathered forces and braced for the next attack.

It came from left field, surprising them with an assault on the personal instead of the corporate front. Sarah saw it in a gossipy column masquerading as business news in the *Woodland Cliffs Spectator*. By the time Sam had finished sending Moira off for a half day of nursery school and settled down to her usual breakfast and newspaper, the item was already missing.

"Hey, what's happened to the paper?" Sam asked, holding up the torn page.

"Oh, sorry," said Sarah, hastily getting up from the table, "there was an ad I wanted."

"Don't we have another paper?"

"No."

"How come? We usually have four."

"I don't know, Sam. Do I look like the paper boy?"

Sam poised for a retort, then thought the better of it. They'd all been on edge lately. There was no point in exacerbating it. "I just wish you had waited until I'd read the paper before ripping it up," was all she said.

"I'm sorry," reiterated Sarah with undue emphasis. "Do you want me to give you back the page?"

"No," Sam backed down, not wanting to make a federal case out of nothing. "It doesn't matter."

"I've got to head out," said Sarah, already at the door. "Are you ready to go yet?"

"No, I'll take my own car."

Sam sighed, remembering the early heady days of their partnership when they all seemed to share the same ideals and the same schedules. Since the start of the subversion at DMC, they'd evolved different time frames and agendas, their paths crossing and diverging throughout the day. Drew went to work before her, wanting to be at the plant before the early shift arrived, leaving her to greet Moira alone each morning. At night, though they tried to spend time with their daughter, work they brought home from the office frequently separated them immediately after she'd gone to sleep.

Ian and Sarah, too, seemed preoccupied with the mounting problems at DMC. Dinners, which, by their own choice, never attained the ceremony of

Mathilde's formal affairs, had usually been a happy gathering for the four of them, plus guests on occasion, in which they exchanged information and opinions in the casual bonhomie of family partners. But now, even though they were all quick to acknowledge that they were in this together, the tension had risen to the point where being in each other's company only made it worse.

Sam finished her coffee and got up from the table.

"You'd better take an umbrella, Miss Samantha," Robert said. "They're predicting rain."

"Okay, Robert." Sam smiled. He had been the butler for Forrest and Mathilde for twenty years, but he'd had no difficulty in switching allegiance from father to son. At the beginning he had called her Mrs. Symington, but Sam kept thinking he was talking to Mathilde. She had tried to get him to call her Sam, like everybody else, but even though he had accepted that the household under the younger generation would be less formal, that was going too far. In the end, they had compromised on Miss Samantha, which echoed the way he'd been addressing Sarah and Drew since they were small children and made Sam feel like she belonged.

In the hall, a huge ceramic umbrella stand filled with all patterns and varieties of umbrellas invited her to make her selection. She started to pull out a large Italian floral, only to feel it catch on something inside the receptacle. Assuming it was another umbrella, she pulled and heard the crunch of paper. Curious, she looked inside and saw a page of newspaper had been casually crumpled and tossed into the stand, where it had been pierced by the spokes of her chosen umbrella. She reached in and pulled it out, wondering if some new maid had mistaken the umbrella stand for a wastepaper basket. But a moment later, the absurdity of her assumption struck her. And then she noticed the date on the top of the page.

"I don't believe her," Sam said aloud. "She rips up my paper because she says she needs something, then throws it away. What a nerve."

"Beg pardon, ma'am?" Robert was at her arm, responsive to her every mumble.

"Oh, nothing, Robert. I'm just talking to myself." He turned to go, and then it struck her. "Robert," she said, stopping him, "what happened to this morning's papers?"

"Miss Sarah told me they weren't needed and I should throw them out. But I'd better tell the truth," he amended guiltily. "Since they were today's, I distributed them to members of the staff. Is that a problem?"

"No, Robert. Not at all. You did the right thing."

He nodded, certain that he had. "May I take that from you?" he asked, reaching for the crumpled page in her hand, assuming it was garbage.

"Uh . . . no, thank you. I'll . . . uh . . . just hold on to it. There's an ad on it I want to see."

He nodded again and moved away, sensitive to even the gentlest of dismissals. She lay the page on the hall table and smoothed it out, glancing at first one side, then the other. There were no ads that could have been of any discernible interest to Sarah. She began to scan the articles, wondering what the hell had gotten into her sister-in-law, and then she spotted it in the "Business on the Move" column. It was only a paragraph, halfway through the column, but she knew it was the reason that Sarah had tried to prevent her from seeing the paper.

"With all DMC's problems, you'd think that heir Drew Symington would be too busy to be dropping in on old flames. But we have it on good authority that although he's married to gorgeous auto genius Samantha Myles, the beleaguered CEO is looking for a little tension relief with former fiancée Bethany Havenhurst. Like they say, it's the exception that proves the rule. Even with steak at home, some guys still crave that occasional hamburger."

She read it three times before the rage hit her. She was angry at both of them: Drew for betraying her and Sarah for trying to cover for him, although she realized she might have done the same thing for Melinda if called upon. She was angry at herself as well, for believing she had become immune, that all their past mishaps had somehow inoculated them against heartbreak. But there was no vaccine against betrayal. She thought about how their schedules had evolved in the past few months, about Drew's insistence on going to the plant almost every night for an hour or two, ostensibly to surprise would-be saboteurs. But when he returned home, of course, there was nothing to report, and now she wondered if perhaps those forays into the night had more to do with making mischief than stopping it. She was tempted to go upstairs and pack, stop off at Moira's little school and pick her up, then drive away.

She was still standing in the foyer when Robert

came to her, carrying a telephone. "Your husband, madam," he said, holding the phone out to her.

She shook her head. "I can't speak to him now."

"Shall I tell him you are on your way into the office? He wanted to know."

"You can just tell him to go to hell," she said and, turning her back, stormed up the stairs.

"I'm sorry, Mr. Drew. She doesn't seem to be able to come to the phone right now."

"Is she coming to work?"

"I can't say, sir."

"Well, did you ask her?"

"Yes."

"What did she say?"

"She said I should tell you to go to hell."

"Oh, shit," said Drew. "She didn't happen to be looking at the newspaper, did she?"

"Not exactly, sir. Although she did have a page of it . . ."

"Robert, whatever you do, don't let her out of the house until I get home."

"How am I going to be able to do that, sir?"

"I don't know. You're a butler. You're supposed to be resourceful." And without another word, he slammed down the phone.

Fortunately for Robert, Sam had barricaded herself in her room and had made no attempt to leave the premises when Drew arrived just fifteen minutes later. Racing up the stairs, he pushed his way into their room, not bothering to knock. He found her staring at an open suitcase, half-filled with clothes, which she started to pitch at him the minute he walked through the door.

"Stop!" he shouted, dodging the flying underwear.

"Get out. I don't want to see you," she yelled back at him, looking for something else to throw now that the suitcase was empty again.

"Are you crazy, Sam? What are you doing?"

"Getting away from you." She saw a pair of socks she had missed on the floor and lobbed it at him. He caught it with one hand and threw it back. It landed softly in her lap. She was tempted to throw it back, but she already saw the beginnings of a smile on his face and had no desire to turn her anger into farce.

"Why are you doing this?" His voice was quiet, gentle. It took the wind from her sails.

"As if you didn't know," she mumbled, tears welling in her eyes for the first time since she'd read about his perfidy.

Seeing her rage was abating, no longer afraid of a violent attack, he came to the bed and sat down beside her. She shrugged him off when he tried to put his arm around her, but she did not move. He took it as a good sign.

"Sam," he said with dead seriousness, "I'm ashamed of you."

She looked at him in shock, her mouth agape. "Me?! You're ashamed of me?! I'm not doing anything!"

"Neither am I," he said matter-of-factly.

"Oh, no? You'd better tell that to the press."

"I will."

"You've been seen with Bethany, for God's sake. What the hell is that about?"

"I have no idea. I haven't seen Bethany in years. And I have no desire to."

"But it said . . . ," she trailed off. They both knew what it said.

"Did it ever occur to you it might not be true? Did it occur to you to even ask me?"

She stopped short. He was right. Something was happening to them all and it was making them lose perspective.

"Is it true?" she asked a little meekly.

"No."

"Then why did Sarah try to hide it from me?"

"Because she's paranoid. Like the rest of us. I don't know if she thought she was saving me or you, but it was stupid and unnecessary."

Sam felt like an idiot. As quick as she had been to accuse Drew, she was now willing to admit that she had been wrong. She had no idea why she had leaped to the assumption that a paragraph in a slimy gossip column was all the proof she needed to end her marriage. Except that, like Drew said, they were all paranoid.

"It's not paranoia," she amended. "Someone really is after us. This little item was planted to upset us. And maybe our stockholders, too. Oh, God, Drew. I'm sorry."

"Never mind," Drew said, accepting his wife's apology with a kiss. "I've talked to Sarah. She's issuing another statement."

"That will probably just make it worse. People will just pay more attention."

"Maybe. But she thinks it's better to nip it in the bud. And it's her department, so I said okay."

"This is so crazy, Drew. What's going to happen to us next? It's getting really scary."

Although he was just as nervous as his wife, Drew tried to reassure her. "No, I think it's turned the corner. Increased security must be working, if whoever is doing this has been reduced to planting blind items attacking our personal lives in the gossip columns. They can't get at the plant. They can't get at the stockholders. Now, if we just make sure they can't get at us, we're going to force them to give it up."

"Do you really think so?"

"I'm sure of it."

"You're lying."

"Okay, I'm not completely sure. But I hope so."

"You're not lying about anything else, are you?"

"Samantha!"

"Okay, okay, I believe you. I was just checking."

"Anyway, you should be grateful about one thing in that smarmy little article."

"What's that?"

"You were referred to as the steak."

They laughed and kissed. He helped her collect her clothes from the various corners of the room and put them back in her drawers. She was too embarrassed to leave the mess for the staff to clean up.

"We'd better get to work," she said when they were done.

"Well," Drew lingered. "It is lunchtime, and we're already here."

"Do you want lunch?"

"Not exactly," he said with a smile. "But I do want my steak."

She came to him and let him draw her down on the bed. Time and opportunity hadn't decreased the pleasure that they took in each other one iota. They made love with passion and commitment, and this time with a little more abandon than usual. They were both aware, though neither one of them would admit it, that the future was not as certain as they had once supposed.

5

Even in her eighth month, Melinda looked like a movie star. She carried the baby high, like a beach ball, wedged between voluptuous breasts and still shapely legs. At the beginning of her pregnancy, as her belly grew and her body altered, she had felt undesirable, certain that her husband would find her overripe form disgusting. Instead, he had basked in her pregnancy, savoring the feel of her skin stretched over the mound that would one day be his child. And, in the end, he had made her come to see its beauty, to enjoy the grace of her roundness and relish the changes that signified impending motherhood.

Preoccupied as she was with her own development, Melinda stopped focusing on what was happening in the country. Encouraged by Diego, who insisted she ought not to be upset or distracted and who promised that he understood her humanitarian concerns and shared them, she stopped involving herself in San Domenican politics. With her pregnancy as an excuse, Diego turned down all requests for his wife to appear in public. And although, at first, Melinda had felt a little confined by his overzealous concern for her, after a while, she grew to appreciate it. And, as with many pregnant women, she found that the act of growing her own child was fulfillment enough for the time being.

For the celebration of the third anniversary of independence, Melinda thought perhaps they should make an exception. Feeling fit and looking fine, she thought it would be a positive gesture for her to appear at Diego's side for the inevitable parades and speeches. She had expected to have to woo Diego to the idea, but to her surprise, even Clara, the nurse that Diego had assigned to watch over her and who had become her closest companion in the months of her seclusion, was also dead set against it.

"But why, Clara? Don't you think it would be good for the people to see me after all this time? I mean, they must be wondering why I suddenly disappeared from public life."

"Everyone knows you're pregnant. You're in your last month, for God's sake. No one expects you to appear."

"All the more reason why I should. I don't want anyone to think I feel I have to hide because I'm pregnant. It's an important occasion for San Domenico. I should be there."

"Don't go," Clara said with such vehemence that Melinda became suspicious.

"What aren't you telling me?"

"Please," was all Clara would say. She had grown to love her patient, but she knew, more than Melinda, that in the presidential palace even words had become dangerous.

Knowing there was more to tell but sensing Clara's fear of speaking, she decided not to press. Instead, she waited for Diego.

Their lives had evolved into separate spheres, with Diego preoccupied with affairs of state, and Melinda contenting herself with preparation of the presidential household for the approaching birth. But each night, he returned to their private quarters and came to her bed. At the beginning, she had tried to question him about the political situation, but he resolutely refused to discuss it, insisting, warmly, fondly, that he only wanted to talk of her, of the baby, of the future of their family. And after a while, touched by his affection, she had given in to his tenderness and restricted their conversation to the things that happened between them.

She waited until the night before Independence Day, knowing that if Diego were to grant his permission, it would be a spur of the moment display of affection, a desire to please her that might momentarily prevail over his usual systematic analysis of every situation. But he came to her later than usual, clearly exhausted.

"I thought you would be sleeping, *mi amor,*" he said, wearily stripping off the camouflage green uniform he continued to wear as a symbol of his revolutionary beginnings.

"I wanted to wait for you."

"It's not good for the baby. You need your rest." He placed his hand on her belly as he climbed into the bed beside her.

"I'm fine. The baby's fine. You're the one who needs rest."

"It's the plans for tomorrow. Sometimes, I wish we could just cancel the whole thing and go on about our business. It costs too much in time and money."

"Actually, that's what I wanted to talk to you about. Since you're not canceling, how would it be if I made an appearance?" she asked lightly, trying to make it sound like no big deal.

The ploy didn't work. "Out of the question," was all Diego said.

"But why? I'm not talking about marching five miles. Just to stand beside you in the reviewing stand, hear a speech or two. Let the people see me. What's wrong with that?"

"Don't ask me. And don't speak of it again."

Forgoing their usual ritual of nightly kisses, he turned away from her without another word and in seconds was asleep. She had to admit to herself that it was no more than she had expected. But even more than disappointment, she felt a stirring of alarm. First, Clara's refusal to discuss it, then Diego's, led her to believe there was a lot more to the situation than she was being told.

By the time she woke up the next day, Diego was gone. Clara had already arrived and was silently laying out breakfast. From her window, Melinda could see the people beginning to gather, filling the streets beyond the palace walls. And if she peered out over the balcony, she could actually see a corner of the reviewing stand that had been set up in the main square outside the presidential palace.

"I take it you are not going to the parade," Clara said, pouring her some herbal tea.

Melinda looked at Clara disgruntled. "Of course he was dead set against it."

"Good."

"What's so good about it?"

"Don't be a child. There are going to be huge crowds. You don't need to be eight months pregnant in a mob."

"Number one, I wasn't planning to be in the mob, just watching it. And number two, this is a celebration. It's not as if these people are dangerous."

Clara gave her a look.

"What's that supposed to mean?"

"Melinda, you were shot once already in an attempt on Diego Roca's life. Do you think there can't be another?"

Melinda felt the small pit of alarm that had settled inside her the day before take root. "Is that what everyone's afraid of? Do you know something?"

Clara turned away, unable to meet her eyes. But Melinda followed her, forcing her to stop fussing with the tea and look at her. "Please, Clara, if you love me, don't do this. Tell me what you know. Is Diego in danger?"

"Every leader is in danger. You know that."

"More than usual?"

"It's not him I'm worried about."

"Then who?"

"Demonstrators. They're organizing rallies."

"Antigovernment?"

Clara nodded. "There are rumors, threats."

"What kind?"

"That if they appear anywhere near the official proceedings, the protesters will be shot."

"That's ridiculous. Diego would never allow that. As long as they're peaceful demonstrations. People are allowed to express their opinions," she said adamantly, aware that she was speaking as much to herself as Clara, hoping as much as maintaining a fact.

Clara would say no more about it, and they spent the rest of the morning in tense silence, both sitting on the balcony, peering into the distance to see the tanks and troops, looking like a phalanx of green ants, cut their way through the flag-waving crowd.

When the parade had ended, the speeches began. Leaning over the wrought-iron railing of the balcony, Melinda found that with a pair of powerful binoculars, she could actually see the features of the speakers at the podium. The sound, projected through a series of loudspeakers over miles, was too garbled to differentiate the words, but through the shield of bulletproof glass that he now used at all public functions, she could see Diego, looking proud and handsome, as he addressed his people.

The demonstrators came from behind the square. Focusing her binoculars on them, Melinda estimated the crowd to be thousands strong. They carried banners protesting the repression of the new regime. Zooming in on their faces, she could see that they were shouting, although she could not make out the words. Nervously, she turned her attention back to Diego. She could tell that he now heard their chanting, too, for he had stopped speaking and his face was drawn into a ferocious scowl. There was a sudden silence that disoriented her until she realized that the loudspeakers had been turned off.

Like watching a silent movie, she stared through the powerful binoculars and saw expressions changing, actions being taken, fingers pointing, mouths moving. But she heard nothing until the shooting began. And then, punctuated by a distant *rat-a-tat* that sounded more like firecrackers than machine guns, she watched in horror as bodies fell, blood spread, mouths opened in silent screams. She watched the people cower and then run in all directions, trampling each other and their fallen comrades as they tried to escape the flying bullets.

She blinked rapidly to clear her eyes of the tears that were clouding her vision and forced herself to move her point of focus from the demonstrators to her husband. Diego stood on the review stand, motionless in his protected field. For a moment, she saw him cringe, and she thought, good, he is still human, he will stop it now. But then, his face set in a grimace of determination as he watched his lieutenants shooting at his countrymen.

She didn't know when she had begun to cry in earnest or when Clara had forced her inside to sit while she appropriated the binoculars and, riveted, hung over the terrace and wept herself at the sight of the carnage. Only an insistent knock at the door brought Clara back inside, and barely controlling her sobs, stopping only to make sure that beyond the tears Melinda was unhurt, she went to answer.

"What is it, Clara?" Melinda asked, shocked out of her own grief at the sight of Clara's ashen face.

"They came to tell me about Gabriel."

"Your son?"

Clara nodded. "He was shot," she added, her voice choking.

"Oh, my God. He was one of the demonstrators."

"I begged him not to go," Clara sobbed, wringing her hands. "I was afraid. That's why I didn't want you . . ." She couldn't speak anymore.

Melinda's head cleared. Tragedy was too difficult for her to handle, but she knew how to deal with trauma.

"Where is he?"

"They brought him to the palace. To the basement where the service staff comes in. They didn't know what else to do. If they took him to the hospital, they would arrest him. I'm sorry. I have to go."

"We'll both go."

"But you . . . you're the wife . . . Roca will . . ."

But Melinda was already halfway out the door. "I saw my share of bullet wounds during the revolution. I haven't done it in a while, but I'm hoping it's one of those things you never forget."

"Bless you. God bless you," Clara whispered as she followed her.

Melinda took her hand as they raced down the corridor together. She had never imagined that she would need to call on the triage skills she'd learned on freedom's battlefield. And never, in all her life, would she have dreamed that it was Diego Roca who would make it necessary.

In a dark pantry in the basement of her palatial home, watched by her silent staff, the president's pregnant wife removed a bullet from the leg of a young man who had dared to defy her husband. Her nurse, the boy's mother, assisted, whispering benedictions for the woman who had been her patient and had become her son's savior. When the wound was cleaned and dressed, Clara sent her son home with his friends, extracting promises from them that they would stay off the main streets and out of sight. To keep from arousing suspicion, Clara would return with Melinda to her room and stay until her usual hour of departure.

When they were alone again, waiting tensely for Diego's return, Melinda turned to Clara. "I can't stay with him, you know that," she said flatly.

"Don't talk crazy," responded Clara. "Where will you go? In your condition. You've done what you can."

"If I stay, people will think I condone what he's done. I could never . . ." Her voice choked at the memory of the people falling, the blood spilling.

"No," Clara was adamant. "You saved Gabriel. Everyone knows that you are not like him."

"They don't, Clara. And you can't tell anyone. It will just put you and your family in danger. Me, too."

Clara was silent for a moment. She knew that what Melinda said was true.

"He wouldn't hurt you." Much as she loathed Diego Roca, a man she had once revered, she had seen in the past few months that no matter how cruel he had become, he still loved his wife, and she felt it needed saying.

"Because of the baby," Melinda acknowledged.

"He loves you, too."

"Only if I support him. I can't do that anymore. He's changed. He's turned into a monster. I don't know him."

Clara nodded. She could not disagree. An entire population had watched it happen. Absolute power had, indeed, corrupted absolutely.

"You have to help me, Clara. You have to help me get away from him."

Clara's face filled with dread. "How? He only lets you out to walk in the garden. And if I . . ."

She couldn't go on; she didn't need to. Melinda immediately understood what she had been asking. "Of course, I'm sorry. I shouldn't even be talking to you about this. You don't need any more trouble."

Clara sighed. How could she refuse the saintly woman who had just saved her son.

"No," she reversed herself. "I will help you."

Now Melinda protested. "Forget about it. I shouldn't have even said anything to you."

"For the baby," Clara amended, knowing it was the only way to get her to agree now. "Just in case. I should be nearby until you're safe. You don't want to take any chances."

"Thank you," said Melinda simply, knowing that whatever courage she had for herself, she must be even braver for her baby.

There was no time to make a plan. Even though the rallies had long since ended and the crowds dispersed, Diego had not yet returned to their private quarters, and Melinda did not expect him for many hours. The crisis had closeted him with his fawning officials, devising more restrictive measures to keep the people from voicing their dissatisfaction. The effect on Melinda or the household could not be guessed at—or gambled on. If Melinda were going to go, she would have to go now.

Listening to the news, they ascertained that the official tactic was to declare the demonstration and the violent aftermath a nonevent. Government-sponsored announcers were proclaiming that there had been only a minor skirmish with a small fringe group and that the country was functioning as normal. The cover-up worked in their favor. At least, they knew the airports would be open, and the daily flight to Miami would depart on schedule that evening.

"What about your people in America? Do you think if you call them, they can help?" Clara was clearly worried.

Melinda shook her head. "Diego knows who I call. He'd find out and stop me. But if I go now, tonight, before he's had a chance to suspect anything or pass any decrees, maybe I can get away with it."

"He doesn't even let you leave the palace grounds."

"You and I know that. But the airport personnel don't. If I just show up there, minutes before the plane is to take off and say that I'm on official business for my husband, who's going to argue with me? They won't have time to check. Besides, they won't have any reason to suspect there's a problem. Diego is very careful with his public image as far as I'm concerned."

Clara was thoughtful. "I can say you need air and walk you in the garden. I can get a message to

Gabriel's friends. We can get you out the way they brought him in. They owe you."

"Yes, oh, yes. Thank you, Clara. I have to do this. Not just for myself, but for my child as well."

"I know," Clara said, and Melinda heard the sadness in her voice.

Melinda looked at the woman who had been her almost constant companion for six months. "Clara, do you want to come with me?"

"I couldn't come back."

"No, you probably couldn't."

"I was born in San Domenico. My children, too." She shrugged helplessly.

"I know," said Melinda, understanding. "But I had to ask. I'm afraid of what will happen to you when I'm gone."

Clara grinned with feigned bravado. "Oh, don't worry. Like I said, I was born here. I know as many people as Diego. Maybe more. They like me more than they like him. He won't get his hands on me."

"I wish I could believe you," said Melinda, knowing Clara was as frightened as she was but also knowing there was no choice.

At dusk, arm in arm and smiling as though they hadn't a care in the world, Melinda and Clara left the palace for a stroll in the pleasant evening air. In the garden, obscured by the thickets and shaded by the sinking sun, they made their way to a small back gate, overgrown with vines and bolted with an ancient lock. It had recently come to the attention of certain members of the presidential palace staff that rust had eaten through the lock, and though it looked secure, in fact, it was easily removed. It was through this gate that Gabriel had been brought to his mother, and it was now through this gate that Clara hurried her charge to an old jeep, a prerevolutionary relic, that her son's friends had been able to requisition for their escape.

Since they didn't know who might see them on the road, they decided Melinda should stay out of sight until they reached the airport. Once there, they would drive straight onto the runway and deposit her at the door of the plane with all the authority they could muster. Melinda had no doubt that she could convince the airline crew that she was hastening to the States on official business. She was not an Academy Award–winning actress for nothing.

Huddled on the floor of the backseat under a blanket, head resting on the mound of her belly, Melinda could hardly breathe. Picking her head up every now and then for a gulp of fresh air, she thanked God for the moonless night and prayed that no one would pay attention to the couple in the old jeep, driving toward the airport with a heap of old clothes in back. She looked at her watch. Judging from the amount of time they'd been on the road, she estimated they would arrive at the airport in twenty minutes. Except, suddenly, they were slowing.

"What's going on?" Melinda hissed, moving aside the blanket for a peek and a breath of air.

Quickly, Clara covered her again. "It looks like a road block. Stay down."

Melinda felt the panic swell and threaten to take over. She looked at her watch again. The plane to Miami would be departing in less than an hour. There was not much time. She rubbed her stomach as though it were a talisman and forced herself to calm down. She needed to think clearly.

"They're not looking for me," she finally breathed to Clara. "Diego can't even have missed me yet. They must be looking for demonstrators."

"What's the difference?" Melinda could hear an echo of her own fears in Clara's voice. "They're going to find you anyway. Damn. We should have anticipated this. Maybe if we had disguised you—"

"No," Melinda said, cutting her off. There was no time for recriminations. Keeping the blanket over her, she lifted her head high enough to survey the area around them. "We have to get off the road."

"What?" asked Clara, confused. "We don't have time to wait out the blockade."

"I know that. We're going to go around it. Tell the driver that there's a dirt turn off about a hundred meters away. Take it."

"But that just leads into the jungle," Clara protested.

"That's the point. It's exactly the part of the jungle I know. It's the way we got from the rebels' camp to the airport when we took it over from Guzman's thugs. The road can't have been used for years, but it must still be there."

She ducked back down, as traffic, slowed by the road block, began to pile up around them. Hunched in the back, the air was hot and stale. She held her breath and waited until she felt the jeep veer to the right and bump its way into the jungle. Concealed by the foliage, she allowed herself to peek out and look around. Even in the dark of night, she knew instantly where they were. Without the rebels' constant traffic, the road had been overgrown. But there was still a distinguishable path, and she knew it would lead them directly to the airport.

"Do you think it's safe for me to get up?" Melinda asked plaintively.

Clara was already reaching over to help her onto the seat. "There's no one here to see you. Are you all right?"

Melinda tried to smile. The fumes from the jeep seeping through the floor had made her nauseous, and she'd forgotten just how bumpy the jungle road had been even when it had been carefully preserved. Now, after years of neglect, reclaimed by the jungle, it was almost unbearable. She locked her arms around her belly, trying to cradle the baby from the jolting movement.

"I'll be fine as soon as we get to the airport," she said.

And then, she screamed. It came without warning, a sharp, searing pain, knifing through her gut.

"Oh, my God, Melinda, what is it?" Clara was completely turned around in her seat, reaching out to Melinda in the back.

Sweat beaded on Melinda's brow as the pain subsided, and she could speak again. "I'm sorry. It must have been the bumping. I'm okay now."

But she had spoken too soon. Seconds later, the pain was back, ripping her apart, so overwhelming that while it lasted, nothing else existed.

"Stop the car, stop the car," she heard Clara commanding as it began to recede again and consciousness returned.

"We can't," she protested. "We'll miss the plane. Just keep going. I'll be fine." This time when the pain hit, she tried not to scream to convince Clara and herself that it was tolerable, that she could make it. But it was no use.

"You're having the baby," shouted Clara. "You've gone into labor."

"I can't. It's too early," she insisted, but even as she spoke, she knew that Clara must be right. She began to cry.

"We have to get you back to the palace," Clara was saying, and Melinda could feel the car reversing, jerking forward, reversing again as the driver tried to turn on the narrow road. It was more than she could take and even though she had forbidden them to stop before, now she begged it.

She could hear the panic in Clara's voice. "Oh, my God, Diego will have me killed. I'll kill myself. We don't even have water."

"Up ahead. There's a freshwater lagoon. We used it for the camp. It's clean," she forced herself to tell Clara before succumbing to another wave.

And then, mercifully, they were stopped. The pains were coming faster now, but the blanket that had covered her was now under her, and she was lying on the ground, looking up at the sky that had begun to clear. She turned her head to the side and saw they had placed her by the water, near the spot where she and Diego had first made love. If she had not been suffering so, she might have appreciated the irony.

Living only between waves of agony, Melinda did not know how much time had gone by. But at some point, the nurse in Clara had taken over. Crouching beside her patient on the ground, she held Melinda's hand, breathing with her through each pain and crooning words of comfort while they waited for the next. Clara's cotton skirt had already been torn into rags, and the driver was boiling water he had drawn from the lagoon in his canteen on a fire of jungle brush. When it came time to push, she closed her eyes and, focusing singularly on Clara's voice, did what she was told. And when the pain had stopped, and she heard a cry that was not her own, she opened her eyes to see the stars falling from the sky and her son lying in her arms.

They were all laughing and crying at once, Melinda and Clara and even the driver who had had to hold the baby while Clara cut the umbilical cord.

"Is he okay?" Melinda asked when she could catch her breath.

"He's perfect," Clara assured her. "Maybe a little puny because he came out a few weeks early, but he's got everything he's supposed to have. And you can hear his lungs are fine."

"Oh, God, Clara. Thank you." She took the time to really look at him. They had washed him with the boiled lagoon water and swaddled him in a piece of Clara's torn skirt. Melinda counted his tiny fingers and toes and watched his rosebud lips making sucking motions.

"Melinda," Clara delicately interrupted her reverie, "We have to go back to the palace. He's okay, but he needs to be checked by the doctor. We shouldn't keep him out here any longer than we have to."

For the first time since the pains had started,

Melinda remembered the mission she'd been on. "I guess we missed the plane," she joked ruefully, trying to push back a surge of fear. How was she going to explain to Diego that his son had been born in the jungle?

Clara's mind was working on the same lines. "He doesn't need to know where we were. I will say I was with you in the garden. We were walking when labor started so suddenly I couldn't even leave you to run back for help."

"He won't believe that."

Clara shrugged. "What does it matter? He won't be told anything else. Besides, when he sees his son, everything else will fly out of his mind. You'll see."

"You're right," said Melinda bravely, knowing there was no choice. The baby had taken away all her options.

Gingerly, they helped her get up and climb into the jeep. With Clara's help, she held the baby onto her breast and sighed with relief and pleasure as he began to suckle. Cradling him in her arms, crooning softly to him as he lay affixed to her, the bumping no longer affected her. And when they got back to the road, they were pleased to see that the passing hours had cleared the traffic, and while the airport road remained blocked, heading back to the palace, there was no one to challenge them.

They sneaked back into the palace the way they had gone. Thankfully, the baby was asleep. The same staff members who had turned a blind eye when she left understood what would have to be done for her return. After sighs and murmurs over the infant, they informed Melinda that Diego was livid over her absence and that he was closeted in his office, instituting a secret but sweeping search.

By the time Diego was told of Melinda's return and her condition, Clara had cleaned the baby more thoroughly and helped Melinda to bathe herself. Aware of effect as only an actress could be, Melinda had dressed in a nightgown of white lace and swaddled the baby in soft folds of palest blue. No acting was necessary for the heavy-lidded exhaustion that could not hide the peaceful pride with which she cradled her sleeping child.

"Diego," she called softly as he stormed into the room, not giving him a chance to say anything, "come see your son."

Clara had been both right and wrong in anticipating Diego's reaction. Taking the baby from his wife's outstretched arms, the fury left his face, replaced by a tender frown of concern as he drew the tiny bundle close.

"He's okay?"

"Perfect," she smiled.

"And you?"

"Tired, that's all."

Still holding the baby, he sat on the edge of the bed and took her hand. "I wanted to be there," he said sadly.

"I know," she answered as hurt as he was that she had not been able to share it with him—and sadder that she would share no more in the future.

The doctor had been summoned and came quickly, cutting off any further conversation for the moment. He checked out mother and child, pronouncing them both remarkably fit considering the ordeal they'd just been through.

When the examination had been completed, Diego announced that he would like to be alone with his wife.

Clara immediately protested. "She is very tired. She really needs to get some sleep. Perhaps—"

Diego cut her off. "Thank you, Clara. I am very concerned for my wife. You can be sure I won't hurt her." His tone was not impolite, but it was clear he would tolerate no dissent.

"It's okay, Clara. You must be exhausted yourself. Go home. I'll see you tomorrow," Melinda said with far more serenity than she felt.

"I should stay the night," Clara attempted. "The baby will wake up in an hour or two. He'll need to be changed. You shouldn't be left alone."

"She is not alone," Diego said with heavy emphasis, and she knew she had said exactly the wrong thing. Now, there would be no use in persisting.

Melinda gave her a small nod, trying to reassure her, even though she did not feel very secure herself.

"I will be back by seven," Clara warned as she backed out of the room. Diego gently placed the baby back in Melinda's arms, followed Clara to the door, and locked it with a snap the minute she had exited. Tension gripping her throat, Melinda forced herself to smile as he walked back to the bed and sat facing her.

"Do you want to tell me how this happened?" he asked quietly. His voice was more sorrowful than angry. She felt her heart breaking. He knew as well as she did that the dream was gone.

She forced herself to sound composed without

being too casual. "It all happened so suddenly. We were just walking in the garden and I went into hard labor. It was so fast, I couldn't get back."

"I looked for you in the garden," he said quietly. There was no accusation, but her heart beat faster.

"We were off the path. I was looking for wild orchids in the uncultivated part."

"How could you walk there? It is very overgrown."

"I know. I shouldn't have done it. It was stupid of me. That's probably why I went into labor. I'm sorry."

"Melinda, *mi amor* . . ." He had called her that many times before, but there was a subtle difference in the way he uttered the words, a hint of steel beneath his velvet tone. "I am not a fool."

She tried not to panic. "I know it sounds incredible, Diego. But ask Clara. She was with me."

He raised his hand and shook his head. She immediately stopped talking.

"You are my wife. And I love you. Because I have never been so happy as when I saw my son, we will never again discuss the circumstances of his birth. Do you understand me?"

"Yes," she whispered, her throat so constricted it was no more than a sigh.

The baby began to cry, first a small whimper, then a highpitched howl. Without a word, Diego took him from her arms.

"Shu-shu," he sang to him, rocking him as he took him to the infant area, complete with bassinet and changing table, that Melinda had insisted be installed in a corner of their room. The squall returned to a whimper as the president crooned to his child, sticking his little finger in the baby's mouth to suck on while he expertly changed his diaper. Watching her husband, suffused with love for his son as she knew he would be, Melinda ached even more for their shattered hopes.

He brought the baby back to her, watching with quiet satisfaction as she placed him on her breast and he nursed hungrily. Then, slipping out of his own clothes, he climbed into bed beside her, just as he had every night of their married life. Melinda looked from her husband to her suckling child, and her throat caught with the beauty of them both. They were the picture of serenity, the three of them together, just as she had imagined them so many times over so many years. But like a gourd that retains its beauty while its insides die and rot, leaving nothing but a hardened, shiny shell, something had happened. And as she brushed away a tear to keep it from falling on her baby's head, she knew that somehow, some day, she would have to get away.

"I think the reason I can't get pregnant is because I don't want to."

Ian looked at his wife. There were dark circles under her eyes, and he could see what a strain the past months had been. Still, he was disappointed and would be lying if he didn't admit it.

"Maybe you're right, honey," he began. He stopped to choose his words carefully. So much of what he said these days Sarah would misinterpret. He didn't want this to be the cause of another argument. "With everything going on at DMC and the bad dreams you've been having, things have been really tense.

Maybe you should just stop seeing Horvath. It's not working anyway. It's just getting you upset. Let's just let things slide for a while. Once the situation eases up, we can talk about it. And then, if we decide to go ahead, we can go to the fertility clinic like we originally planned."

"Jesus, you don't listen, do you?"

Ian took a deep breath. Obviously, he hadn't chosen his words carefully enough. Sarah's fuse was shorter than he'd ever seen it. Sometimes he felt like she was turning into a different person.

"Sarah . . ." he began, putting a gentle hand on her shoulder. But she shrugged him off.

"I . . . don't . . . want . . . children!" She paused between each word, adding heavy emphasis the way people spoke to the very deaf or the very stupid. "Look around you. What would be the point? My father didn't care about us when he was alive, and my mother couldn't wait to get away from us the minute he died."

"Your parents are not exactly the best examples."

"Oh, and yours are? Your mother gave you away, for God's sake."

He stared at her, his hurt apparent. "Why are you doing this?" For a moment, he thought he saw her falter, but then her jaw went rigid with contempt.

"Because I don't want to live in a dream world like the rest of you. I don't want to pretend that everything is okay when it's not."

"We don't have to talk about this now," he said, defeated.

"You're right, we don't!" she responded and slammed out the door.

It took her fifteen minutes to drive to the bar in Oakdale. She parked in her usual spot out front, under the pool of light from the sign, a flashing neon beer bottle, that marked the place.

"What am I doing here?" she asked herself out loud. But the answer came quickly.

"You know damn well what you're doing, so stop you're fucking whining and let's go get a drink." She laughed a short, ugly guffaw and got out of the car, not even bothering to stop and lock the door.

Inside, green-shaded lamps hung from the low ceiling, casting dirty circles of light in the prevailing shadow. The fake wood veneer was peeling from the walls around the edges. Sawdust hid the grime on the floor and left footprints where the few patrons had walked. She breathed in the stale smoky air and felt instantly at home.

"Hey, Sunny," the bartender called convivially, "haven't seen you for a while."

"You're telling me. I couldn't get away."

"Family?"

"Yeah. Might as well be jail," she snorted.

He poured her a shot of no-brand whiskey, and she drank it down in one gulp and put her glass down on the bar for another. It was their ritual, and they performed it with the same ceremony as a return to communion.

"Anyone interesting here tonight?" She cast her glance into the back room, where a few desultory pool players moved some balls around. A man sat alone at a table, watching but not participating. The bartender followed her eye.

"Yeah, he's new."

"Know anything about him?"

"Nope.

"So much the better."

"You ought to be careful, Sunny," he offered. "These days, you don't know—"

"Don't worry." She laughed. "I'm horny, not stupid."

He shook his head and smiled ruefully as she picked up her drink and made her way to the back room. She'd been coming to the bar once or twice a week for several months. She was hard drinking and tough talking, but still, there was something about the way she looked that made him think she wasn't from around those parts, and not just geographically either. She never wanted anything except the cheap whiskey, but she looked like she was used to better things. He'd tried to ask her once what she did and where she was from, but she just said she was from around and did whatever she could, and that was that. After that, he figured it was her business and left it alone. He watched her now as she slid easily into the seat beside the stranger and wondered what it was about her that could let her act like a whore and still look like a lady. He could tell from the look on the guy's face that he saw it, too.

"What are you drinking?" the man said by way of introduction.

"Whiskey," she answered, and he immediately motioned to the bartender to bring her another.

Her eyes moved over him from head to toe as she made no attempt to hide the fact that she was studying him. His face was hard and told her little, but his body was good, not like a bodybuilder, but like a man who did physical work. She reached out and took his hand, turning it over in her own, feeling the callouses and confirming her appraisal. She liked that he made no protest and no comment. She could feel that he was willing but not overeager, that he would let her stay in control. And that was all she needed to know.

"They call me Sunny," she informed him. "Isn't it ironic?"

"I don't know yet," he said, raising an eyebrow. She was pleased that he understood. They didn't always.

"Do you have a name?" she asked.

"Doesn't everyone?"

She shrugged. It didn't really matter to her if she knew it. She wouldn't remember it anyway.

"Call me whatever you want. You won't remember it anyway."

She laughed. "That's just what I was thinking, Mac."

"Mac it is. See, Sunny. You're pretty easy to read."

"Oh, yeah? Do you know what I'm thinking now?" She looked at him through half-lowered eyelids, her lip curled.

"Yep."

"So how about it?"

"Where?"

"I got a car."

"Nope. I need room to move."

She laughed again. Usually, men were so thankful to get lucky that they were already out the door panting the minute she made the approach. Mac was different. He was letting her lead, but he wasn't going to follow so easily.

"Got any ideas?" She expected him to ask her to go home with him. They sometimes did. She always refused.

"There's an alley out back."

"What? Are you kidding?"

"Nope."

"What if someone comes by?"

"We got there first." He stood up. "Coming?"

She realized she wasn't leading any more. She was tempted to let him go alone. The point was to stay in control, and she wouldn't be if she followed. Her breath came more rapidly, and she could feel the struggle going on inside. She clenched her jaw. If she gave in to the voice inside, the voice of fear, that would be admitting an even greater loss of control. She'd rather let Mac have his way than give in to the gutless wonder inside. She got up and walked with him out the front door and around to the back of the bar.

It was dark in the alley. No moon illuminated the grim proceedings as he picked her up and unceremoniously deposited her on top of a garbage can. He reached under her skirt and with one twist ripped off her panties, throwing them on the ground behind him. He lifted her feet off the ground, pushing her back against the hard brick of the building, so that all he could see in front of him was the dark space between the white V of her parted legs. Propped on her elbows, she saw him open his fly and release his cock, hard and straight.

"Wait a minute," she said. "You've got to use a condom."

He looked at her like she was crazy. "Do you think

I'd put it in a bitch like you? I don't know where the hell you've been."

She started to get up, insulted. "Who do you think you are . . . ?" she began. But he pushed her back hard, and she gasped in pain as her head hit the wall. He held her legs apart with one hand, so he could see what she offered. And then, quickly, he closed his other hand around himself and, with a strong stroke, brought their encounter to an end.

Leaving her soiled and humiliated, he turned to zip up his fly. He heard her make a sound in her throat, interpreted it as a rattle of disgust instead of the growl of indignation that it was and, feeling neither remorse nor compassion, didn't bother to turn around. He didn't see her eyes roll back into her head for a moment or her teeth bared in fury as she leaped at him. But he felt the pain as she raised her knee between his legs with such force that he doubled over in screaming agony, feeling like his scrotum had been kicked halfway to his chest.

"This should teach you there's a lot more to safe sex than condoms, mister," she said. "I could have killed you, but then, it would have just been a wasted lesson."

Then, pushing her way between the garbage cans, she wiped off what she could with a tissue and ran to her car.

Ian found her at dawn. Waiting for her to come home, he had fallen asleep with his clothes on, on top of the covers. His sleep was troubled but deep, and he didn't hear the car pull up the gravel driveway and come to a stop. He woke with the first rays of the sun, startled to find himself fully clothed and still alone.

Peering out of the window, hoping for some sign of his wife, he had been happy to see the car parked in front. Quietly, so as not to wake the still-sleeping household, he ran downstairs and out the door to greet her.

She was asleep in the driver's seat, her head lolling to one side as she snored. Her arms and her legs were covered with dirt, and a sticky stain was spattered over her dress and even in her matted hair. She stank.

"Sarah?" Ian called softly, almost afraid to touch her.

There was no response.

"Sarah," he repeated a little louder this time, adding a shake to the shoulder.

She opened her eyes, blinked them shut as if she was unwilling to accept her waking state, then opened them again. She looked at her husband, staring anxiously at her through the car window, then down at herself. Then she began to cry.

"Honey, what happened to you?" Ian asked, his own anguish obvious as he opened the door and tried to gently help her out. As she stepped out of the car, he saw that she wore no underpants. She saw it, too, and knew that he had noticed. She cried harder.

"Sarah, talk to me. Where were you?"

"I don't know," she sobbed.

"What happened to you?" he pressed, not accepting or understanding her answer. "How did you get . . . like this?"

Unable to speak, not knowing what to say, she shook her head. He stood staring at her, leaving a distance between them, and she could see the disgust and confusion on his face. She felt the same way.

"I want to die," she whispered as much to herself as to him.

"No!" he said, galvanized. "No. We'll figure this thing out, whatever it is."

He came to her and, ignoring her rankness, put his arm around her. Embarrassed by her own condition, she tried to pull away, but he wouldn't let her.

"Together," he said as he led her into the house.

"Together," she responded, wanting to believe him, not knowing if she could.

She showered for a long time and afterward showed him the bump on her head, which she had painfully discovered while washing her hair.

"You have no idea how you got this?" he asked. It was a sizable egg, not something that could have happened without being noticed.

"Maybe that's why I don't remember anything," she said. "I must have fallen or hit my head on something and got some sort of concussion that made me forget."

He could see she was searching for an answer—or an excuse, he couldn't be sure. "We'd better get you to the doctor."

"Ian," she said quietly, "I'm not making this up."

"I know you're not, sweetheart," he said. But the truth was that he didn't know anything, and he hadn't for a long time.

6

The call came in the early evening when Sam and Drew had retired to the west wing to give Moira her bath and play with her until her bedtime. Normally, the staff was under instructions to take messages for calls that came in at that hour. They had agreed to try and keep that family time sacrosanct on the assumption that, unless it was an emergency, it could wait until after Moira was asleep. So Robert's appearance at the door of the nursery with a telephone was an immediate cause for concern.

"What is it?" Drew asked nervously as Sam gripped her husband's hand and told Moira, squealing with delight over some game they had been playing, to hush for a minute.

"Sorry, Mr. Drew," Robert said quickly, seeing they were anxious and wanting to allay their fears.

"It's for Miss Samantha. From San Domenico. I just thought you might want to take this one right away."

Sam leaped to her feet and grabbed the phone, a big smile on her face. "You were absolutely right, Robert. Thank you."

Robert bowed and left the room. Drew took his turn at hushing Moira while Sam spoke loudly into the receiver.

"Hello? Hello?" She waited a few frustrating seconds before she heard her sister's voice.

"Sam, is that you?"

"Melinda, hi. I'm so happy to hear your voice. Is everything okay? . . . It's your auntie Melinda," she whispered an aside to Moira, whose new game was trying to grab the phone from her mother.

"Yes, fine . . ." Sam thought she heard a strain in her sister's voice, but she let her go on. "Sam, you're an aunt."

"Oh, my God!" screamed Sam. "But I thought the baby wasn't due for another couple of weeks."

"He came a little early."

"He? It's a boy?" she asked rhetorically. Grinning at her own family, she announced, "It's a boy. Melinda had a boy." There were cheers from Drew, and though she wasn't entirely sure what all the glee was about, Moira clapped, too.

"You're okay and he's okay?" Sam asked before letting the full extent of her joy unleash.

"Yes, yes," Melinda said, "we're both fine."

Sam couldn't be sure, but she thought there had been a nanosecond of hesitation before her sister's response. "What aren't you telling me?" she asked.

"Nothing, really. He was a little small. Six pounds,

eight ounces. Because he was early. But he's healthy and he has all his fingers and toes. He's got lots of hair and big dark eyes."

"Like his father."

"Like his father," echoed Melinda, sounding, Sam thought, a little forlorn.

"I'm coming down there," Sam said. It had popped out of her mouth before she had even thought it out or talked to her husband about it. But once having said it, it made perfect sense. "Drew can stay home and take care of business. I'm bringing Moira, and we're coming down to see you and the baby." She looked at Drew questioningly; he nodded his enthusiastic approval.

Moira was pulling the cord. "I want to talk. I want to talk."

"Wait," Melinda began, but Sam had already given in to Moira's entreaties and put the receiver in her pudgy hand.

"Aunty Minna?" came the plaintive little voice.

"Oh, Moira, sweetheart. You sound like such a big girl. I miss you."

"Do you have a new baby?"

"Yes, I do. He's very little and he's very cute."

"Can I come and see him?"

"Well, yes, of course you can, one day. But not—"

"Mommy, Aunty Minna says I can see the baby." Having accomplished what she wanted, Moira was already handing the phone back to her mother.

"So, it's settled." Sam laughed into the phone. "We're coming to San Domenico."

"No, Sam, wait . . . I don't think . . . I can't . . ." Her voice ran out.

"Melinda? What's the matter?" She waited for what seemed an inexorably long time. Again, Sam couldn't be sure, but for a second there, it had sounded like Melinda might be crying.

"Sam, it's Diego here." Sam heard her brother-in-law's voice, mellifluously accented, quietly controlled. It was not hard to remember that she was talking to the head of a small nation.

"Congratulations, Diego. I was just telling Melinda that I'm going to come and see your new son."

"That would be wonderful." He sounded most sincere. "But I think not just yet. The birth was a little hard for Melinda."

"Were there complications?" Sam asked, anxious again.

"Not anything that couldn't be handled. But as you know, babies are demanding. And Melinda is exhausted."

"Of course. I can help—"

"I don't think so," he cut her off before she was finished. "Of course, she has all the assistance she needs, I've made sure of that. But she needs to avoid excitement. Your visit would just make her want to do too much. It wouldn't be fair to have you here and tell her she must rest. You see that, don't you?"

Sam didn't know what to say. In fact, she did not see the logic in what Diego was saying. But the iron in his voice, even encased, as it was, in a sheath of honeyed charm made it clear that no argument was possible.

"Can I talk to Melinda again?" was her only reply.

"Of course. My best regards to all your family. And I look forward to seeing you when Melinda and the baby are better equipped for company. We'll let you know."

"What the hell is that all about?" Sam asked without preamble when Melinda was back on the phone.

"Diego's right," Melinda said quietly. "It would just be too much for me right now."

"Why? What's wrong with you?"

"Nothing, really. I . . . I . . . just need to rest. Leave it alone, okay, Sam? You call Mom and Dad. Tell them about the baby. I'll be in touch with you all again real soon, and we'll figure out when to get together."

"If that's what you want," Sam agreed, not at all sure it was.

"Yes. That's how it has to be right now."

"What's his—" Before she could finish her question, the high-pitched tone told her that Melinda had hung up. She put down the phone, a look of stupefaction on her face.

"I want to see the baby," Moira announced, oblivious to the frown on her mother's face.

"Me, too," said Sam, sighing.

"Now. Let's go now," demanded Moira.

"I wish we could, sweetheart. But we have to wait until we're invited."

"I want to go now." Moira began to cry.

Sam hugged her daughter and looked at her husband. "Something's wrong, Drew. She didn't even tell me his name."

While Drew soothed Moira and got her to sleep, Sam called her parents. Not wanting to adulterate their pleasure at the birth of their second grandchild, she didn't reveal how disturbed she had been by the conversation with her sister. When Diane wondered why Melinda hadn't called them herself, Sam explained that they were having trouble with the phone lines in San Domenico. Harvey, who had always believed that the United States was the only place in the world where things worked, accepted the explanation without question.

For Harvey and Diane, working-class people all their lives, placing a call to the presidential palace of a foreign country had proved too daunting for regular communication with their daughter. Even a year after Sam had moved into Belvedere, they had been so uncomfortable at the idea of speaking to a butler that they had preferred to drive the half hour to her house rather than telephone. So Sam was able to deflect all their questions, many of which reflected her own, by promising to bring Moira to visit the next day, so they could telephone Melinda together.

"Do you think she's going to want me to come down there and help out?" Diane asked nervously.

"What the hell does she need you for?" Harvey bellowed on the extension. "Her husband is president of a goddamn country. She's not getting up in the middle of the night with the baby. So why should you?"

"A girl's mother is different," said Diane, hurt.

"Let's just wait until we talk to her before we make any plans," Sam intervened. Silently, she hoped that by the time they talked to Melinda again, she might have changed her mind about seeing them. She doubted it, but she wasn't going to say anything to her mother to cause concern before she understood what was really going on.

By the time Drew had finished putting Moira to bed, Sam had hung up with her parents and was on the phone again.

"Who are you calling now?" he asked, kissing the top of her head.

"Jack. He's not in, so I'm just logging into his pager. Maybe he'll call me back."

"What can he do?"

"I don't know," said Sam, hanging up with a sigh. "Maybe nothing. Maybe give us some information. He's in the State Department. Maybe he has some insight into what's going on. And if there's anything that needs to be done, Jack will do it. Let's face it. Except for the family, he's still the best friend Melinda ever had."

Jack was having dinner in Daisy's pristine apartment when the message came. He felt the beeper vibrating against his waist and, with a look of apology, picked it off his belt. He recognized the number immediately.

"Is it an emergency?" Daisy asked. He saw the look of concern on her face. She had already taken the individual Valrhona chocolate soufflés out of the oven, and the peak period of consumption was now or never.

"It's not the White House, so we're not at war. I guess it can wait for dessert."

"Yum," she said, licking her lips as she carefully pierced their powdered chocolate tops and poured just a little crème anglaise into each crevice. Jack smiled, not sure which was more delectable, the pudding or its preparer.

In the past few months, Jack had been spending more and more of his free time here. After his first unexpected visit, he had stayed a week, leaving only to go to his office at State, do his work, exchange a few guilty words with Griffin, certain that the signs of sin must be all over his face, then stopping into his own place for a change of clothes before coming back to Daisy's oasis with more relief than either one of them was willing to admit.

At the beginning, they had both been hiding. From the possible accusations of the outside world, their connection coming so close on the heels of word of the breaking of Daisy's engagement to Griffin. And from self-inflicted indictments, neither one of them caring to expose their all-consuming appetite for each other to the light of day. If their reasons for being together were less than direct, what did it matter? It felt too good to scrutinize.

Carefully, with calculated nonchalance, Jack mentioned that he'd run into Daisy a couple of times and was inordinately relieved when Griffin responded with a list of his new girlfriend's assets, comparing her favorably to the one he'd clearly already left behind.

Suddenly, there was nothing to hide. Examination seemed beside the point. There was comfort in each other's presence, pleasure in each other's passion. They talked more but didn't make love any less. They also discovered each other's skills outside the bedroom, that they both cooked well in entirely different styles, that they both had learned to tap dance for no discernible reason, that they both told a good joke and could make each other laugh without restraint. And even though there was nothing to stop them from going out together, they found that what they really wanted to do was stay home together. And so they did.

When they had practically licked their little ramekins clean of their near orgiastic chocolate contents, Jack felt another quivering at his belt. Reluctantly, he laid down his spoon, and Daisy piled her plate on his and started carting them to the kitchen.

"Go on, call. I'll load the dishwasher. Then when you're done, we can play," she said without the least rancor. Jack marveled that no matter how odd his hours, how inopportune the interruptions, Daisy never seemed to have a problem with his schedule. She had been raised a diplomat's daughter, and for her, there had always been a blur between life and work. The spillover seemed to be what kept both interesting.

Sam picked up on the first ring. Obviously, she had been waiting for him to return her call. He felt instantly guilty.

"Sorry it took me so long to get back to you." He didn't elaborate. He wanted to apologize, but he didn't need to explain.

"How are you, Jack?" Sam asked with genuine affection and concern. He realized he missed her. They hadn't spoken that much since she'd left Washington, although he'd called her after he'd heard about the explosion at the plant just to make sure they were all okay.

"I'm really good, Sam. Working hard, same as usual. But things are going well."

"I'm glad. I wouldn't be surprised if we pick up the

paper one day and see you've been appointed deputy secretary of state or some such thing."

He laughed. "Don't bet on it. What about you guys? Everything okay?"

"Well . . ." She hesitated.

"More trouble at DMC?" he prompted.

"Yes, unfortunately. There's some kind of industrial sabotage going on. We think it's someone on the inside."

"Do you have someone investigating?" She could hear the concern in his voice.

"Yes, of course. It's hard to smoke out, but I think we've got it under control. But that's not why I'm calling. I need to talk to you about Melinda."

There was a heavy silence on the line. She felt as if he was holding his breath.

"She's had her baby," Sam went on. "A boy."

"Really? That's wonderful. Mother and child doing well I hope?" She could tell he was being careful. It was impossible to tell what he was thinking.

"The baby was a little early, but he's okay. But I'm worried about Melinda."

"Why?"

It was just one word, but this time, she knew without a doubt that she had scared him.

"Well, I talked to her, and she just didn't sound like herself. When I said I wanted to come down and see her, she said not to. And when I insisted, Diego got on the phone and said she was too exhausted or something and they'd let me know when it was convenient."

"Is there something wrong with that?" Jack asked, sounding almost irritated.

"Yes, of course there is. You know me and Melinda. There's no way in the world she wouldn't want me there. Especially if she was tired. She knows I'd help."

"She's the wife of the president, Sam. My guess is they've got plenty of help for her."

"That's what Diego said."

"There you have it."

"If they've got so much goddamn help, then what would be the problem of my going to see my sister and her new baby."

"Maybe she's just not up for company."

"Company?!" Sam was outraged. "Me?! Come on, Jack. You know us better than that. The only way she would tell me not to come down there is if Diego was making her for some reason."

"Are you suggesting he held a gun to her head?"

Sam was furious. "Why are you making me sound like I'm crazy?"

"Why are you turning this into a melodrama? It's not so unbelievable that a woman who has just given birth to her first child might not want her family to descend on her immediately."

"That's not the way we think," she said adamantly, and he could hear that she was hurt.

He gentled his voice. "People change, Sam. I know the two of you were close, but you can't forget that she's living a different life now. San Domenico is farther away than Hollywood. She's married to the president. It's not a part she shuts off at the end of the day."

"It's not her," she said, and he could tell she was holding back tears. "It's him. He's making her do this."

"Okay, let's surmise for a minute that what you say is true. What can we do about it? When she said she wanted to leave, I offered to help her. I made all the arrangements and, excuse me if I toot my own horn here for a minute because no one else ever did, at quite a good deal of trouble for myself."

"I know, Jack. You were wonderful, and I never told you how much I appreciated what you tried to do. I was just so upset when she decided not to come."

"It's okay. That wasn't really my point. What I wanted to say was Melinda could have come back. There would have been no way for Roca to stop her. She chose not to. She chose to stay with her husband because she was going to have his baby. It's not an unreasonable choice. And it's not up to us to make those decisions for her."

"You're probably right," Sam said, her voice very small. "I'm sorry I bothered you."

"Don't be silly. You can bother me any time. There's just nothing I can do about it. I tried. She didn't want my help. If she ever does, you can ask me again. Okay?"

"Okay."

They hung up even though it was clear that neither one of them was satisfied with the conversation.

"Is everything okay?" Daisy put her cool hands on his throbbing temples, and suddenly, everything was.

He sighed. "That was my friend Sam."

He had often spoken to her about life in Oakdale and Woodland Cliffs and his friends there. She knew who the Symingtons were and had passed by Sam and Drew at a reception or two during their days in

Washington. He'd also given her a sketchy outline of his relationship with Melinda, not the details, just enough to know that she had broken his heart and it wasn't until Daisy had come along that it had begun to mend.

She tried to keep herself from asking but couldn't. "Was it about her sister?"

He nodded.

"Problems?"

He nodded again. Then he slammed his fist on the table and said, "Shit!"

She jumped a little, and he saw that he had startled her.

"I'm sorry," he said, "I shouldn't be here. There's no reason to inflict this on you." He stood up to go.

"Don't be silly," she said. "If you want to go, that's fine. But if you think you have to just because your dealing with an issue that involves an old girlfriend, then sit down."

He thought about it. "I don't want to go," he declared and plopped down on the sofa.

She came and sat beside him and took his hand. "You know, I was never one to subscribe to the theory that as soon as you met someone new, you had to pretend there was never anyone else before. It's okay to be concerned about someone you love or loved, even if it's not me."

He smiled at her gratefully, increasingly aware of how special she was. "I feel like an idiot," he said.

"Why?"

"Because every time Melinda walks away from me and gets into trouble, she calls me to bail her out. Like a shmuck, I go. Which would be all right. Except there's always something in the back of my head that says maybe this time, if I fix whatever it is she's done, maybe this time, she'll be so grateful, or better yet, it'll be so obvious, she'll stay with me. But she never does. She just walks away and does it all over again."

"But this time, when she called, you didn't go."

"She didn't exactly call. Her sister did."

"And if Melinda had called herself, would you have gone?"

Jack looked at Daisy. She looked like a white willow, pale and beautiful, fragile enough to break in a strong wind. But her eyes shone with a clarity of focus that belied any weakness. He did not want to hurt her, but he owed her the truth.

"I don't know," was all he said finally.

For a long time, she didn't say anything, and he wondered if perhaps she was offended. But when she spoke, there was no recrimination and no self-pity in her voice.

"Well, we really have two issues here, don't we?" she said, matter-of-factly assessing the situation.

"Which are?" He was interested. He didn't always agree with what she said, but he always respected it.

"First, there's the issue of responding to a friend in need. No matter what passed between you and Melinda, or maybe because of it, she is someone who has a place in your heart. There's nothing wrong with that. And since you're the kind of guy who would go out of his way to help a stranger, it's not surprising that you'd feel obliged to help someone who was so much more. There's no shame in that.

"But then there's the issue of harboring an unrealistic desire to have something that has already been denied to you. Now, there's no saying that if you attempt to get it over and over again, you might not very well succeed. But you have to decide if its worth dedicating yourself to the quest or whether it might not be time to let it go and find another crusade.

"So then the question becomes why did you refuse to help this time, and why did it upset you to do so? Are you concerned that Melinda might be in danger? Or are you afraid that you've blown your chance for a reconciliation?"

He looked at her admiringly. "Have you been moonlighting at the Rand Corporation? I've been grappling with this for years, and I've never even come close to describing the problem so succinctly."

"Maybe you're a little too close to it," she allowed. "Can you answer the question?"

She wasn't going to let him off the hook, and she was right. She deserved to have an answer.

"Yes," he said, and it suddenly became alarmingly clear. "I refused to help because I'm not convinced that it's what Melinda wants. I offered to help her get out of San Domenico once and she refused. Sam could just be overreacting."

"That makes sense," Daisy said. "What about part two?"

He thought about it. "I'm upset because I feel guilty, pure and simple. I don't like to turn people down when they come to me for help, whether I can do anything or not. As for Melinda, I didn't blow anything with her. There's nothing to blow. It's over."

And having said it, he felt truly for the first time that it was.

"In that case, forget about it. I've never found guilt

to be a very productive emotion. No one can do what is required or requested of him all the time. It's just another form of arrogance to expect that you can."

"Jesus, Daisy, you cut right to it, don't you?"

She smiled ruefully, "Makes you want to run, doesn't it?"

"No, actually. It makes me want to marry you."

"Very funny."

"I'm not kidding."

"Well, then, it's very sweet. But I've already been engaged, and it didn't work out too well. So if you don't mind, I think I'll pass."

"Who said anything about getting engaged. Let's just get married."

She looked him in the eye. He did not waver. "You're serious, aren't you?"

"Yeah, why not. I adore you. You're beautiful, sexy, brilliant, and can read me like a goddamn book. And if you feel about me half the way I feel about you, it'll be a marriage made in heaven."

"Seventy-five percent," she teased.

"Then I say we do it."

"Okay." She laughed.

He kissed her then and, strangely, felt something break loose inside him. As if a bird, held on a long, slender tether that allowed him to fly, but never to soar, was suddenly freed, the thread that bound him to earth severed.

She sensed it, too, in the intensity of his kiss, the heat of his embrace.

"Let's not get married tonight, though," she whispered. "Let's just go to bed."

* * *

The baby was named Sebastian Nicholas Vincenzo Roca after their maternal grandfathers and the doctor and hero of the revolution who had been a friend to them both. But he was such a small thing that Melinda couldn't bring herself to call him by such a big name and addressed him, instead, as Nico.

In spite of his adventurous beginning, Nico turned out to be a sweet and docile baby, eating and sleeping regularly, quickly adjusting to six hours of undisturbed rest at night, kicking and gurgling appropriately for his adoring parents in his waking hours. For her part in the unconventional circumstances of his birth, Clara had been summarily dismissed, although Melinda had begged for a promise from Diego not to harm her or her family. Seeing how upset his wife was becoming and genuinely concerned for her well-being, Diego readily agreed, but Melinda had no way of knowing if he had kept his promise.

As a proud father and doting husband, Diego's behavior was exemplary, far more involved than even the average male of his background and culture. Somehow, between cabinet meetings and diplomatic functions, he managed to find time to lavish attention on his family. That he loved his son and his wife was obvious and never in question. That he kept Melinda a prisoner, severely restricting her contact with the outside world, was something only discreetly and surreptitiously observed.

"I would like to see my family," Melinda said simply. "I want them to meet our baby."

"In time," Diego responded affably. "You need to regain your strength."

"The only thing that keeps me weak is your refusal to let me see anyone."

"Don't be ridiculous. You're surrounded by people all day long."

"I mean anyone I care about."

"And what of the baby?" There was an element of accusation in his voice. It was the tone he employed whenever he wanted to indicate her problems were of her own doing.

"Don't do this, Diego. You know I love Nico."

"And so do I." He softened, reaching out to caress her cheek and push a wisp of hair from her face. "He needs us both, *mi amor.* And I need you as well."

She shrank away from him. She had begun to fear his tenderness more than his anger.

After the call to Sam, she did not eat. It wasn't a willful decision. In fact, she wanted to keep up her strength for the baby's sake and dreaded the thought that her breasts might dry up and be unable to supply him with the sustenance he needed. But try as she might, she could not force herself to swallow more than a few bites at each meal. Under worrisome instructions from Diego, the kitchen tried to entice her with all manner of delicacies. But it was no use.

Soon she refused to appear at mealtimes. There was no point in sitting at a table that held no temptations. Diego summoned the doctor. There was no classic diagnosis. She didn't try to disguise her lack of appetite or binge and vomit. Indeed, she seemed as distressed as the rest of them at her inability to consume. But there was nothing she could do about it. She had simply lost all desire to eat.

It was then Diego brought back Clara. The two women wept when they saw each other. Clara cooed at the baby and remarked at how much he'd grown in the month she hadn't seen him. Then she warned Melinda that Diego had made a deal with her. As long as Melinda ate regular meals, Clara could stay. But if her weight loss continued, Clara would be forced to leave again. Melinda had not contrived her fasting to use as leverage, but from that point on, she ate whatever was put on her plate.

The days took on a semblance of normality. With Clara by her side, Melinda walked in the garden, played with Nico, read, or watched the occasional American video, imported for her by her husband. Diego's desire for her happiness was genuine, and it pleased him to watch her regain her healthy glow. With no one daring to contradict him, he had convinced himself that it was possible to keep his personal and political lives separate, to be two disparate personalities as the situations demanded. On the official front, he continued his autocratic policies, insisting that his mission was to deliver San Domenico from its undeveloped status at any cost, even if it meant ruthlessly eliminating anyone who did not agree with him. In the name of progress, promises were forgotten, principles abandoned, friends denied.

In the private quarters of the presidential palace, Diego continued to maintain that nothing had changed. And indeed, on the surface, there was a pleasant serenity. Melinda had ceased to question him about his political operations, aware that that road would only lead to conflict. Instead, she secretly kept abreast of his maneuvers through Clara, who quietly delivered the latest on the president's exercise of his powers, the freedoms revoked, the atrocities perpetrated, all in the name of a better, if embittered, San Domenico. When they were together with their child, Melinda focused all her attention on Nico, limiting her observations of Diego to his loving and growing attachment to his son. But when they were alone, she pleaded exhaustion, unable to reconcile the heartless despot she heard about during the day with the devoted husband who came to her at night. She knew she wasn't fooling Diego, that one day his patience would expire and that his love would turn to anger.

Clara knew it, too. "He won't put up with your holding back from him forever. He's a very virile man."

They were walking with the baby in the garden, the only place Melinda was allowed to go without Diego's supervision. Even though he had never really been able to prove that Nico's birth had occurred during an attempted escape, all the gates leading to the palace grounds had been reinforced and protected by either lock or sentry. He told Melinda it was to keep their enemies out, but she knew it was to keep her in as well.

"I can't help it. Every time he gets into bed with me, I think about the women who are waiting for husbands, lovers, sons, they'll never see again. Because of Diego. It makes me hate him."

"Well, it had better not make him hate you. Because you know what happens then."

"He wouldn't hurt me. Because of Nico."

"I'm not so sure," said Clara, and the dread in her voice made Melinda shiver. "I think soon it won't be safe for you here. Not that it's safe for anyone."

"There's nothing I can do about it."

"What about your family in the United States? There must be a way for them to get you out. They must have friends of influence. Why don't they help you?"

"They don't even know I need help. He won't let me speak to them."

"If they did know, could they help you?" She said it so slyly that Melinda understood instantly that Clara must have a plan.

"Yes, I'm sure they could. Somehow. But what are you saying, Clara? I'm sure Diego is watching you as closely as he's watching me. He's not going to let you make contact with anyone."

"I know that. Not me." She lowered her voice to a whisper. "My cousin Ottavio was trained as a pilot during the revolution. But since the restrictions, he's been speaking out against the government. We tried to get him to shut up, but he's always been a big mouth. First, they took away his passport. Now we think he's next in line for a disappearance. He's got to get out of San Domenico."

"How can he do that if he doesn't have a passport."

"He still knows how to fly. He's been secretly fixing up an old plane. He's going out tonight. He can take a letter."

Taken aback, Melinda was confused. Although she had begged Diego to let her call her family, it somehow suddenly seemed shameful to write to them that she was being held prisoner by her husband.

"If you wrote," Clara added as if divining her thoughts, "maybe you could also ask them to help my cousin to stay in the United States."

It was the focus Melinda needed. "Of course," she said and had to laugh when Clara instantly whipped out paper and pen from the pocket of her dress.

To the happy gurgling of her baby, as Clara threw Nico into the air and caught him, Melinda wrote. Aware that it might be necessary for the letter to be shown to a number of officials, Melinda kept the tone formal.

"Dear Sam, I pray you get this letter, because if you do it means that Ottavio has reached safety in the U.S. He is the cousin of the woman who nursed me and saved Nico when I gave birth in the jungle. Help him stay in the States, because if he comes back here, he will be killed. Diego has changed. He has people tortured and imprisoned for speaking their minds. He loves the baby and he hasn't hurt me, but we are kept virtual prisoners in the presidential palace. Though I long to see you, I guess it can't be for a while. I love you all."

She started to sign, but Clara, who was by now reading over her shoulder, stopped her with a hand over the page.

"You're not finished," Clara protested.

"I just need to sign," said Melinda, trying to move the paper from under Clara's hand.

"What about yourself. Tell them you need help. Tell them to come and get you."

"They can't do that," Melinda objected. "Diego would never let them. I don't want them to do anything that would endanger them."

"Please, Melinda. They're Americans. They'll know what to do. They can find a way."

Melinda raised her eyes to Clara. She desperately wanted to believe what the nurse was telling her. But she was afraid—for herself, for her baby, for her family, for all of them.

"Tell them. Let them decide."

Clara took away her hand. Melinda took a breath and began to write again. "Nico and I have what we need, but more than anything, I wish I could bring him home and watch him grow up with the independence I never truly understood or appreciated until it was gone. Please, please, don't put yourselves at risk. But if you can, help me. I am afraid."

She paused for a minute, then added, "Myles Militia forever." It was their secret sign-off. If Sam saw that, she would have no doubt that it was Melinda herself who was writing. She folded the paper and put it in the envelope that Clara provided.

"You've thought of everything." She smiled.

She wrote Sam's name, address, and phone number at Belvedere as well as her office at DMC on the envelope and sealed it tightly.

"Wherever he lands in the United States," Melinda instructed Clara, "tell him to insist he must speak with Samantha Myles Symington. Any American official will know who she is and how to get in touch with her. He must not show this letter to anyone else."

Clara nodded solemnly. "I'll tell him. Don't worry, Melinda. If he gets to your country, he'll get to your sister. I promise."

They hugged each other hard enough for the baby,

who was squeezed between them, to squeal and then, laughing nervously, broke apart and headed back to the presidential palace, glad that no one could see their beating hearts.

Diego came back to their private quarters earlier than usual, anxious to spend some time with his son. Clara took her leave, and the two women exchanged a quick look but said nothing. Both knew that tonight, more than any other, everything must appear normal.

Watching Diego play with Nico reminded Melinda of every reason she had ever loved him. He was gentle, fun, inventive, and openly affectionate, and it was clear that the baby adored him.

"I'll give him his bath," Diego announced, stripping off his shirt. He stood for a moment, holding the naked baby in his arms, nuzzling his little neck, while the child twisted his tiny fingers in his father's black hair. Melinda caught her breath at their beauty and felt the tears well up in her eyes. For a second of insanity, she thought maybe she could make it different. Maybe she could find a way to bridge the schism that had separated the man of compassion from the man of ambition.

"What is it, *mi amor?* Look, Nico, Mommy's crying. What's wrong?"

Quickly, she wiped away a tear and tried to laugh it away as Diego came to her, and the baby reached out his pudgy arms. "It's stupid," she said. "I was just remembering how it used to be before. I was happier in our leaky tent than I am in this whole palace."

She hadn't meant to tell the truth, but somehow it had slipped out. Maybe in the hope that Diego might suddenly agree with her and walk away from the trappings of a tyrant. She saw him stiffen and knew instantly that she had made a mistake.

"I can't believe that you still romanticize the poverty and deprivation that led to the revolution."

"That's not what I'm doing at all. I was just thinking about us. We *were* happy."

"I was at war. You were a movie star having an adventure."

"That is absolutely not fair. And you know it. I was out there in the trenches, too. Vincenzo died in my arms."

"Then you should understand that we cannot allow this for our son. He will have what my people never had. He will know things they never had a chance to know."

He turned on his heel and went into the bathroom. She could hear him cooing to the baby as the water ran into the sink that they used as his tub.

"But he will never know freedom," she said quietly to herself. "Not if he stays here."

7

Ian had insisted on coming with her, although Sarah had been reluctant. In the end, they agreed to talk to Dr. Horvath together and then let him decide what should be done. They took turns telling him what they knew, although Sarah's part was mostly about what she didn't know. Ian said they had had an argument and that Sarah had stormed out of the house. He had waited for her all night, but when she didn't return, he'd fallen asleep for a few hours. At dawn, he'd looked out the window and seen her car parked in front with her asleep inside. She was dirty and had been drinking but said she didn't know what had happened to her. He brought her inside.

Sarah said she remembered starting to talk about having children and thinking maybe the reason she wasn't getting pregnant was that she didn't really want to. She assumed that she had come to this possibility through the work she was doing with Dr. Horvath. She didn't remember having a real argument or storming out. She didn't remember anything that happened to her during the night. Her first recollection was Ian waking her and the horrible feelings of shame, disgust, and utter confusion. She told the doctor that she had found a bump on her head and wondered if perhaps she had fallen and knocked herself unconscious, which would account for her appearance as well as her amnesia. The doctor had examined her and said that even though she'd received quite a knock, he didn't think she had a concussion, and if her amnesia were a physical problem, it was neurological and she would have to go to another doctor. Sarah had had a CAT scan, but nothing had shown up. Which brought them to Dr. Horvath.

Dr. Horvath listened attentively. He didn't take notes when they talked; he never did. But he always seemed able to remember whatever had been said during the session. Sarah suspected he took notes after she left and looked them over before she arrived. He told Sarah that he wanted to speak to Ian alone for a few minutes and then send him away so they could have their regular session if that was agreeable with her. Trusting them both as she did, she had no objection.

When she'd gone into the waiting room, Dr. Horvath turned to Ian. "With your permission, I would like to be direct."

"Of course."

"Has Sarah had these blackouts before?"

"Not that I know of."

"Is it possible that you might not know? Could she hide it from you?"

His first instinct was to scoff. They shared everything; why would she? But then, he thought again. "We both work at DMC, in separate areas, of course. But we used to go to the office and home together. Lately, she's taken to using her own car. She says she needs more flexibility. So I suppose it's possible. But I find it hard to believe she wouldn't tell me about it. We're extraordinarily close."

"Does she drink a lot?"

"No more than average."

"What constitutes average. Cocktails at lunch? Before dinner? Wine with the meal? A nightcap after?"

"All of those are possible but not regular. There are days when we'll have a drink before dinner and then wine. Other days when we won't drink at all."

"What about when she's not with you?"

"I've never seen her drunk if that's what you're suggesting."

"I'm asking because Sarah's experience could be a classic blackout. Alcoholics tend to deny that they drink so much they don't know what they're doing. They hide the amount they drink and, when they're caught, try to cover with sometimes bizarre stories. You understand, this may not be Sarah's problem. But it might be wise just to keep an eye out, look for hidden bottles, that sort of thing."

"Her mother is a pretty heavy drinker. Sarah told me there was once a family scandal that involved her driving drunk and hitting someone."

"Unfortunately, we don't really understand alcoholism as well as we'd like to. But there does seem to be a hereditary propensity toward it. In the meantime, I'm going to keep working with Sarah to try and uncover other root causes. But let's keep in touch."

"Thank you, Doctor. I appreciate your help. I'm really worried about her."

"It's good for Sarah to know that you care about her, and I can see that you do. That puts her way ahead."

Sarah came back into the room, looking questioningly from one to the other.

Dr. Horvath didn't wait for her to ask. "Sarah, I was speaking to Ian about my concern that you might be drinking too much and that might have led to the incident."

"But I don't even remember taking a drink. Wouldn't you think that if I went out to get drunk, which I didn't, I'd at least know where I'd gone?"

Ian reflexively reached out for her hand. He could tell that the suggestion had upset her. But he couldn't help wondering if it bothered her because it wasn't true—or because it was. Dr. Horvath seemed to take it in stride.

"We're just going to examine every possibility until we get to the bottom of this thing. Which we will. I'm sure of that."

Sarah seemed a little reassured. At a nod from the doctor, Ian stood up to go.

"Do you want me to wait for you, honey?"

"No, thanks, really. I'll be fine. You go ahead; I'll just take a cab home."

"I don't mind waiting."

"Actually, I'd rather you didn't. I'm afraid that if I

know you're out here, I might not be able to concentrate on the hypnosis, and today of all days, I think I need to do that."

He kissed her, understanding, shook the doctor's hand, and headed out.

"Do you think if you hypnotize me, I will remember what happened that night?"

"Truthfully, I don't know. It all depends on why you don't remember it now."

"What if it doesn't work?" She was already envisioning a slow descent into madness, untold escapades to unknown places, and he could hear the terror in her voice.

"Then we'll try to find out what's blocking it. That may be the more crucial thing to know."

She lay on the leather recliner as she had done many times before. By now, it took very little to put her into a deep hypnotic state.

Dr. Horvath snapped his fingers and said simply, "Deep sleep." Instantly, she closed her eyes and felt every muscle in her body relax. It almost made her smile, her response was so instantaneous. As usual, she was in her bilevel state of consciousness. One part of her obeyed the doctor's directives, while the other watched, fully aware of what was going on. He counted to ten and made her breathe deeply and say "Far away" while he pressed his fingers on her eyelids. He told her he wanted her to sleep more deeply and relax more completely than she ever had before, to go farther away than she had ever been.

"I want you to think about that night," he said to her, his voice quiet, soothing. "Remember where you were and what you did. Can you do that?"

"Yes," she answered. It was already in her mind. The picture had come on his command.

"Where are you?"

"I don't know. I see it but I don't know where it is."

"Can you describe it to me?"

"It's a bar. An ugly, dirty dive." There was genuine disgust in her voice.

"Do you know this place?"

"No."

"Have you ever been there before?"

"I don't know."

She was becoming visibly uneasy. He decided to keep the scope of his questioning small, to limit it to the night in question. If she could tell him what happened that night, then they could worry about whether it had happened before.

"What are you doing?"

"I'm having a drink. Talking to the bartender."

He nodded, though with her eyes still closed, she could not see. The pattern was falling into place, and his suspicions were being confirmed. He was not surprised.

"Is there anyone else in the bar?" he asked her.

"Yeah. A man."

"Who is he?"

"I don't know. I don't like him. I don't want to do this."

Her agitation was growing.

"What don't you want to do?" He wasn't sure if she was referring to something she was remembering or the remembering itself.

She was upset now, moving around in the chair,

unable to sit still. He asked her again, "What don't you want to do, Sarah?"

"For Crissake, leave her alone," she barked at him, taking him aback.

"What did you say?"

She was quiet again, "Please, can we leave it alone."

"I thought you said leave *her* alone."

"No. This just isn't working for me."

"Do you want me to bring you out?"

"Yes, I do."

He counted to five, and her eyes blinked open. He tried to ask her about the bar she had seen while she was under hypnosis, but all she could suggest was maybe it was something she had seen on television or in a movie. It certainly wasn't any place familiar. When she insisted that following this line was just a dead end, he dropped it, aware that her resistance was too great to penetrate. Then, he tried to focus on what had bothered her about his line of questioning, but she was too restless to concentrate on what he was saying.

"I'm sorry," Sarah said. "I must be tired. I really can't think of anything specific right now."

He saw that there was no use in prolonging the session; she was already gone. "All right. Why don't we call it a day and make an appointment for next week?"

Sarah watched him consult his calendar, leafing through the pages. She felt as though she was going to suffocate.

"I'll call you. I . . . I don't have my schedule." She excused herself and headed out. He stopped her at the door and pressed something into her hand before she escaped.

Outside, she stood with her face into the wind and took a few deep gulps of air. She glanced down at the folder in her hand. "Facing Addiction" it said in big black letters.

"That reminds me. I need a drink." She laughed out loud, crumpling the folder and tossing it into the nearest waste basket. "Got to watch out, Sunny, my girl," she continued to herself as she walked away. "You almost gave away the game."

The call came at midnight. Drew was still at DMC at an all-night security overhaul meeting. Sam had taken the opportunity to go to bed early with a book, but after half an hour of forcing her eyelids to stay open, she'd given in to fatigue, turned off the light, and gone to sleep. Startled by the sudden ringing, she found it disorienting to reach across the empty space on Drew's side of the bed to get to the phone.

"Is this Samantha Myles Symington?" an unfamiliar voice asked in response to her mumbled greeting.

"Yes, what is it?" She was instantly alert. There had been too many cataclysmic occurrences lately for her not to be alarmed by a midnight caller.

The caller heard the consternation in her voice and had the grace to reassure her. "Nothing's wrong, ma'am, and I'm sorry if I've alarmed you by calling at this hour. My name is Mark Sutpin and I'm with the INS in Miami, Florida. A man claiming to be from San Domenico and seeking political asylum has just performed an unauthorized landing on an airstrip near here. He has on his person a letter addressed to you, which he claims is from your sister."

"Oh, my God. What does it say?"

"Ma'am, we don't know. The letter is sealed. We do need to know the contents, but since it's addressed to you, we thought it appropriate to inform you first. If you can get down here today, we will hold off any action until you've had a chance to read it for yourself. Otherwise—"

She didn't even let him finish. "I'm taking the first plane I can get. I'll be there by this afternoon."

"That's fine, ma'am."

"You'll keep him there, right? The pilot? I want to be able to talk to him."

"He'll be here. We're not sure what we're doing with him yet. What's in the letter might even make a difference."

"Okay. Thank you, Mr. Sutpin, for calling me. If you give me a number where I can reach you, I'll let you know when I'm arriving as soon as I've made my arrangements."

There was a plane to Miami from Chicago at six A.M. She would need to leave by three to allow for the two-hour drive to O'Hare and enough time to buy her ticket. She called Drew and got him out of the meeting to tell him what she was doing.

"Why didn't you just ask him to read the letter to you over the phone?" he asked.

"I don't know," she said. "I was afraid of what it might say, I guess. I wanted to see it myself. And I wanted to speak to the pilot. Maybe he knows something that he's not telling the authorities. I don't know. It was just a gut reaction. I have to go."

Hearing the anxiety in her voice, Drew understood how important this was for her and dropped his argument. "Okay. I'll be home by the time Moira gets up, so don't worry about that. Call me when you know something."

A flood of affection for her husband swept over Sam. "Thank you, Drew. I'll probably be home tonight. But I'll call you in any case."

"Do you want to get a driver to take you to the airport? You're pretty nervous."

"No, I'll be fine. It'll give me something to occupy my mind."

"Okay. Drive carefully. I love you."

"I love you, too. Kiss my baby good morning for me."

"I will."

She hung up and sat for a moment to organize her thoughts. Then she swept into action, dressing quickly and throwing a change of clothes and a toothbrush into a bag just in case it took longer than she anticipated. On the way out, she tapped gently on the door of Halsey's room next to the nursery. Apologizing profusely for waking her up, Sam explained what was going on and asked her to keep an ear out for Moira. Drew would probably be home by the time she woke up, but in case she got up early, Sam didn't want her running to her parents' room like she did every morning and finding the bed empty.

"I'm leaving my door open," said Halsey. "Don't you worry about a thing. We'll get on just fine."

Sam thanked her and blessed the day that she had walked into their lives and replaced the upheaval left by Natalie with her serene, well-organized presence.

Driving through the dark streets toward Highway 55, which would take her right to the airport, she tried to keep her imagination from running wild. It had been months since she had heard from Melinda. All attempts to call her at the presidential palace had been rebuffed. She was always told that her sister was out, that she was busy, that she'd call her back. But Sam never doubted that someone was keeping Melinda from her against her will. It was totally inconceivable that either one of them would not want to communicate with the other. Since they'd made their pact as the Myles Militia when they were children, they had shared everything, both good and bad. There was no reason and no possibility that Melinda would voluntarily cut her off now.

Forcing herself to keep her mind on her driving instead of envisioning a scenario for disaster, Sam focused on the road and realized she had absolutely no idea where she was. Frustrated and angry at herself for not heeding Drew's advice and getting a driver to take her to the airport, acutely aware of the time going by, she pulled over to the side to consult a map, only to discover there was none. She cursed quietly, remembering she'd taken the map out of the glove compartment when she and Drew had taken Moira to the country for a picnic last summer, and as she'd had no occasion to use it since then, she'd forgotten to put it back.

She peered out the window and tried to see the name on the street sign, barely illuminated by the dull glow of a lone street lamp. The name told her nothing except that she was in a part of town that every decent kid in Oakdale knew to avoid. She considered just driving around until she found an open gas station or at least a familiar landmark, but looking at the clock, she realized she couldn't afford the time.

She got out of the car and surveyed her immediate surroundings. The area was run-down and appeared to be mainly old warehouses. No one was on the street. Up ahead, she saw a sign, a beer bottle flashing a neon red welcome. Quickly, she got back into her car and drove the two blocks to the bar.

Intent on getting directions from the bartender, Sam didn't even notice the other patrons at first. It was only as she was on her way out that she heard a familiar laugh. She turned to see an unsavory-looking character, gray thinning hair hanging in a greasy ponytail down his back, tattooed arms emerging from a studded motorcycle jacket, pulling a woman onto his lap, causing the outburst of drunken hilarity.

Sam laughed at herself. For one insane moment, she had thought the woman was Sarah. But immediately, she remembered where she was and realized how absurd it would be for her sister-in-law to be here. She started out the door and then stopped in shock as she heard the woman, speaking in the blaring timbre of someone too drunk to know or care how loud they're speaking, say, "Forget it, George. I'm not going to fuck you right here in the bar. You want to get laid, you get us a room."

It was definitely Sarah's voice, and it was just as definitely not something Sarah would ever say. Sam peered into the dark corner of the dingy bar. The woman did have a certain resemblance to her sister-in-law, but her hair, her makeup, and, even more important, her demeanor were poles apart from

Sarah's look. Ready to continue her journey, Sam told herself she'd have to remember to tell Sarah that somewhere in Oakdale she had a doppelgänger.

Then the woman stood. Sam gasped. She recognized the woman's blouse. It was three buttons more open than she usually saw it, but she knew it well. It had been her gift to Sarah last Christmas. Unable to move, not knowing what to think, Sam stood there until the woman, feeling strange eyes upon her, turned and saw her staring, mouth agape.

"Well, well. Look who we have here." She grinned. "What is it? Slumming or spying?"

"I . . . uh . . . I got lost. I'm on my way to the airport. I got lost. I needed directions."

"Running away from home?" Sarah mocked.

"Who's the bitch?" George asked cordially, putting his arm around Sarah and squeezing her breast.

"Shut up. She's my sister-in-law," Sarah said, wriggling out of his grasp.

"No kidding. She looking for a good time, too? I got a friend."

"Hear that, Sam? Want George to call his friend?"

The two of them had made their way to the door where Sam had remained riveted.

"He's got a thing for redheads," George said. "He says they're really hot. Is that true?" He reached out a dirty hand to touch her hair, and Sam snapped out of her daze and violently twisted away.

"Sarah," she said, unable to keep the horror out of her voice, "what are you doing here?"

Sarah was unperturbed. "Isn't it obvious?"

"I don't understand."

"You want it spelled out for you? Okay. I'm having

some goddamn fun. That's what I'm doing. I'm getting goddamn drunk, and then, with George's help, I'm going to get goddamn laid."

Sam tried not to let her shock show. Obviously, Sarah was drunk. She knew things had been tense between Sarah and Ian lately, but she couldn't imagine how it could lead to this state. "Sarah, I don't know what's happened to you or why you're being like this, but I'm sure Ian must be worried." She looked at her watch. "I'd take you home myself, but I have to catch a plane. Let me call you a cab."

"I can take care of myself."

"No, I don't think you can."

"Fortunately, I don't give a shit what you think. You and your little moralistic family make me sick. You like to act so smug and good. But let's get real. First your mother fucked my father. Then your sister fucked my father. And God knows what you and your boring brother are doing. So you can just fuck off."

Sam resisted the temptation to just slap her face and walk out the door. *This is not Sarah talking,* she told herself. *This is someone who needs help.* "I'm sorry, Sarah. I don't have time for this. Either you let me put you in a cab right now or I'm calling Ian to come and get you."

"No," Sarah said quickly, and Sam saw the threat was the first thing that had disconcerted her. "I don't want him coming here."

"Fine. Then go home."

"Don't let the bitch push you around, baby. I'll get us a room."

"Shut up, George. You're too dumb and too late."

Sam saw she'd won the round, but she had no idea

how this incident calibrated with either the past or the future. She didn't have time to figure it out now. She asked the bartender to call a cab.

The cab arrived in mercifully short time. Sam gave him twenty dollars and instructed him to take Sarah to Belvedere. Then she gave him an extra fifty and told him to make sure she got to the door and was taken in by someone in the house. For added security, she took Sarah's purse and emptied it of money and credit cards.

"Hey, you can't do that," griped Sarah.

"Just want to make sure you've got nowhere to go but home. I'll give it back to you later."

"You're going to be sorry you did this. You're going to wish you minded your own business," mumbled Sarah as Sam pushed her into the car.

"I don't think so," said Sam, knowing that Sarah's resentment wasn't the real problem. They'd have a lot more to deal with when she returned from Florida.

Sam watched the cab pull away, then got into her own car and, realizing she had a half hour to make up, speeded toward the highway.

Inside, a bewildered George stood at the bar. "What the fuck was that all about?"

"Beats me," said the bartender.

"And why'd she keep calling her Sarah? I thought her name was Sunny."

"Beats me," said the bartender again, having long since realized it did him no good to figure things out.

8

Jack found the letter at the bottom of a thick pile of papers in his "things to do" file. With his background in union negotiations, he'd been drafted by his superiors at the State Department to help review trade agreements that were coming up for renewal, and everything else had fallen by the wayside. Even his relationship with Daisy had been put on hold while he worked late nights at the office, trying to meet his deadlines. Now, with the end in sight, he'd decided to go through his slush pile to see if anything required immediate attention.

A quick glance told him that the letter was, in fact, a form letter, with the heading "Dear . . ." and a blank space where his name had been filled in by a computer with a similar, but not exactly identical, print. His automatic reaction was to simply toss it in the wastebasket without even reading it, but the Amnesty International logo on the top of the paper caught his eyes, and he fished it back out of the garbage to look it over. He saw that he was being informed that an Amnesty International delegation was leaving for San Domenico in ten days and that since they knew of his "interest" in the country, they would welcome any information or contribution he could make to their investigation of rights abuses. He thought about his last call from Sam and her fears for her sister and wondered if perhaps he should try to write Melinda a letter and send it with the delegation. He glanced at the date at the top of the page, then at his own calendar. The letter had been written nine days ago. If it had been mailed on the same day it was written, then the delegation would be leaving tomorrow. If it had sat on someone's desk or at the post office for a day or two, the delegation would already be gone. He reminded himself of the point he had been so careful to make to Sam. Melinda had chosen to stay in San Domenico. If she chose to leave, she would find a way to make her wishes known. For all he knew, trying to contact her might just upset her own delicate balance and make things worse. He crumpled the letter and threw it back into the wastepaper basket.

He thought about calling Daisy, then looked at his watch and realized it was already past eight. She'd be gone already. She had invited him to a concert at the Kennedy Center, but there had been a meeting to review the changes that the team of legal advisors proposed, and not knowing how long it would take, he had had to decline. As it turned out, there had been little argument over the suggestions, the meeting had broken up early, he'd had time to go through his papers, and still an empty evening stretched ahead.

"Shit," he said to himself. "I should have called her before."

He drove home, not even bothering to turn on the radio. He had to keep reminding himself not to take the familiar route to Daisy's Connecticut Avenue apartment, where he'd been spending most of his nights. He yawned and then thought it was just as well that he had not gone to the concert. He would have been asleep before intermission.

He felt fatigue settle around his shoulders as he parked his car and walked up the stairs to his townhouse apartment. He noticed a faint light was peeking from under his door. He was surprised at himself. Ecologically minded, he was usually so careful to turn off all his lights when he left. He unlocked the door and wearily let himself in. He started to chuckle.

His lights were still off. The glow was coming from a string of small votive candles that lined the walls of the corridor. Strewn between the candles was a drift of rose petals, turning his hallway floor into a sweet-scented blood red path. The configuration of his small apartment being what it was, he assumed the path led to the bedroom. Throwing off his clothes as he went, he followed his floral destiny.

"Welcome home," came the familiar husky growl, not from the bedroom as he had expected, but from the bathroom.

He pushed the door open. The lights were off here, too, and the room was aglow in more candlelight. She was in the tub, surrounded by an aura of bubbles. Her white blond hair was pinned to the top of her head, but silky wisps trailed down her neck, licking at the water.

"Get in," she said. "The water's fine."

In seconds, he was naked, easing himself into the steaming water opposite her. He leaned back and closed his eyes: hot, liquid heaven.

"I thought you were going to a concert," he said.

"I didn't want to go without you." Her foot had found him.

He sighed. "I'm glad. I was just thinking how much I was going to miss you tonight."

After that, he couldn't talk for a while. But he understood that there was more than one meaning to being fast on your feet.

Daisy made them omelettes, and they ate in bed, watching the news on television. She took the plates back to the kitchen, promising to come back with milk and cookies, but by the time she returned, Jack was already fast asleep.

In the morning, he woke up with her beside him. He had slept long and well. He reached over and pulled her to him. She turned to face him, warm and pliant.

"Doesn't this feel incredibly comfortable?" he asked as she nestled in his arms.

"Hmmmm," she murmured in assent, still half asleep.

"Don't you feel like you could do this every morning of your life?"

"Hmmmm," she said again.

"Then why don't we?"

"Okay," she replied sleepily, burrowing into the space between his neck and his shoulder, her soft breath brushing his skin.

He sat up and reached for the telephone, leaving a cold empty air space where his body had been.

She groaned. "What are you doing?"

"Calling the office and telling them I'm not coming in for a few days."

"Can you do that?"

"Sure, why not? We finished the trade agreements, thanks to my eighteen-hour days. There's nothing pressing. I'm up for some personal time."

"Oh, good." She was sitting up now, too, fully awake. "We can play."

"No," he said solemnly. "We can't."

"Why? What else do you have to do?"

"Get married." He saw her mouth drop open. "You want to, don't you?" he asked worriedly. "I mean, we did talk about it . . ."

"I know. I guess I just didn't expect to do it today."

"Is there any reason why we shouldn't?"

"Well, we'd need a license. And I think there's a waiting period."

"Not in Maryland. We could drive over, get married, find an inn, disappear for the weekend, and come back as Ma and Pa Kettle."

She laughed. "I'll settle for Mr. and Mrs. Jack Bader. Although, officially, I'm keeping my own name."

"Deal!"

"And there's one other thing."

"What? Anything."

"I'm not getting married in the clothes I wore yesterday."

"Fine. Go shopping."

"No, I don't need to do that. I just need to go home

and get a bag with some stuff. Especially if we're going to stay away for the weekend. And I've got to get someone to cover at the soup kitchen. And water the plants."

"Okay, listen. You go home. Do what you have to do. Pack a bag and don't forget ID, like license, passport, whatever. I'll call the office and get myself cleared. Then meet me back here in, say, two hours. And we'll go get married. Want to?"

She didn't even have to think about it.

"Yes," she said, throwing her arms around him. "Yes, yes, yes."

After she left, he washed the dishes and made the bed. He took a shower, shaved, got dressed. He looked at his watch. He still had an hour before Daisy was due back. But he had a feeling that she'd be early.

"What am I doing?" he asked himself, dropping into an overstuffed chair that had come with the furnished apartment. He was pleased that no waves of panic threatened to drown him in a sea of self-doubt or remorse. In fact, although he had to admit it might have been wiser to do his thinking before his impromptu suggestion to Daisy, marrying her made a lot of sense. Since their passionate meeting over a year ago, he'd had no interest in anyone else. She was the only one who had ever come close to filling the void left by his breakup with Melinda. It was time to move on, and Daisy was the person who could help him do it.

The ringing of the doorbell called him back to the present. He looked at his watch and laughed. Still a half hour to go. He had known she'd be early. It was only as he was opening the door that he wondered why she hadn't used her key.

"Hello, Jack." Sam was smiling at him from his threshold. It must have taken longer than he thought to register, because she went on. "I apologize for just dropping in this way. I tried to call from the airport but your line was busy, and I didn't want to waste any time."

"That's okay. Come on in, Sam. It's good to see you," he ushered her in, trying to cover his astonishment.

"It's been a while, hasn't it?"

"It certainly has."

They looked at each other for a moment and then, wordless, went into a hug. They'd been avoiding each other, and they both knew it. Ever since the troubles in San Domenico had started, no matter what they talked about, Melinda was always the unspoken subject between them. Sam could not bear to skirt the issue, and Jack could not bear to confront it. So, even though they had been friends for a long time and cared about each other deeply, it had been understood without either one of them articulating it that it would be best to limit their contact.

"How are you, Jack?" Sam asked, truly pleased to see him no matter what the circumstances. "You look great."

"I am. Really great. What about you? Everybody okay?" He had kept it general, afraid to ask, knowing she would not just drop in on him without a reason, and in due time she would tell him what it was.

"Pretty much. I left Drew with Moira back in Woodland Cliffs. They're fine."

He nodded. "That's good. Hey, do you want some coffee? Something to eat?" He was being polite, but he was also stalling for time. Whatever brought Sam to Washington, he was already certain he wouldn't enjoy hearing about it.

"No. I had some on the plane."

"Well, at least come in and sit down."

They moved into the living room, and Jack sank back into the chair where he had been sitting when she arrived. Sam perched on the end of the sofa, too nervous to even sit properly.

She took a deep breath. "It's about Melinda."

"I had a feeling."

"Remember you said that if she ever wanted help, really needed it, you'd be there."

"I've said it more than once. I still mean it."

She handed him the letter. He read it silently. She saw his eyes scanning from top to bottom, then start at the top again.

Finally, he asked, "Where's this pilot—Ottavio or whatever his name is?"

"Immigration has him. He landed his plane on an airstrip in Florida. INS officials found the letter on him and called me to come down there. I tried to get them to let him come with me to see you, but it was too complicated. But I got him a lawyer. I expect he'll be granted asylum."

"Is he for real?"

"Definitely. And so's the letter. I recognize Melinda's handwriting."

"So do I," admitted Jack. "Still—"

"She wrote this of her own volition, Jack. You know it. If she didn't mean this, she would never have said anything about the Myles Militia. That's our code. This time, I think she's really scared and she wants to get out. And she's got the baby."

He didn't say anything. He agreed with Sam. Melinda was in trouble. The baby wasn't going to make it any easier.

"I don't know what to do, Jack. Who to go to. I'm afraid if I go public and turn it into an international scandal, Roca will just take it out on her somehow. He won't let me talk to her. I don't know how to get to her."

"I do," said Jack, his wheels suddenly beginning to turn. He picked up the phone. "Liane," he said when his secretary picked up, "no, I'm still not coming in. Listen to me. I want you to go to my wastepaper basket and get something . . . Don't be squeamish, it's all trash. It's a letter from Amnesty International. There's a phone number on it. I need it."

Sam looked at him questioningly.

"There's a delegation going to San Domenico."

"That's great," said Sam, heartened. "Do you think they could do something for Melinda?"

Before he could answer her, he was listening to the phone, scribbling information. "Tell me again what's the date on that? . . . Yeah, that's what I thought."

He hung up. He stood there for a moment, thinking, hesitant.

"Are you going to call them?" Sam asked, encouraging.

"There wouldn't be much point."

"How do you know unless you try?" She was getting angry, and she made no attempt to hide it. She knew that things were problematic between Jack and her sister, but she never thought he'd balk at saving her life. "Damn it, Jack. If you don't want to get involved, just give me the goddamn number and I'll call myself."

She reached for it, ready to grab it from his hand, but he pulled it away from her. "Take it easy, Sam. The problem is they've gone already. The letter said the delegation was leaving today."

Sam looked at her watch. "They're not gone yet. There's only one plane to San Domenico a day from Washington. Believe me, I know. It doesn't leave for another couple of hours. We could get them at the airport. Come with me."

"Sam, I . . ."

He heard the key turning in the lock. He knew he had a lot to explain, but there didn't seem to be any time.

"Honey, I'm home," trilled Daisy in her best *Leave it to Beaver* voice. She stopped, embarrassed, when she saw he was not alone.

"Daisy," he said before she could say anything else, "you know Sam Myles, don't you?"

"Of course," said Daisy, all practiced graciousness as she set down her bag and came to greet her. "By reputation if nothing else. Jack has told me about you and your family."

Almost imperceptibly, Sam's eyes swept over Daisy, and Jack could see her taking it all in as they shook hands. True to her word, Daisy had changed her clothes. She was wearing a soft beige suit, with a long fitted jacket over a very short, flippy sheer skirt. Her pale blond hair was pushed behind her ear on one side and curved down her face in a modified Veronica

Lake wave on the other. She was carrying a small Vuitton overnight bag. She looked ethereally beautiful and, Jack thought, exactly as though she were about to get married.

"I'm so sorry to have just popped in this way," Sam apologized, either not noticing what seemed so obvious to Jack or, more likely, choosing to ignore it. "I'm afraid I've got a family emergency and I've come to Jack for help."

"Well, then," Daisy said, looking Jack straight in the eyes, "you must help."

"But, we . . . ," Jack began, helplessly.

"I'm sure Sam wouldn't have come unless it was important. And I know you well enough to know you wouldn't be able to live with yourself if you let her down."

The minute she said it, Jack knew it was true. He looked at his watch. If they left for the airport now, they could find the AI delegation, talk to them about what could be done for Melinda, and then he and Daisy could still be on their way to Maryland by noon.

He picked up Daisy's bag and his own, which he had left at the door in preparation. "Come on," he said. "We've got to go to the airport. I'll explain what's going on along the way," he added to Daisy, aware from the look on Sam's face that for her, no explanation was necessary.

They didn't have any trouble finding the AI delegation at Dulles Airport. San Domenico had already been placed on the travel advisory list by the U.S. government, so there weren't a lot of tourists to contend with. As it happened, Jack had worked with one of the delegates on another matter and recognized him. With the two women in tow, he rushed over to the group just as they were getting ready to embark.

Corey Winthrop greeted him cordially. He was a little older than Jack, a Peace Corps graduate who had successfully made the transition to the world of business, only to find that he could get no satisfaction unless he felt like he was doing some good for humankind. Jack had admired him for giving up his six-figure salary for something he really believed in, fully aware that he himself had gone in the opposite direction.

"I've got to talk to you, Corey," Jack said after they'd exchanged pleasantries and Jack had introduced Sam and Daisy.

"Well, Jack," said Corey, aware that Jack hadn't waylaid him in the airport to talk about the weather, "I've got a plane to catch. You're going to have to make it fast."

Jack nodded to Sam, and she handed Corey the letter. He read it quickly, then looked back at them. "Is this authentic?"

"Definitely. She's my sister. I know her writing," said Sam.

"I'm glad you showed it to me. But I'm not sure what you expect me to do."

"Neither am I," admitted Jack.

"Get her out of there," said Sam without hesitation.

Corey started to speak, then paused while a final boarding call was announced over the PA. "Mrs.

Symington," he said politely, "I understand your concern about your sister. But she's also the wife of the president of San Domenico. Amnesty International has a limited mandate. We're allowed to observe but not to interfere. It is that assurance that gives us access. I can't jeopardize my mission or the organization."

Tears sprang to Sam's eyes. "But there's got to be something you can do. I'm afraid that if we don't act now, it could be too late. I don't know what he'll do to her."

"She says that he hasn't harmed her," Corey pointed out.

"Not yet. But he won't let her contact anyone in the States. And who knows how he'll react if he finds out she's tried. She's got to get out of there. She's in danger and so is her baby."

Sam was openly crying. She couldn't help it. Jack put an arm around her, and Daisy gave her a tissue. "Jack," she sobbed, "I'm really afraid. I've never felt this way before. I just know something will happen to her if we don't get her out of San Domenico."

Another announcement came, telling them that all passengers should be aboard. One of Corey's colleagues peeked out from the passageway door and warned him to hurry up.

"Could I go with you?" asked Sam excitedly, suddenly getting an idea. "What if I just went as part of your delegation. Maybe I could find a way at least to see her."

"You mean right now?" asked Corey, taken aback.

"Yes."

"Do you have your passport?"

Sam's face fell. She'd forgotten about that little detail.

"I've got mine," Jack spoke before he could think.

"Oh, my God, Jack. Will you go? If you could see her, talk to her, I'm sure—"

"Wait a minute." Jack was backing off. "I can't. Not now. The only reason I even have my passport on me is I'm supposed . . ."

"Jack," Daisy interrupted before he could say more, "maybe you should. If it's a matter of saving someone's life—"

"Daisy, thank you," said Sam fervently, fully aware of what she was being offered. "Maybe if you tell him . . ."

"Okay, Jack. If you want to do it, I can put you on my manifest. But you've got to decide right now."

"I need to talk to Daisy for a minute." He took her arm and led her a few feet away. "I don't have to do this, honey," he told her. "I don't know that this is a matter of life and death."

"You don't know that it's not," she said quietly. "And what if you don't go and we go off to Maryland and blithely get married, and then something does happen to her. Then your whole life you'll be thinking, 'Oh, shit, if I hadn't married Daisy, then everything would be different.' I couldn't stand that. Our marriage deserves a more auspicious beginning."

"You're right," he said. "And you're wonderful. I love you. More than ever."

"You'd better. Because I'm only letting you go for a little while. You owe me a wedding."

"And a lifetime," he promised as he brushed the wandering lock from her eye and kissed her.

"Anyway, it's probably better this way. Daddy would have been furious if we eloped. This was all probably designed to thwart our running away."

"I've learned my lesson. After this, no more running away. We'll tell your parents, make a big announcement, have a huge wedding, whatever you want."

"I just want you to come back," she whispered ardently as she buried her face in his neck.

"Jack?" Corey was calling him. "They're closing the doors."

"I'm coming," he said, kissing Daisy once more.

"I don't know how I can ever thank you," said Sam as she hugged him.

"Don't thank me yet. I don't even know what I can do. I'll be in touch. With both of you," he added as he hurried after Corey onto the plane.

"Where's Mommy?" demanded Moira as Halsey brought her back to the house after her morning at nursery school.

Robert had opened the door for them, then excused himself to return to the kitchen. It was silver polishing day, a task traditionally undertaken once a month that required all household hands.

"She had to go to Washington, love, but she'll be home soon," the baby-sitter promised.

"She was going to play with me," Moira pouted.

"I know. And she will when she gets back."

"I want her to play with me now," insisted Moira with her child's logic.

Much as she loved school, the mornings away from home were still new and tiring for Moira and Halsey could see she was a little cranky. She wished she had asked Robert to bring her a treat before they'd come upstairs. She considered calling the kitchen on the intercom, but she'd never before worked for a family where she wasn't the sole employee, and she still felt awkward issuing orders to other staff members.

"I'll tell you what," said Halsey patiently. "You wait here, and I'll go get you some milk and cookies from the kitchen. Then I'll play with you. How will that be?"

"Okay, I guess," said Moira, not entirely happy. "Chocolate chip?"

"Absolutely. Is there any other cookie?" At that, the child brightened, and relieved to see her charge return to her usually sunny self, Halsey hurried off to the kitchen.

"Now, you stay right here until I get back," she added for insurance, even though she knew that Moira, sweet, compliant child that she was, wouldn't even think of leaving. Besides, she was already happily preparing "dinner" for her dolls on her little stove, a pastime that would definitely keep her busy for the few minutes it would take Halsey to go to the kitchen and get her snack.

From behind the powder room door, Sarah watched Halsey go down the stairs. Then she quickly stepped into the nursery.

"Hi, Aunt Sarah," Moira greeted her happily. "Do you want some salad?"

Sarah smiled benignly at her niece. "No, thank you, Moira. I already had my lunch. I'm going outside to play. Do you want to come with me?"

"Now?"

"Sure."

"Halsey is bringing me some cookies."

"Oh, well, I have licorice right here in my pocket. You could have that if you came with me."

"Okay. I love licorice."

"Let's run," said Sarah, and she swooped the giggling child into her arms and raced down the stairs and out the door. The entire staff was in the kitchen cleaning the silver. She was certain that no one saw her.

Once outside and away from the house, Sarah put the little girl down and let her walk. She skipped ahead, stopping to pick flowers or look at a butterfly perched on a tree stump. Just as she was beginning to complain that she was tired, Sarah saw the rundown building ahead of them. She picked up Moira and let the child ride the rest of the way on her shoulders. She hadn't forgotten how far the last half mile seemed to a small child. She had walked it herself too many times.

At the door, Sarah put Moira down again.

"Do you know where we are?"

"This is where the horses used to live."

"That's right," said Sarah, holding the little girl by the hand as she led her into the stable. It smelled damp, of old hay and animals long gone.

"It stinks," said Moira.

"Not as bad as it used to when the horses were here," Sarah said, laughing.

"Ugh. I don't want a horse."

"Well, I didn't want one either. But my daddy said I had to have one and I had to take care of it myself. But I'll tell you the truth, I didn't really like it here. I was afraid."

"Why?"

"Because this is where my daddy brought me to be punished."

Moira's eyes went wide. "Punished?" She knew the meaning of the word, but it was a foreign concept.

"Yes. When I was bad. What does your daddy do to you when you're bad?"

Moira thought for a minute. "I'm never bad," she answered confidently.

"Oh, no. All little girls are bad."

"I'm not," insisted Moira. "What did you do to be bad?"

"Nothing. I was just a little girl. Sometimes, if my mommy did something my daddy didn't like, then I got punished, too. Your mommy did something I don't like.

Moira began to cry. "You sound different, Aunt Sarah. I don't like what you're saying. I want to go home."

"I'm not your aunt Sarah," came the chill rejoinder.

Confused, the little girl cried even harder. It was easy for her to believe that this bad woman who was scaring her was not her aunt Sarah. She had started out being the aunt she knew, the one who always played with her and took her to buy ice cream. But something had happened to change her, and now, Moira understood without really understanding that she was somebody different.

"I want to go home," she sobbed.

"You can't. I have to teach your mother a lesson."

"No!" screamed Moira as she realized what was happening. She ran to the double doors, but it was too late. They were closed, and she was alone in the dark. She pushed on the door, crying, but it didn't move. She heard a click outside and had no idea it was the padlock but sensed somehow her confinement was complete.

"I wasn't bad," she sobbed, objecting loudly. "I wasn't bad." But there was no one to hear.

When Sarah walked into the mansion, the entire staff was in a panic.

"What's going on?" she asked Robert who was wandering in and out of the rooms, still wearing his apron and rubber gloves.

"It's Miss Moira. She's gone missing."

"What? How's that possible?" She was incredulous, genuinely shocked.

Frantic, Halsey ran up to her. "Oh, my God, Mrs. Taylor. I was hoping maybe she was with you."

"I just came in. Where are Drew and Sam?"

"Sam's in Washington. Drew is on his way. I just called him at the office. Oh, God, what am I going to do?"

"Take it easy, Halsey. What happened?"

"I don't know. I left her in the nursery to go down to the kitchen and get cookies and milk. When I got back she was gone. Just like that."

"She must be somewhere in the house."

"That's what I thought. But then I couldn't find her. And then the rest of the staff looked with me, and we still couldn't find her."

"Maybe she wandered outside."

"She can't open the door by herself."

"Well, maybe she can now. She's getting pretty big."

Before they could investigate that possibility, they heard a car pull up outside and stop with a screech of its wheels. Trying to get Mrs. Halsey to calm down so she wouldn't unduly scare Drew, Sarah opened the door to her brother. Ian was with him. He greeted his wife with a kiss, while Drew made Halsey tell him every detail of what had happened from the moment she had arrived home with Moira.

"She's got to be here somewhere," Drew said, refusing to panic. "Maybe she got scared by all the commotion and she's hiding. We're just going to have to find her."

Dividing into groups of two, Drew with Robert, Ian with Sarah, Halsey with the cook, they began at the top of the house and took turns combing through the rooms, each one covering the other so no area could be inadvertently overlooked. Keeping their voices soft and casual, they called to her, trying to coax her out with promises of ice cream and presents. It took them over an hour to go through the mansion, but when they were done, they were certain Moira was nowhere in the house.

"I'm calling the police," Drew said.

"Are you sure?" Sarah questioned. "What if she's just on the grounds? She could have wandered out and be playing somewhere."

"Too much time has gone by. If she had wandered off by herself, she would have come back by now."

"You don't know that," Ian said. "She's pretty small and the grounds are pretty big. She could have gotten lost."

"Or stuck in one of the outbuildings," suggested Sarah helpfully.

"Okay, we'll look," agreed Drew. "But I'm still calling the police."

By the time Sam arrived home, three police cruisers were blocking the entrance to Belvedere. Nervously, she pulled up to the gate.

"What's going on, officer?" she asked the cop who shone a flashlight into her car.

"I'm sorry, ma'am. Can I ask your business here?"

"I live here. This is my house," Sam said, annoyed. "What's *your* business?"

"Oh, excuse me, ma'am. You must be the mother. Go right ahead."

He motioned her on.

"What the hell does that mean?" she cursed. "What kind of a stupid thing is that to say to a mother whose house is surrounded by police cars." But even though her heart had stopped, she kept the car moving.

Drew was at her side before she'd even parked. She refused to let the distraught look on his face register in her consciousness. She would not presume something was wrong until she was told.

And then, when he told her, she started to scream and couldn't stop.

9

They kept a vigil through the night. The police had been over the house half a dozen more times, but as they gathered silently in the downstairs study, the family knew she wasn't there. Mrs. Halsey had been put to bed with a tranquilizer, immobilized by remorse and guilt and no help to any of them. The mere threat of a sedative had been enough to quiet Sam's hysteria. She refused to be less than present for the entire ordeal. She insisted on remaining fully conscious until her child was back in her arms. They had called Harvey and Diane on some off chance that somehow, incredibly, Moira might have ended up at her grandparents. Instead, the grandparents had ended up there, sitting up with them, waiting for a phone call that never came.

"If she's kidnapped," said Sam, forcing herself to

say the words, "why isn't someone demanding a ransom?"

"Sometimes they wait a while," volunteered one of the men. He was a plainclothes detective and seemed to be the one in charge. Sam had forgotten his name. "And sometimes," he went on, "if something goes wrong, they don't ever bother to get in touch at all."

Sam and Drew looked at each other but said nothing. They didn't need an explanation for "if something goes wrong." Seeing the tears start to gather in his wife's eyes again, Drew quickly went over to her and put his arm around her.

"For Crissake, stop carrying on like she's dead, will you?" snarled Sarah her voice so full of derision it was barely recognizable.

"Sarah!" Ian admonished his wife as the others stared at her in shock.

For a moment, her eyes went dead as though she could not see them. Then, she blinked and, registering their reaction, said, "What?" in a tone so completely baffled she left them at a loss for words.

Sam looked at her sister-in-law. Sarah had spoken entirely out of character, but maybe she was right. Maybe it would be better to talk as though they were dealing with an ordinary, everyday crisis instead of a looming disaster. Maybe focusing on impending doom would invite it. Maybe if she acted normal and expected a normal reaction in return, then only normal things would happen. Sam was willing to make the attempt.

"I'm sorry, detective," she said, trying to sound affable, "I've forgotten your name."

"It's Brian, ma'am."

"Is that your first name or your last name?"

"Actually, ma'am, it's both. Brian Bryan. First name with an *i*, last with a *y*. My parents had quite a sense of humor."

She smiled, although she couldn't help thinking it must have been less amusing for the young Brian Bryan when he was teased in grade school. Then, she couldn't help wondering if Moira would ever get . . . She forced herself to stop thinking. It was no use trying to be normal.

More policemen came in from trampling over the grounds with flashlights and dogs.

"Nothing?" asked Sam.

"Afraid not. We checked the outbuildings. She's not in the boathouse, the guest house, the pool house, or the gazebo. We couldn't get into the greenhouse, the toolshed, or the stables because they were all locked."

"Those buildings have been closed for years. If you couldn't get in, neither could Moira," said Drew, aware he was stating the obvious.

"All right," said Bryan. "I think we've pretty much established she's not on the property. And if that's the case, in all likelihood she was removed. She could have been carried off forcibly, but that seems unlikely, considering the number of staff you employ."

"Obviously not enough," said Drew bitterly. "My father was big on security. There were always armed guards, dogs, the whole works. I was always carrying on about being raised in a prison. And I felt so righteous when he died, I let things go. Well, looks like he was right, and I'm a goddamn idiot and my child is suffering for it."

"Stop it, Drew." Sarah came to her brother's

defense. "You did the right thing. We hated those guards. No one can blame you for not wanting Moira to grow up like that. You don't know what happened, and for all you know, an entire patrol couldn't have stopped it."

"Your sister's right, Mr. Symington," Bryan interjected. "It's more likely that your daughter knew whoever took her away and went willingly. Can you give us the names of anyone who had something against you or members of your family? Any acquaintances who are short of money? Anyone with whom you might have had a falling out recently?"

"There's no one," said Drew, not even needing to think about it. "No one we know would do anything like that."

"No one we know," echoed Sam, but there was something in her voice that made the detective turn to her.

"Ma'am?"

"Someone *is* after us," declared Sam.

"Who?" Bryan wanted to know.

"I don't know, but someone. Things have happened at DMC. There was an explosion, and then those fake letters went out to the shareholders. Someone is trying to undermine us."

"But that's business," said Ian. "Even an unscrupulous competitor wouldn't stoop to kidnapping a child."

"You'd be surprised by what people would do," Bryan said politely. "I've seen a lot worse for a lot less."

"Think about it." Sam was vehement. "If someone is trying to destroy DMC, they're after us. Sure, we've got stockholders, but really, *we're* the company. By taking Moira . . ." She couldn't go on, but they all understood.

"That bastard deserves to die," proclaimed Harvey. Startled, they looked at him. He and Diane had been sitting so quietly in the corner, everyone had forgotten they were there. Sam went over and hugged her parents, aware through her own anguish that this was painful for all of them.

"All right, here's what we're going to do." Bryan was pacing, working things out as he spoke. "For the present, we're going to discontinue searching the grounds. It is possible police activity has scared the kidnappers off, and they're waiting to get in touch. We'll set up a tracer on the phone, and I'll stay here with you. Otherwise, I want anyone who doesn't belong on the premises to leave."

There were some mild protests from Harvey and Diane, but Sam convinced them that it would be better for them to go home and get some rest. If they were in this for the long haul, she'd need their strength later.

After seeing Sam's parents out and closing the door on the last contingent of police, Robert returned to the study. His face showed nothing, the impassive visage of a man trained in service. But his voice cracked as he offered to make fresh coffee and sandwiches. Sam looked into his eyes and saw a reflection of her own pain.

"Thank you, Robert," she said, touched more than she would have imagined. "But we can manage. Why don't you go to bed? It's been an awfully long day for you."

"If you don't mind, Miss Samantha, I couldn't sleep with little Moira out there somewhere. I'll be in the kitchen if you need me. For anything," he added with emphasis.

She nodded and grasped his hand. He squeezed hers just a little, and she smiled, strangely comforted that Moira's disappearance affected them all so strongly.

Sarah sat in an armchair, her head leaning back, eyes closed, lips moving slightly. Ian watched his wife and thought she must be asleep, conversing in her dreams. He went to her and touched her shoulder.

"Sweetheart," he spoke softly into her ear so as not to startle her, "maybe you should go up to bed." He knew only exhaustion could have made her utter her earlier harsh words.

She silently mouthed another word or two before she opened her eyes. "No," she said, standing up, "I have to help find Moira."

"Honey, there's nothing you can do right now. I'll call you if they need you or if anything happens. I promise."

He put his arm around her and tried to steer her toward the stairs. She shrugged him off.

"They need me now," she said, heading over to the corner where Drew and Sam huddled with Detective Bryan. Ian shook his head. It was pointless to argue. The tension had obviously rendered his wife less than logical. Quickly, he followed her, ready to step in with a little damage control before she said something else to upset Sam and Drew.

"You should look in the stable," she said quietly as the three of them turned to her.

"It's padlocked," Drew answered his sister. "There's no way Moira could have gotten in."

"My men went over the grounds pretty thoroughly," Bryan added reassuringly.

Sarah's head jerked back. "Your men are idiots," she barked.

"Sarah!" Ian said sharply. "I'm sorry, guys. She's very tired. Come on, we're going to bed. We're not really helping here."

"Maybe you're not, asshole. I am."

They gasped in unison and stared at her. She smirked at them for a moment and then seemed to shiver.

"I'm sorry," she said, her voice modulated to an entirely different tone. "I *am* tired. I'll go up now. But don't stop looking."

They watched her leave the room and head up the stairs. Ian started to apologize again. "It must be the strain. She's not herself."

"It's okay," Sam said quickly. "We're all under pressure. Why don't you go with her. There's not much anybody can do right now. We're just waiting."

He looked uncertainly from one to the other, then up the stairs. They were obviously more in control than Sarah. "Maybe I'd better," he said. "But promise you'll get me if you need me."

Sam nodded and Drew shook his hand. Detective Bryan gave him an edgy smile before turning back to the list he had been making with Sam and Drew of their possible enemies. He was glad that the study had finally emptied of extraneous people. He needed the Symingtons to concentrate, to think of who might possibly have taken their child and for what reason.

Because, experienced as he was, he also knew that the longer Moira was missing, the less likely she was to be found—alive.

"All right, let's go over this again," he said, calling them back to attention.

But Sam couldn't stop thinking about what Sarah had said. "Maybe we should look in the outbuildings again."

"Honey," said Drew kindly, "we've been through that. What's the point of wasting time? Even if Moira had a key, she couldn't have opened the padlocks."

"We did check, Mrs. Symington. The locked buildings were all secure. And the dogs went over the open buildings very thoroughly. If someone had been there, they would have picked up the scent. I really think that right now the most productive thing we can do is come up with this list. If we can zero in on the right person, we can find your child."

Sam tried to focus. She offered the name of Bethany Havenhurst, Drew's fiancée before her, who had once tried to undermine both their marriage and their business. But it had been years since they'd heard from her, and somehow, Sam couldn't see Bethany willingly dealing with a child, even for the purpose of revenge.

"I'm sorry," she said. "I don't want to be a pest. But couldn't we just go look at the stable again. Maybe Sarah had a feeling. A premonition or something. She was acting very strange tonight. Maybe it was like a psychic phenomenon."

"You don't believe in that stuff," Drew chided her softly.

"I know I don't," she admitted. "But she said it, so

I just can't ignore it. Please. Just so that I can get my mind off it. Can't we just open the door and look?"

Drew looked at Detective Bryan. "It couldn't hurt. The stable is pretty old and hasn't been used in a while. There might have been a loose board or something that Moira could have gotten through to get in, then couldn't find her way out."

Bryan shook his head. He knew they were grasping at straws and losing precious time. But they were the parents. It was important to accommodate them in any way he could. He picked up his flashlight.

"Do you want to get a jacket, Mrs. Symington? It's gotten kind of cool out."

"Thank you," she said as she ran to the closet. She knew he was humoring her, that the likelihood of a happy outcome was slim, but she was grateful nonetheless.

As they tramped across the garden under a moonless sky, Sam looked back at the mansion. There was a light on in the kitchen, where she assumed Robert was keeping his vigil. The west wing looked strangely dark, and she felt a stab in her heart as she realized that it was the hall light outside of the nursery that was missing. Even when the entire house was asleep, there was always a faint glow around Moira's room. Not tonight. The east wing, too, was dark. But she thought she saw a shadow standing at the window of what must have been Ian and Sarah's bedroom.

Drew led the way, holding Bryan's flashlight, even though he would have had no trouble finding it in the dark. Like everyone in his family, he had ridden since he was a child, although he had never quite succumbed to the allure of horses and the hunt, always bothered by the cruelty and bored by the pageant. It had been Sarah, he remembered, who was always going off to the stables with their father, immersed in the riding and the grooming and the bonding over sport that Drew had never shared. It had surprised him when Sarah had called them in Washington one day to ask if he had any objection to her selling the horses. Since he was rarely home and, when he was, had little desire to ride, he made no protest. And the stables had been locked ever since.

Now, pushing the key into the padlock so many years later, he was surprised at how easily it maneuvered. Doing this to satisfy Sam's impulse, he imagined he heard her heart beating, then realized it was his own. They pushed open the doors. The stale odor of horse manure concentrated by years of airlessness was overwhelming.

"Whew," said Bryan. "No wonder the dogs stayed clear of this place."

Everything was deathly still. Although the night was cool, as Bryan had said, there was no breeze, and even the cicadas were silent. The beam of the flashlight vibrated over the empty stalls, and Drew realized he was shaking. They saw nothing.

Sam tried not to be overwhelmed by the disappointment. She told herself it was no worse than they had expected. She told herself it didn't mean anything beyond the logical conclusion that a little girl couldn't get into a locked barn. She told herself it wasn't an omen; it signified nothing. But still, she was almost crushed by the despair that closed around her like a vise. They turned to go.

"Mommy?"

She stopped. She thought she must be going crazy. She looked at the others. She saw from their faces that they had heard it, too.

"Moira?" she called quietly, breathing hard to keep from screaming or sobbing. "Is that you? Where are you?"

"Over here," came the littlest voice from the farthest alcove of the stable.

"Wait," shouted Bryan, grabbing the flashlight from Drew's hand and shining it in the corner, afraid that it might be some sort of trap, that someone might be there, holding the child, poised to do harm.

But it was too late. Sam and Drew were already running across the stable. And when the light revealed nothing but a tiny girl huddled on a bale of rotting hay, Bryan was running, too.

"Baby, baby," crooned Sam over and over again as she cradled her little girl in her arms. "What are you doing here?"

"I was sleeping," said Moira, taking the question literally.

"But how did you get here?" asked Drew, putting his arms around both his wife and daughter, patting her dear little head.

"Aunt Sarah brought me."

Sam felt a chill and not because she had taken off her jacket and wrapped it around her little girl. She knew the others were having the same reaction. She could hear Drew struggle to keep the shock out of his voice.

"Not the Aunt Sarah who lives with us?"

"Oh, Daddy," said Moira, convinced that now that her parents had found her she was fine and open to teasing, "she's the only aunt Sarah we have."

"I . . . I don't understand," stuttered Sam. She could see Drew's face over Moira's shoulder. He was as distressed and confused as she was.

Until that moment, Bryan had let them have their reunion. Now, he stepped in. He needed specifics. "Did your aunt Sarah open the door and bring you in here, then leave you all by yourself?"

Noticing the stranger for the first time, Moira suddenly lowered her eyes in shyness, refusing to look at him.

"Is that what happened?" Drew encouraged.

She nodded.

"Why?" blurted Sam, aghast. "Why would she do that?"

"She said I was bad," mumbled Moira shamefacedly, afraid perhaps that she had been. "But I'm not, am I, Mommy?"

"Oh, no, pumpkin. Of course you're not. You're a very, very good girl. And I love you very much."

"She said you were bad, too," Moira offered carefully, still afraid that there might have been just cause for her ordeal. "And I had to be punished."

Drew exploded, "What sh—" he started to say, then caught himself and finished, "What hogwash."

"Hogwash," echoed Moira, laughing, happy to be reaffirmed good, safely ensconced in her parents arms.

"You and Mommy are the best there is," said Drew. Sam could feel him seething with rage, even though he kept his voice even. "You're both my good girls. Always were and always will be."

Moira smiled and burrowed into his chest. The finality of his words pleased her. "But why," she wanted to know, "did Aunt Sarah say that? Why did she leave me in the dark?"

"Because," said Drew, lifting his child in his arms and carrying her out of the dank, stinking barn, "your Aunt Sarah has a big problem."

Respecting Drew's wishes, Detective Bryan waited downstairs while Sam and Drew put Moira to sleep in her own bed. Halsey, awakened from her drugged sleep by the jolly commotion, showered the little girl with kisses, gratefully accepted the Symingtons' absolving her of blame, and pulled the mattress off her own bed so that she could sleep on the floor near the girl's bed.

When Drew knocked on the east-wing bedroom door, Ian opened it.

"She just fell asleep," he said in a hushed whisper when Drew announced that Sarah was needed downstairs. "Can it wait until morning?"

"We found Moira," Drew explained, realizing that Ian would not have heard them from the other side of the mansion. He watched for his reaction.

Sheer joy filled Ian's face as he grabbed his brother-in-law in a bear hug. "That's wonderful. Where was she?"

"In the stable. She said Sarah locked her in."

Ian let him go and looked at him. He knew he had not heard wrong, but what he had heard made no sense at all.

"That's ridiculous."

"It's what she said."

"Drew, be reasonable. You saw how upset Sarah was. Why in God's name would she do something like that. Moira must have gotten mixed up. Maybe she had a dream or something."

"Maybe." Exhaustion and confusion made him sound emotionless. "That's why we need to talk to Sarah. Detective Bryan is waiting downstairs."

Moments later, Sarah swept into the study, her robe tied tightly around her. Like Ian, who came in right behind her, there was no mistaking her relief at the news that Moira was safe. As Sam and Drew had agreed before she arrived, they let Bryan question her. But it was obvious to everyone that either Sarah was the best actress in the world or she was as baffled as they were about Moira's claim that she had locked her in the stable.

"I never even go to the stable myself." Sarah was vehement. "Why would I take Moira there?"

"I understand you used to love riding," said Bryan conversationally. He never liked to challenge possible perps in their stories. It only made them more intractable.

"I don't know that I loved it," answered Sarah honestly. "I did it when I was a kid. But it hasn't appealed to me much in recent years."

"Why is that?"

"I don't really know. I just wanted to stop, so I stopped."

"But you rode a lot as a kid?"

"To tell you the truth"—her exasperation was showing—"I don't remember all that much about it. It was a long time ago. And it certainly has nothing to do with Moira ending up there, since I didn't take her."

"She seemed very certain it was you. She said you said she was bad and had to be punished."

Tears sprang to Sarah's eyes. "Oh, that poor sweet thing. That's so awful. She must have been so scared." She looked at Sam and Drew, her emotion clearly genuine.

"You never said anything like that to her?"

"Of course not." She was getting angry now. "Why would I? Moira is a darling child. She's never even slightly naughty. We all adore her. You can't help it."

"Somebody doesn't," Bryan pointed out, shaking his head. "She couldn't get into that stable on her own."

Sarah turned to her husband, then to her brother and sister-in-law. "You don't think I would do something so awful, do you?"

"It's just that Moira said . . ." Drew trailed off, not knowing what he believed. Ian looked close to tears himself.

"You can't be serious," Sarah shouted, chagrined. "How could you even think I would do something like this? Do you want me to take a lie detector test? Will that make you believe me?"

Bryan stepped in again. He would get no information if he didn't control the situation. "That might be useful, Mrs. Taylor. We could set one up tomorrow."

"Fine. The sooner, the better." This was depressing her. Somehow, she felt like victim and criminal at the same time.

"By the way," Bryan said, gathering his things as if he were ready to go, "what made you suggest we look in the stable? We would never have found her if you hadn't led us there." He made it sound like praise, but for the first time, Sarah faltered.

"I . . . I . . . don't know. Voices."

"I beg your pardon?"

"Voices in my head. It was like people were talking in my head."

"Really," said Bryan as though he were interested, but it didn't much matter. "What exactly did they say?"

"I . . . I'm not sure. It was sort of like one voice was saying the cops were stupid and it was their own fault they couldn't find her. And then another voice kept saying, 'You have to tell them to look in the stable.' So I did."

She shrugged and blinked back tears, painfully aware it sounded like a fiction, desperately wanting them to believe it was the truth.

Bryan looked like he was going to ask more, but Ian, with an apologetic look at his sister and her husband, intervened. "Detective, do you think we could continue this tomorrow? Sarah's been under a lot of pressure lately. She's seeing a therapist, and maybe all this stuff is connected. But we've all been through a long and awful night. And maybe we could accomplish more if we got a little sleep and worked on it tomorrow?"

"I'll need to see her, Mr. Taylor. Right now, she's under suspicion for attempted kidnapping."

Sarah gasped but said nothing.

"I'll bring her in, I swear it. Just give us a little time. Moira's okay, and I promise you, I won't let Sarah out of my sight."

Bryan looked at Sam and Drew. "You're the parents. How do you feel? I could take her in now . . ."

Without even consulting each other, Sam and Drew shook their heads no.

"Thank you, Detective Bryan," Drew volunteered. "Ian's right. The main thing is that Moira's home. Obviously, this is going to take some figuring out. Maybe we all need to sleep on it."

The detective took his leave, shaking hands with Ian, nodding cordially at Sarah. But though she said nothing, she read the skepticism in his level gaze. As Sam and Drew showed Bryan to the door, Sarah turned to her husband.

"I'm scared, Ian," she whispered, collapsing on his shoulder.

"I know you are," he answered, "So am I. Something weird is going on, and we're going to have to find out what it is."

There was no way to reach her. The Amnesty International delegation was tolerated on the island, but they were categorically denied access to the presidential palace. The president refused to allow them to meet with him or any members of his staff. Interviewing his wife would have been out of the question. The only way to for him to see Melinda would be to sneak into her quarters.

"I'm warning you, Jack," Corey threatened when he heard Jack's plan, "if you jeopardize my mission in any way, if you so much as whisper your connection to AI . . ."

"Don't worry, I won't. It could only hurt."

"You're right about that." Corey sighed. "From

what I've heard, Roca's not too thrilled to have us here."

"Who are your sources?"

"What?"

"If you're hearing things from inside the palace, obviously you have sources. Who are they?"

"I'm not telling you." Corey looked at him as though he'd asked for an act of indecent exposure.

"I'm not going to compromise you. I just need to know who goes in and out of the place. When they do it. How they do it. What security is like."

"Security is good. I promise you that."

"That's a given. But it's a big palace. You need a staff to run a place like that. And somehow, I don't think Roca's the kind of guy to skimp on the help."

Finally, Corey had given him the name of a man, supposedly loyal to the government but angling any way he could to get safe passage out of the country and an assurance of political asylum. The man, one of Roca's low-level aides, told Jack that as far as he knew the only person except for Diego Roca to have regular contact with Melinda was the nurse, Clara. Only Jack's insistence, coupled with proof that Jack worked in the State Department and a small lie that suggested he was somehow involved in the granting of political asylum, convinced the man to drive Jack to Clara's village. But, dropping Jack off on the edge of town, he resolutely refused to even identify her house. With Jack's rudimentary language skills, it wasn't difficult to figure out that he was an American, and the first person he spoke to immediately directed him to Clara's front door.

He knocked and was greeted warily by a woman in

her forties. Her face was stern, but her eyes were kind, and he hoped that she was the woman he was looking for. He asked if she was Clara, and she simply raised her chin as if to ask who wants to know.

"Do you speak English?" he asked, suddenly afraid that his search would all come to nothing if he couldn't make himself understood.

Again, she answered with a noncommittal tilt of her head. *She's smart,* he thought. *She's not going to tell me anything until she knows who I am.*

"My name is Jack Bader," he began. And in the next moment, she had grabbed him by the hand, pulled him into her house, and thrown her arms around him.

Looking heavenward, she crossed herself in what must have been a gesture of thanks. "You came," she sighed. "I prayed you would come."

He was overcome, touched to see such faith placed in him; afraid of what had called it into play. He didn't know how to begin. "Uh . . . we got a letter . . ."

"He is safe, my cousin? The Americans have accepted him?"

"He's fine. We're working on getting him what he needs to stay in the States. He'll be all right."

She crossed herself again, and he hid a smile. The woman had obviously been doing a lot of praying.

"I made her write," she said proudly. "She didn't think it would help. But I knew her family would not let her suffer. You love her as we do," she stated unquestioningly.

"Well, I'm not exactly family—"

"I know who you are," Clara interrupted. "Melinda

has spoken about you. You have a special . . ." She knotted her fingers together, searching for the word.

"Bond," he supplied, a little taken aback. "I guess that's true," he added, picturing Melinda, a lifetime away, talking about him to this woman. He shouldn't have been surprised. He could not forget; why should she? And yet, he was. Surprised and pleased. More than he expected. Or wanted.

Sizing him up with her eyes, Clara began to pull clothes out of a bag in the hall and hand them to him: a rough cotton shirt, loose pants, a rope belt.

"You are staying at the Reef?" she asked as she went through a bag of sandals, estimating fit.

He nodded.

"It's the only hotel left. The are others are too broken for foreigners."

"The Reef's not doing too great either. It looked a lot nicer when I was here for the wedding."

"Everything looked a lot nicer then," she remarked sadly, but this was no time to reminisce. "Tomorrow, put these on," she went on, indicating the clothing she had given him. "But put your own nice things over so no one sees. You are driving?"

"I can get a car," he said, hoping he could. Everything was in short supply in San Domenico, and he had been sharing one with Corey.

"Good. Drive toward the palace on the main road. But five, maybe six kilometers before the walls, you will see a road that leads into the jungle. Be careful. It is overgrown and easy to miss. Take it. Drive two kilometers. Wait. Someone will come."

"To get me inside the palace?" he asked, excited at

the prospect, amazed at how sure she was that she could arrange it.

She seemed to divine his thoughts. She gave a self-deprecating shrug. "The gardener is also my cousin. Sometimes he brings a helper."

Jack nodded. "I'll be in the clothes and ready."

She grinned. "It's good my *abuelita* was very . . ." Struggling for the word, she moved her hands in a circle in front of her belly.

"Fertile," supplied Jack, smiling in return. "Thank you, Clara."

"Thank *you,* Jack," she responded with a solemnity that both touched and dismayed him. And while she went to find yet another relative who would drive him to within walking distance of the hotel, he couldn't help wondering what was at greater risk in this rescue mission: his body or his soul.

In the morning, he had to argue with Corey about the car.

"I need it," Corey insisted. "We're collecting statements from the families of the 'disappeareds.' "

"Ride with one of the other guys."

"Hey, you're here courtesy of the AI, and this is an AI mission, remember?" scowled Corey, balking at having his authority unsurped.

"Well, as I remember it," said Jack, his voice gaining in sarcasm what it lost in patience, "Amnesty International's mandate is to assist prisoners of conscience. So unless you want to be remembered as the asshole who refused to help Melinda Myles until *after* she disappeared, give me the fucking car!"

He missed the side road the first time, and when he

saw that he was closer to the presidential palace than he should have been, he had to make a U-turn and slowly retrace his route. Clara had been right. Overhanging vines curtained the entrance to the road, and had he not been going at a snail's pace, he would have missed it again. He was glad that gasoline was scarce enough on the island to keep the traffic to a minimum, and he hoped that if anyone had seen him lurching and stopping, they would simply assume that, like everybody else in the country, he was having trouble with his car.

He barely had time to strip off his suit and take the sandals out of his inside pocket before a rickety truck clanked into sight. For one generously insane moment, he considered offering Corey's rented car to Clara's cousin, but he realized it would only arouse suspicion to see a laborer in a vehicle that worked. Since the man spoke no English, and Jack was far too nervous to try his schoolboy skills, an exchange of smiles, nods, and gestures was enough to get the journey started.

As they approached the palace walls, Jack could feel his stomach churning. The old man reached over and put Jack's hat over his face and gave a couple of snores.

"Sí, sí," said Jack, getting the picture as he stretched himself out, hat covering his eyes, and pretended to be asleep.

They drove a little farther and then stopped. Jack didn't dare to peek and see where they were. He heard an exchange of words that he could not understand. The truck bounced on. They stopped again. Clara's cousin got out. Still, Jack made no move. A moment later, his door was opened, and he was being pulled out. As his hat fell to the ground, he saw that he was inside the walls, in the garden, facing the back of the palace. Crunching his hat back onto his head, he ran a little to catch up to the gardener who was cutting a brisk path through the flowers, slicing birds-of-paradise to the left, orchids to the right, until they had reached the palace itself. Then, he thrust the bouquet, vibrant with color and fragrance, into Jack's arms and left him standing alone.

Only a second passed before a door opened, and Clara pulled him inside. Carrying on a rapid-fire patter in very loud Spanish, she clicked her heels down the hall, as Jack, hat pulled low, arms full of flowers, obediently followed. She opened doors, he entered and waited while she closed them behind him. He did not raise his head to see where they were going.

"What beautiful flowers."

Her voice had not changed nor its effect on him. Miles and years evaporated in that one mellifluous moment. He took off his hat.

She gasped but did not say his name. He had not time to say anything before she was in his arms. He held her, and again, as before, his body had instant recall of her every curve and sinew. This time, he realized, she felt a little different: softer, fuller, rounder. Time had not stopped. She had a baby. And he, he reminded himself, had Daisy.

"I told you he would come," said Clara proudly as though the saying had made it happen.

They broke apart.

"You look wonderful," he said, meaning it. "Motherhood suits you."

He had said it without reflection, but in the hollow space that followed his words, he knew that both of them were thinking that by all rights, this child could have been his.

"Do you want to see him?" Melinda asked, deliberately breaking the silence.

Clara brought Nico, and Jack held him, trying not to think of what might have been. The baby began to fuss, and Melinda took him from Jack's arms and, settling into a chair, held him to her breast. Jack could hear him suckle but kept his eyes on Melinda's face, whether out of respect for her modesty or fear for his resolve, he didn't dare to ask himself.

While the baby nursed, Melinda asked about her family, and Jack assured her that except for worrying about her, they were all well. Then she asked about him, and both loyalty and perhaps a need for self-preservation made him tell her about Daisy. If he had wanted to be completely honest with himself, he might have admitted that her seemingly genuine happiness over his good fortune made him a little sad.

He began to question her about her situation, but before she could answer, she noticed the baby had fallen asleep, the nipple still in his mouth. Gently, Melinda eased him off and, with a feathery kiss on his tiny forehead, handed him to Clara.

"I'll put him in his crib," the nurse said, pointedly closing the door behind her and leaving them alone.

She sighed deeply, and though she was still extraordinarily beautiful, he noticed that she looked not so much older, but less innocent. There was a weariness around her eyes that he guessed came not so much from late-night feedings as from daily dealings with a harsh reality.

"Diego has changed," she said without preamble. "When I married him, he was full of idealistic zeal, and I have to admit now, it fueled my passion for him. To be so close to someone who cared so much was, I don't know, a privilege. It sounds hokey, but for me it was true."

"Story of my life," he said with mock annoyance, purposely trying to lighten her mood. "As I recall, when I was the one with idealistic zeal, all you wanted to do was go to Hollywood. Now that I've joined the establishment, you've become the crusader."

"Fighting a revolution will do that to you every time." She laughed, and he was happy to see that she still could.

He was sorry to have to return to the serious matters at hand. "Things have gotten bad here?" He made it a question, although he already knew the answer.

"You can't imagine," she said, sighing. "Power has turned him into a different man. Democracy? Forget about it. He says the people of San Domenico aren't ready for it."

"Colossal arrogance, wouldn't you say?"

She shrugged. "Maybe. But I think he really believes it."

"Please," he said with disdain, unwilling to grant his former rival even a modicum of morality. "He's got the power, he's not giving it up. It's that simple."

"The two aren't mutually exclusive, you know."

It was a mild reproach, and he recognized that he deserved it. It was anything but simple, and Melinda had grown far more savvy than the naive starlet he had known. She was telling him it was possible for Diego to be good and evil at the same time. And it was possible for her to love and hate him for it. But she still wasn't telling him what she wanted to do.

"Where do you fit in all this?" he asked, wondering, in fact, where *he* fit in.

"I've thought about it a lot," she said. "I could become Evita to Diego's Juan Perón. He'd allow me to do all the good works I wanted, provided I never questioned his policies. But I can't see myself throwing pesos to the poor while he threw opponents into prison."

She paused, breathing deeply, and he saw that this was hard for her. She didn't come lightly to turning on the man she had loved and married. He guessed that was good, although he resented it as well. He was not the selfless friend that Clara envisioned.

"And there's Nico," she finally went on. "I . . . I can't see myself raising him as the son of a tyrannical dictator. Even if he's a fabulous father. I'm just too American for that. Does that sound stupid?"

"No," Jack responded. "It's not the kind of thing I hear every day, I'll admit. But it's not stupid."

She smiled wanly, appreciating his attempt to cheer her but too troubled to respond in kind.

"I have to leave him, Jack," she finally said, and he knew the statement made him happier than it should. "It's either that or stop being myself and pretend I agree with everything he does. Otherwise, I don't know what will happen."

"Do you think he might . . . hurt you?" This was her husband he was talking about, and he had to be careful with his accusations.

"Not physically, if that's what you mean. I'm almost more afraid of what I might do to myself. He's already taken away all my freedom. I can't see my friends or family. I can't call home. Since Nico was born, I haven't even been allowed to leave the palace grounds."

"If I get you out of San Domenico," Jack said, never doubting that he could, "you probably would never be able to come back. You would never see Diego Roca again. Nico would never know his father except from newspaper accounts. Are you prepared for that?"

It was the truth, but to Jack it was also a test. When he had seen her last, she had loved Diego Roca more than life itself. He wanted to know, more for his own sake than hers, if she could spend the rest of her life without him.

Her eyes filled with tears. "I have no choice," she said.

It was an I-told-you-so moment, replete with the corollary now-it's-too-late. They both knew that had they stayed together in the beginning, as sometimes it seemed they should have done, none of this would be happening. But past choices had led them to separate futures that could not be derailed. Jack was going to marry Daisy just as Melinda was going to leave Diego.

It was a revenge of sorts, but it was not sweet.

10

Clara knew of the plan but, for her own safety, not when it would be carried out. It was decided that trying to sneak Melinda and the baby onto an airplane would be too risky, so Clara put Jack in touch with a man who had a boat and was willing to sail it to Haiti. From there, they could get a flight to the States. For the cost of a new BMW, her cousin, the gardener, had sold Jack his broken-down truck. Corey only knew that Jack would find his own way out of San Domenico and not to question his disappearance.

For a week before their scheduled departure, Jack, in his peasant clothes, drove to the palace with the gardener every day. On the truck bed, under a tarp, was loaded every piece of equipment, working or not, that could conceivably belong to a gardener. For the first three days, the guards checked under the tarp when they arrived and again when they left. On the fourth day, the gardener gave them a gift of a bottle of Scotch, bought by Jack, and they didn't bother. On the fifth day, Jack drove to the compound alone. Having been coached by Clara on all possible renditions of the question, when the guards asked what had happened to the usual gardener, he was able to answer that he was sick. Since they already "knew" Jack, they had no reason to doubt him, and they let him go on his way. Jack made sure that they saw him at various intervals throughout the day doing the regular gardener's work. On the sixth day, Jack came alone again, and they waved him through. He stayed later than usual that day and left after the sun had gone down. Used to him as they were, no one seemed to notice or care.

On the seventh day, Melinda sent Clara home early. Throughout the day, one piece at a time, in areas not likely to be noticed, Jack unloaded the equipment that he had kept on the truck bed each day. Then, he busied himself with work near the palace walls, his truck parked with its back facing the door where Clara had first drawn him into Melinda's world. Every few minutes he would raise his head, ostensibly to wipe the sweat from his brow, but in truth to ascertain that the coast was still clear and to check and see if the door had opened. As the sun began to set, his anxiety increased until, finally, Melinda emerged, carrying only the sleeping baby in her arms.

"He wouldn't go to sleep," she whispered as Jack hustled her onto the back of the truck and arranged the tarp over her and her child. Then, he climbed into the cab and after two or three terrifying misfires managed to start the engine and drive to the gate.

Having no reason to believe that this night was different from any other, the sentry lifted the automatic barrier and with a bored wave let the truck out.

With his heart in his mouth, Jack drove past the walls of the presidential palace and onto the road to the beach. Choking under the tarp, Melinda cradled her baby to shield him from the bumps in the road and prayed that he would not wake up and start to cry.

If a member of his puppet cabinet had not chosen that day to retrieve his conscience and object to some new restrictive measure that Diego Roca was proposing; if Diego had not become so incensed that he disbanded the cabinet all together and canceled the official dinner he had been planning to share with his closest advisors, if Diego had not been so smitten with his infant son that he believed Nico's small, sweet face was all the solace that he needed, if the confluence of these events had not brought him to his private quarters hours before he was expected, to find his wife and child gone and on his desk a petition from an Amnesty International delegation that included the name of a friend of his missing wife's, then things might have turned out differently.

For the president of a small country like San Domenico, tracking down a foreigner was a simple matter. Corey's blustering threats of repercussions from AI did nothing to dissuade Diego's men from searching Jack's room at the Reef and confiscating whatever had been left there. And the few contacts Jack had needed, who had promised to keep his confidence in exchange for handsome sums of money, terrorized by the sound of the soldiers boots stomping through the halls, suddenly remembered things they had heard or been able to surmise. And while the broken-down truck lurched along a slow and careful route, Diego Roca gathered an armed entourage and sped to the shallow bay where, he had learned, a boat waited to take his wife and son out of the country.

Even in the dim light of a crescent moon, Diego could see them. Unable to traverse the beach, the truck had been parked at the side of the road. Carrying the baby close to her, with Jack supporting her by the arm, Melinda trudged through the sand. A boat, motor lifted to avoid grounding, waited in the shallows.

The soldiers saw, too, and raised their weapons, trying to stand as the jeep's four-wheel drive cut through the sand.

"Don't shoot. She has the baby," Diego instructed. "Just cut them off at the water."

In seconds, the jeep was upon them, and they froze in fear as they saw the soldiers, guns aimed in their direction, escort Diego to his escaping wife.

"This woman is an American citizen with all the rights thereby accrued," said Jack Bader, invoking his most authoritarian timbre. "You cannot prevent her from leaving your country if she wishes to do so."

He knew he didn't have a legal leg to stand on, but he hoped between his conviction and their confusion, he'd win enough time to get them on the boat. He should have known Diego Roca would not be so easily intimidated.

"Take the baby," Diego ordered the soldier beside him, ignoring Jack all together.

"No!" screamed Melinda. "No!"

Diego ignored her as well. "Take the baby," he said again.

Jack stepped between Melinda and the soldier. The cold steel of a rifle muzzle caressed his temple. Behind him, Melinda tried to run. He could hear the waves lashing at her skirt. On the boat, the captain desperately pulled up anchor, then tried to unlock the motor and lower it back into the water. The baby, wakened by the commotion, began to cry, not a small whimper of distress, but a full howl of terror. Panic churned in the air.

"Give me back my baby!" Melinda was shrieking. "Give me back my baby!"

Jack turned in time to see the soldier rip the screeching infant from his mother's arms and bring him to his father. Without another word, Diego turned and carried his son, still crying bitterly and flailing wildly, back to the jeep.

And then, without warning, the shooting started.

Acting more on instinct than reason, Jack did a nosedive into the water, grabbing Melinda by the legs and bringing her down with him. Sputtering, she tried to pull away, struggling against him, still attempting to chase after the soldiers as the bullets whizzed over her head.

"Melinda, stop!" Jack cried. "They're going to kill you!"

"They've got my baby!" she screamed. "I can't let them take my baby."

A bullet splashed in the water near them, and not

knowing what else to do, he pulled her down again, grabbed her in a chokehold, and swam the short few yards to the boat. Gasping for breath, she could not fight him as he pushed her on the boat and jumped on board after her, just as the captain succeeded in finally nudging his rebellious motor into action.

"Go back!" she shouted over the noise of the engine and the slapping of the sea against the hull as they sped away from shore. "I can't leave my baby!"

"Are you crazy?" the captain pulled himself out of her frantic grip. "They'll kill me as well as you. I'm not going back there."

She was sobbing inconsolably.

Jack tried to comfort her. "We'll get Nico back, I promise. We'll find a way to get your baby. But you can't go back there. Roca will kill you."

"I don't care," she cried. "If I can't be with Nico, I'd just as soon die."

She leaned on his shoulder, cold and wet, bouncing over the sea to Haiti and then home. Through the night, he held her and talked to her softly. But all she could feel was the absence of Nico's tiny body in her cruelly empty arms. And all she could hear was his anguished wail imprinted on her soul.

"I was pleased to hear from you, Sarah," Dr. Tibor Horvath said as he ushered them into his waiting room. "I was afraid you'd given up on your therapy."

Sarah smiled wanly. "Actually, I had."

"What made you decide to come back?" he asked, keeping his voice pleasant, professional. She looked at her husband, her eyes pleading for assistance. The doctor was pleased to see that he took her hand and held it tightly before answering. Whatever the problem, the fact that she had strong family support would help.

"Dr. Horvath," he began, looking at his wife with a deep empathy, "we're in trouble, and Sarah needs help."

"Do you want to tell me about it?"

Again, Ian looked at Sarah, and again, she signaled him to speak for her.

"You know those blackouts that Sarah was having?"

The doctor nodded. He had suspected, as they all had, an acute case of alcoholism with a strong denial mechanism.

"Well, she had another one. Only this time, she took her niece, Moira, and locked her in an empty stable. Everyone thought she'd been kidnapped. It was pretty terrifying."

Sarah's eyes filled with tears. "Moira said I did it, but I don't remember anything about it. She said I told her she was bad and had to be punished. Isn't that awful? She's such a sweet child. I could never have done something like that."

"But you did?" Horvath looked from one to the other for confirmation.

Sarah shrugged. Ian said, "It kind of looks that way."

"Were you drinking?" the doctor asked.

"No," said Sarah vehemently.

"She wasn't," Ian corroborated. "I mean, not so as anyone could tell. She was there through the whole ordeal while we were looking for Moira and everything. She just didn't remember. It was like someone else had done it, and she didn't know anything about it."

Horvath took a deep breath. He hadn't had a patient like Sarah Taylor in a long time, but he was surprised that he hadn't suspected it before. It was possible that his assumption of alcohol addiction had not been wrong, it had just been incomplete.

"Mr. Taylor, I think there may be an answer to this. But I'm going to need to talk to Sarah alone for a while."

"I can sit in the waiting room. But I can't leave her. I promised the police I would bring her down for questioning today, and I can't take the chance that she might . . . uh . . ."

"I understand." He rose and opened the door for Ian. "I guarantee you she won't disappear without your knowing it," he added cryptically.

Ian kissed his wife quickly and left. Horvath closed the door behind him. He could see Sarah was trembling slightly. Her fear was understandable. She was on the brink of a terrifying discovery, and she knew it.

"Sarah," he said gently, "I want to put you in an hypnotic trance. Will you let me do that?"

"Do you have to?"

"I know it's scary, but it's the one way to find out what's going on. You want that, don't you?"

She nodded and, after a moment's hesitation, went to the recliner where she had spent their previous sessions and lay down. Conditioned as she was, it was a simple matter to put her into a trance. She knew the ritual, and as he touched her closed eyelids and commanded her to take deep breaths and say "Far away" while he counted, she felt herself relaxing, her body letting go of the anxiety that had kept her bound in a Gordian knot of tension for days.

When he saw that she was under, he began without preamble. "Did you lock Moira in the stable, Sarah?"

"No." It was an honest, quiet response, and he believed it.

"Can I speak to the person who did?" Silence. "I'd like to meet her. I think it's time, don't you?"

He saw her eyelids quiver. Her body twitched as though she was trying to get out of an uncomfortable position. Then, suddenly, she opened her eyes and sat bolt upright.

"You rang?" she said and broke into raucous laughter.

"Who are you?" he asked, struggling to maintain his calm.

"Don't you know? I thought you wanted to talk to me."

"I do. But I'd like to know your name."

"Sunny. Ironic, isn't it?"

He smiled. He could see Sunny was a tough tomato, but she had a sense of humor.

"Do you know who I am?" he asked.

"The shrink with the funny name."

"Close enough. I'm Dr. Tibor Horvath. I'm trying to help Sarah."

"She needs it. That girl is one sorry mess."

"But you're the one who got her into trouble. You're the one who kidnapped Moira and made Sarah take the blame."

"Oh, for Chrissake," Sunny burst out, getting up

from the couch and starting to pace. "I did not kidnap the little fucker. I gave her some licorice and put her in the stable. Big deal. A lot worse happened to me in there."

He registered the comment but decided to let it go for the time being. It was the immediate past he had to deal with first. Now that he had met Sunny, he suspected there would be time to discover why she had been created in the first place. "Why did you do it, Sunny?"

"Why? I don't know. I was pissed off, I guess. I fly off the handle some times. I didn't kill her or hurt her or anything. I just figured she'd be missing for a while, they'd be upset, and then they'd go and find her. I didn't think it was going to turn into a federal case."

"Did Moira do something to make you angry?"

"Nah, I don't have much to do with her. I'm usually not allowed to come out when the family is around," she added with heavy sarcasm.

"So who upset you?"

"Her busybody mother. I'm in my regular bar, having a good time, and who do you think walks in? It's like that line in *Casablanca*—how does it go? 'Of all the gin joints in all the cities in the world, she had to walk into mine.' Then she starts giving me a lecture and ends up pushing me into a cab and sending me home. What a bitch!"

"But if you were mad at her mother, why did you punish the little girl?"

"Well, hey, that's how it works. Do you think I did anything wrong when I got taken to the stable? He couldn't do it to my mother, so he took it out on me."

Horvath nodded. He'd had a feeling she would come back to that herself. "Who?"

"My father, who do you think? The great Forrest Symington himself."

"What did he do to you?"

She started to squirm. "I don't want to talk about it."

He knew better than to push her. It would come out when she was ready. "Does Sarah know about it?"

"No." Sunny was vehement. "And don't you dare tell her either. I'm the keeper of the pain and rage. Sarah's got nothing to do with it."

"So you protect Sarah."

"I guess you could say that. She's such a wimp," she added disdainfully. "No one else will do it."

"I think Ian tries."

"Her husband? He's a bigger wimp than she is. He doesn't know anything about us."

"Us?"

She gave a tantalizing smile and then ran her closed fingers across her lips as if to zipper them shut. There were others, he realized, more fractures in a personality that had been unable to handle some unbearable pain alone.

"Can you tell me about the others? Who they are? What they do?" he tried again.

"No."

He suddenly got another thought. "Do you know them?"

Sunny shrugged. "I know who they are." He saw that she was trying to save face, unwilling to admit that, in fact, she was not the one in control.

"But you don't know what they do," he said, stating a fact rather than asking a question. He didn't want to give her a chance to back away from it.

"Not everything," she whined, unhappy with being put in her place. "But I know more than Sarah," she added, trying to regain some lost ground. "And I'll tell you something else, I'm the only one who knows how to have a good time. The rest of them are so uptight. He got to them. But he couldn't get to me."

"Forrest, you mean."

She nodded.

"I guess that's why they made you keeper of the pain."

She touched her nose with one hand and pointed at him with the other in the charade gesture of you-got-it. "You know what they say. If rape is inevitable, lie back and enjoy it."

"I've heard that," he said, refusing to share the joke, "but I don't think it's funny. Rape is a horrible, reprehensible crime." He decided to take a chance. "And it's an especially evil act when it's carried out against a helpless child."

"Well, excuuuuse me, Mr. Politically Correct," she said, affronted. "But I guess we all deal with these things any way we can, don't we? And isn't that what's great about our wonderful country?!"

He could see he had her on the defensive, and it was making her uncomfortable. His instinct told him that was good. He wasn't going to get all he needed from Sunny, and he wanted her to be so disturbed that she would have to leave.

"You're very sarcastic, Sunny. But I think that's

just a cover because you want me to think you're more in control than you are. I don't think you really know what's happening all the time."

"Maybe not," she said, defiant now. "But I sure know when it hurts."

"But there is someone who does know everything, isn't there? I want to talk to her. You protect Sarah from the pain, but you can't help her get better. I need to talk to someone who can."

"Oh, fuck," said Sunny and punched the wall. But a moment later, when she turned around, Dr. Horvath saw that she was gone, and he was confronting a woman he had never met before.

"I'm sorry, Dr. Horvath," she said in a voice that was strong without being aggressive. "Sunny doesn't like to leave the spotlight."

"The spotlight?"

"That's what we call it. Whoever is going to come out has to get into the spotlight. That's why I let her get so drunk. Then she falls asleep, and it's easier to take over."

"So you're the one in charge." He had read about similar devices in other multiple personalities. There was usually a dominant personality who managed the system of bringing the others into the open, whether it be by way of a spotlight, like Sarah's, or doors opening onto a common corridor that was the representation of the host's body.

"My name is Susan."

"I'm very pleased to meet you, Susan," he said respectfully. In the literature, it was called the self-helper. She would be the one who knew everything.

And if Sarah was ever going to get better, to become one whole person, he would need Susan's help.

"And I, you," she said a little formally in a slightly British accent. Susan clearly had intelligence, composure, and an innate sense of power, like the CEO of a giant conglomerate whose many divisions have been turning a profit for years. The only thing Susan lacked was any emotion that might affect her cognitive process.

"Listen," she went on, "I have to apologize about what happened to the little girl. Sarah really knows nothing about it. I'm the one who told her to tell them to look in the stable, but she's not really aware of my presence. I just let her think it was a voice in her head, something she could interpret as instinct."

"Sarah doesn't know about any of you, does she?"

"Of course not. That would be defeating the purpose, wouldn't it?"

"Which is to protect her."

"Exactly."

"I have to say, Susan," Horvath said, deciding to challenge her a little, "you didn't protect her very well when you let Sunny kidnap Moira."

"I apologized for that," Susan said haughtily. "Sunny carries the rage. She has a right to dispose of it. Usually it's self-directed, but it doesn't hurt anyone except Sunny. The others are safe. I admit in this case with the child it went too far. But obviously, I wouldn't let anything really awful happen. We're not violent—except . . ."

He noticed her faltering. "How many of you are there?"

"Only five. There were more, but I destroyed them. They weren't needed after Sarah married Ian."

"You like Ian?"

"He's helped her. Sunny thinks he's boring, but she doesn't really know what goes on with them. I can tell he really loves her. That's why I let the others go. Except for Stuart. He's the strongest physically. He's all she needs to keep her out of any real danger."

"Let's see," Dr. Horvath counted off. "There's Sarah, the host; you, the facilitator, Sunny, the keeper of the rage and pain, Stuart, the protector. That's only four. Who's left?"

"Just Shana."

"What does she do?"

"Nothing. She just cries. She's only a child."

"How old is she?"

"Four."

Horvath decided to try a guess. "Is that how old Sarah was when Forrest Symington first abused her?"

"Yes. He used to do it to her in the stable. Which is why Sarah, who doesn't know anything about it, has never really liked horses. I let her get rid of the ones at Belvedere first chance she got. I think it made her feel pretty good to sell those horses and lock the place up, even if she didn't know why."

"I'm sure it did," Horvath agreed. "You've done a remarkable job of protecting her without letting her know what she was being protected from. But I think it's something we have to talk about. Can we?"

She hesitated. For a moment, she seemed to go back into her head. Her lips moved a little, and he sensed she was gone from him. Then she focused her eyes on him and began again. "I had to make sure the others weren't listening. I'm really the only one who knows everything, and I'd like them to find out in a more controlled environment."

He smiled. She was a good guardian.

She started to speak almost mechanically with little inflection in her voice, and he sensed that even Susan had to dissociate herself from the emotions to bear the hurt. "Her parents didn't really fight a lot," she began, still speaking of Sarah in the third person as though Mathilde and Forrest Symington were no relation to her. "Her mother was too refined to raise her voice, so she mostly got drunk. Her father blustered a lot, but he was no match for the woman. I think she intimidated him. And I'm certain she despised him. But, of course, she was the one with the money, so there wasn't much he could do about it.

"The first time he took Sarah to the stable, she wasn't scared. She was learning how to ride, and she thought it was fun. In fact, it was kind of thrilling that her father was even paying attention to her. Her mother rarely did. But this time when they got there, he locked the door. He said her mother had been bad, all girls were bad, and Sarah was going to have to be punished. Can you believe that? Doing that to a little kid?"

She didn't try to hide her disgust. Horvath had to struggle not to show his own. He'd heard a lot of horrible stories in his career, but they never lost their ability to shock and sicken. But as a professional, he knew he would have to maintain a distance, keep any hint of his own emotions off his face, if he wanted Susan to continue.

"Sarah had no idea what he was talking about. She

just believed it. Of course, with the hindsight of an adult, I know now it meant that Mathilde wasn't putting out for the old man, so he was going to get his rocks off with the little girl. Sarah couldn't deal with that, and voilà, Shana was born."

"Did Mathilde know what was going on?"

"I'm not sure. I think she was just grateful that he was plugging someone else and wasn't battering down her door, so she didn't ask any questions."

He nodded. It was a classic tactic of the unhappy wives of abusive men.

"Sarah didn't know anything, and poor little Shana thought this was happening because she was bad, so she was too ashamed to tell anyone."

"All she could do was cry," supplied Horvath, unable to disguise his sympathy.

Susan nodded. "That's why we needed Sunny. Sunny can take anything. Nothing bothers her. Really. She can even make the most awful things seem like fun. Blows off the steam. It's quite a talent."

"So," Horvath said, putting the pieces together, "when the pressure was on Sarah, she'd black out. Shana would get upset, then Sunny would take over and, as you put it, blow off steam. If she got in trouble, Stuart would show up and get her out of it."

"You're a very intelligent man." Susan rewarded him with her highest compliment. "You're the only one who has been able to figure it out."

"I owe that to you, Susan. You're the one who was smart enough to know that maybe, finally, Sarah could do a better job of taking care of herself then all of you. You're the one who let me in on the secret. The facilitator, right?"

She smiled wearily. "It's a tough job but somebody's got to do it."

He smiled. He liked this Susan. When they'd put the pieces back together, as he was now sure they could, she would be an attractive part of the whole personality.

"We're going to have to let Sarah in on it," he said, addressing her like the ally she had become.

"I know."

"And her family."

"Do you think that's necessary?"

"Yes, I do. It's not going to be easy for Sarah to accept all of you as part of her. I think her family can help her do that."

"Are you going to kill the rest of us off," she asked nervously.

"Absolutely not. I think each of you has something that Sarah needs to integrate into herself. We're not going to eliminate you; we're going to make you one."

"Perfect." She sighed. "Dr. Horvath," she went on, "I'm going to go now and let Sarah take over. I'm really exhausted, and I need to plan for my early retirement."

He laughed at her little joke, and she laughed with him. And then, her eyes rolled back into her head, and he knew that Sarah had come back.

"What's going on?" she asked.

"We have a lot to talk about, Sarah," he said.

11

It wasn't the reunion they had hoped for. A call from Jack informed Sam of what had transpired and of Melinda's intention to go with Jack directly to Washington to try and pursue a diplomatic solution to retrieving her son. Leaving Drew with Moira, who seemed to have recuperated from her few dark hours in the stable far more quickly than her parents, Sam flew to Washington to be with her sister.

They met in Jack's small apartment and promptly burst into tears.

"Oh, Sam," sobbed Melinda, "what am I going to do? I can't live without my baby."

"Of course you can't," Sam cried with her. "We're going to get him back. Moira's waiting to meet him. We can't disappoint her."

Melinda smiled wanly at her sister's attempt to cheer her. "How could I have let this happen to me?"

"Don't beat yourself up," Sam instructed her. "There's no way you could have known things were going to turn out this way."

"Maybe if I hadn't been so trusting . . ."

"Honey, when it comes to love, we're all too damn trusting. The important thing is to bring Nico to America and put it all behind you."

"We went straight from the airport to talk to someone at the State Department. Jack set it all up."

"Roca doesn't have a great record on human rights since he got into power," offered Jack. "I'm hoping we can approach this as a way for him to redeem himself. We're even offering to try and contain the press until after Melinda has the baby back. That way all his media coverage will be positive. He can get a lot of points for returning a baby to his mother."

"You're amazing, Jack," Sam said, meaning it. "I don't know how this family could survive without you."

"That's me," he joked with a self-deprecating laugh. "Consigliere to the Myles Mafia."

"Actually, we call ourselves the Myles Militia," Sam corrected, laughing, too.

Melinda tried to smile, aware the bonhomie was for her benefit. But there was no lightening her mood.

"Jack has always been there, hasn't he?" she said, and Sam knew it was not a question. For a moment, Jack and Melinda locked eyes, and Sam could almost see the tentacles reaching out from their respective hearts to intertwine in the distance that had grown between them. She could see what an effort it took for Jack to pull away, even though nothing tangible bound them.

"Listen, you two," he said brightly, hoping his cheerful tone might conceal, if not relieve, his disquiet, "I know you've got a lot to catch up on, and you don't need me around for that. It's too late for us to hear anything today. So, I'm going to consign my apartment to you for the night. You can bunk together in the bedroom, or one of you can sleep on the couch. But I'll stay out of your way."

They protested in unison, pointing out the two of them could share the bedroom and he could have the couch.

"It's okay," he insisted, and Sam thought for a minute she saw the tinge of a blush. "I've got somewhere else to stay."

"Of course," she said, remembering Daisy, and looked at Melinda, wondering how much she knew.

Instantly, she got her answer. "You've been so busy with me, you haven't even seen Daisy yet," Melinda said. "She must be worried sick." There was no hint of jealousy in her voice, but Sam knew that didn't mean anything. Melinda was a consummate actress.

"I called her," Jack said. It was hard to tell if he was uncomfortable or just anxious to go. "She's expecting me."

They didn't argue with him after that and sent him on his way with thanks and kisses.

The moment the door closed behind him, Sam had only to look at Melinda, and she burst out, "I can't even think about it, Sam. So don't ask me."

When they were alone, it was as though no time had

passed. They took turns telling their tales, each sister feeling the other's pains and triumphs. Eventually, certain he would not mind, they searched Jack's drawers and, finding T-shirts for both of them, got comfortable. Forgoing the couch, they slipped into his bed together, and whispering as they had done when they were girls, they fell asleep holding hands.

In the apartment on Connecticut Avenue, Jack lay beside Daisy in her bed, wide awake. There had been candlelight and soft music when he had come in. The table had been set for two, and the air had been redolent with the aroma of something cooking, not easily identified, but indisputably delicious. Daisy, dressed in nothing but the kimono she had been wearing the first time he had dropped in on her, was more warmly alluring than she had ever been. They had kissed at the door and held each other a long time, and when they broke apart, she knew without asking that things had changed.

He would have sat down with her at the table, but she said without regret or recrimination that it would be a shame to waste her fabulous food on someone who really didn't want to eat. She was right, and he did not press her, watching her turn off the stove and put the pot on a trivet to cool without even asking her what was inside.

He did not offer to tell her what had happened, and trusting she would hear in good time, she did not ask. Instead, she led him to the bedroom and helped him strip off the clothes he had been wearing since he'd left her at the airport, days, though it seemed like eons, ago. She ran a bath for him and filled it with something aromatic that did actually make him feel calmer after it made him sneeze a half-dozen times. She turned the bed down for him and would have left him to sleep or dream or simply be alone with his thoughts. But he insisted she lie down beside him, and gently untying her robe, she let his hands wander over her body, reminding him of what it was he loved and stood to lose.

They made love, she with passion, he with zeal, as he willed himself to blindness on her snow white skin, burying his face in the scented avalanche of her white gold hair. He wanted to refuel his ardor, to refill the tank of his soul that had been emptied by Melinda's need. And she gave him what he asked for, sensing that his demand was for more than carnal completion, that he was seeking in her body to obliterate a void. They came together, and released, he refused to acknowledge that some small part of him had remained without her.

Sleepless, he held her in his arms through the night, her body sweet with contentment, and told himself that he could ask for no greater gift than to spend the rest of his life with her. And when Daisy woke in the morning and beamed a smile of tender satisfaction to see him still there beside her, Jack kissed her and promised her that as soon as the trouble with Melinda was over, they would have the biggest damn wedding Washington had ever seen.

"Is this your way of getting breakfast in bed?" she asked slyly. "Because it could work."

"Well, let's see." He held his hands in front of him as though each concept could fit neatly in the palm of one hand. "Breakfast—wedding," he weighed them, keeping his hands evenly in balance. "Yeah, that looks fair. It's a deal."

She kissed him and went to make coffee. He let his eyes close, the night's restless speculation having finally, now that it was too late to sleep, worn him down. But a moment later, Daisy was back.

"We may have to wait a while for that wedding," she said, handing him the morning's *Washington Post.*

It wasn't the main headline, but it was a front-page story. "President of San Domenico Divorces American Wife and Keeps Custody of Child."

He scanned the article, mumbling as he read. "In an unusual judicial maneuver, Diego Roca, president of San Domenico, was granted an immediate divorce from his wife, the former American actress Melinda Myles, after announcing that she had left the country, abandoning their four-month-old son. No details were released about events leading to her departure, but a reliable source suggests that Mrs. Roca objected to her husband's increasing intolerance on the island and that she has been kept a virtual prisoner in the presidential palace. The source also says that the child being left behind in San Domenico was the result of a botched escape attempt."

He took a breath. "Damn it. I expected trouble but not this. I figured Roca would at least have the decency to respond through diplomatic channels. And who the fuck is this reliable source who's giving out all this goddamn information."

"Your Amnesty International friend perhaps?" volunteered Daisy.

"Corey? Could be. He was pretty pissed off that I

was on my own mission. Shit." He jumped out of bed. "I better get back to my apartment. If Melinda sees this, she's going to . . . I don't know what."

"I take it breakfast is off?"

"I'm sorry, baby. I've got to get to her before—"

"It's okay," Daisy interrupted. "I understand. Go."

"When it's over . . . ," Jack promised again, grabbing his jacket and throwing it on over his still unbuttoned shirt.

"Kiss?" asked Daisy, trying to waylay him in the hall.

But it was too late. Jack was already out the door and at the elevator. "What?" he called back to her, aware she had said something he'd been in too much of a hurry to catch.

"Never mind." She sighed. "When it's over . . ."

Arriving at his own door, Jack knocked softly as a warning, then let himself in with his key. He had hoped that, exhausted from their ordeal, Melinda might still be sleeping and he would be able to break the news to her gently. He should have known better. He found the two sisters in his bedroom, still wearing his T-shirts, channel-surfing through the morning news programs, gleaning what they could.

The minute Melinda saw him, she abandoned her search, went into his arms, and started crying. From the color of her eyes and the splotches on her cheeks, Jack could tell this was not her first tearful reaction of the morning. Talking on the phone to Drew in Woodland Cliffs, Sam blew him a silent kiss over Melinda's shoulder and shrugged ruefully.

"The guy's a bastard," Jack said by way of comforting Melinda.

"I shouldn't have left, Jack. Not without Nico. It's my own fault."

"Stop it, Melinda. They were shooting at you. Nico doesn't need a dead mother. We're going to get him back."

"How?" she asked simply and saw that he was as stymied as she was.

"Hey, the State Department hasn't even started exerting the real pressure," Jack blustered, trying to recover.

"You know as well as I do that it's not going to have any effect on Diego," she said, blowing her nose loudly. "He doesn't care what the U.S. government thinks. He doesn't care what anybody thinks."

"Still, it's going to be hard for him to get away with using a baby as a pawn in a political game."

"The irony is, I'm sure he doesn't see the baby as a pawn. He loves Nico. He wants him as much as I do. It's something I never thought of before Diego changed. A person can be an absolute monster and still be a loving father."

Sam hung up the phone and joined them. "Well, the press has been working overtime trying to track you down," she informed them. "They're parked in Mom and Dad's front yard, and since they can't get past the gates in Belvedere, they've resorted to calling every hour on the hour. So far all they've got is a universal 'no comment.' "

"It's only a matter of time before the trail leads them here," Jack said unhappily. "You might want to prepare a statement."

"I've been thinking about that," said Melinda quietly. "I think the only thing I can say is that this has all been a gigantic error, and all I want to do is go home to my husband and patch things up."

Jack and Sam looked at her. "Are you crazy?" Sam asked her sister, echoing Jack's thoughts.

"What choice do I have?" Melinda wailed. "Diego is never going to give up Nico. I have to convince him to take me back."

"How do you know he won't just have you shot? Or have you disappear—that's more his style, isn't it?" Jack couldn't keep the scorn out of his voice.

"Not if I tell him I was wrong. Beg his forgiveness."

"For God's sake, Melinda. You weren't wrong. The man is a dangerous megalomaniac. You have no idea what he'll do." Jack could feel his temperature rising, and he told himself it was because he feared Roca's cruelty, not his rivalry.

"He's my husband, Jack. I know it's hard for you to understand, because you just know him from news reports and Amnesty International complaints. I'm not saying there aren't bad things about him. But he wasn't always that way. He was a good, decent man once. A hero. I loved him. Everyone did."

"Excuse me," said Jack, unable to control his rage. "If you think he's so goddamn great, why the hell did you make me risk my life to get you out of there? Just a little trip home to see the folks?"

Silent tears rolled down Melinda's face, and he turned away, feeling like a heel.

"Let's everybody take it easy," soothed Sam, aware that the dynamics between her sister and her friend had as much to do with their past history as their current situation.

"I'm sorry," said Jack. "It's just that . . ." He

trailed off. He was definitely sorry; he just wasn't sure what for.

No one spoke for a minute. Melinda blew her nose, and Jack handed her another box of tissues from inside the night table. She thanked him quietly, then blew again.

Finally, Melinda spoke. Her voice was barely a whisper, and both Sam and Jack leaned in to hear her. "I did love Diego," she asserted as much to herself as the two of them. "But that kind of power does things to a person . . . to him anyway. I know he'll never again be the man I married. And knowing what he's become, I will hate every minute of my life that I have to spend with him. But I *will* go back to him, and I will find a way to make him take me back. Because I have no choice. I will not leave my son behind."

Sam tried this time. "Listen to me, Melinda. If you go back, you don't know what Diego will do, and you know for sure you'll never get out again. Maybe if you stay here, you can work on a way of getting Nico out. Just because Diego rejected the first diplomatic request doesn't mean that he won't reconsider."

"That's right," Jack picked up, encouraging. "Roca is vulnerable. At some point, if you keep working at it from this end, he's going to have to acknowledge there's a problem, and then he's going to have to deal with it. You've got a much better power position as an American citizen in the United States."

Melinda just shook her head. She looked at Sam. "Would you leave Moira alone with someone you knew was evil? Would you take a chance that you might never see her again and this evil person would raise her without you, turning her away from you and everything you believe in? Would you consider it even for a minute?"

Sam was silent. She could not look her sister in the eye. Melinda understood. "Then why do you expect me to be able to do that?" she asked quietly. "If Nico can't come to me right now, right away, then I have to go to him. And if I'm killed in the process, what does it matter? I'm dead without him anyway."

A pall hung over the three of them. There was nothing to say. Suddenly, Jack broke the silence. "What if Nico could come to you?"

"Diego won't let him," she said without emotion.

"I know that. But what if we could find a way? It would be dangerous, but—"

She didn't even let him finish. "That's all I want. To get Nico out of San Domenico and never, ever go there again."

He told them to dress, to stay off the phone and away from the door. He made them promise to make no moves and take no measures. He admitted he was taking a shot in the dark, and his idea might come to nothing, but he sounded so emphatic that they took heart. And when he left, for the first time in days, Melinda smiled.

By the time he returned three hours later, the smile had faded, and Melinda, dressed as she had been instructed to do, was pacing the small living room like a caged animal. Sam had tried to calm her sister with tea, talk, even tranquilizers, but to no avail. When they heard the key in the lock, Melinda almost pounced on the door. She was taken aback for a minute to see he was not alone, but when she realized who was with him, she let out a cry of joy and fell into his arms.

"Ottavio! It's so wonderful to see you."

Ottavio grinned and hugged her back, made bold by their mutual status. In San Domenico, she had been the president's wife. Here she was just another refugee seeking political asylum.

He shook hands with Sam, who also greeted him warmly. "How's the lawyer we set you up with?" she asked him.

"Oh, he is excellent," crowed Ottavio. "We filed all the forms already. It is just a matter of waiting for the interview. But I know it will go well. All of you people"—he swept his arm around the room, indicating the three of them—"have made this possible for me."

"I'm so happy," Melinda beamed, genuinely pleased at his good fortune, even though she was having none herself at the moment. "Clara was so worried about you."

"Now," said Ottavio gravely, "she is worried about you."

"She'd better worry about herself. I'm afraid Diego will blame her for what happened," said Melinda with a shudder.

"He can't," said Ottavio with a sly grin. "He needs her too much."

"What do you mean?" asked Melinda, excited. "Have you spoken to her?"

"When I heard the news, I called my cousins. It seems when Roca brought the baby back to the palace, he was very upset. Roca couldn't make him stop crying. He had to call Clara in the middle of the night. She's the only one who could calm him. Now, they say, he will only let her feed him. Roca doesn't like it, but what can he do? He's worried about the child."

"Poor Nico." Melinda's eyes filled with tears again. "Thank God that at least Clara is still with him."

"For more reasons than one," said Jack.

Sam looked at him. She knew that voice. It was the way he sounded when he had an ace up his sleeve. "What are you thinking, Jack?" she demanded.

Jack looked at Ottavio. There was a hint of question in his eyes, and Ottavio responded with a solemn nod.

"Ottavio has volunteered to fly a small plane back into San Domenico. He says he can get below their radar and land on an abandoned strip that he knows. Clara will meet him there with the baby, and Ottavio will bring them to America."

Melinda gasped. Then she screamed. Then she jumped up and down and hugged each of them in turn. It was only after she'd paused to catch her breath that the reality of what they were proposing struck her.

"Ottavio," she wavered, "this is very dangerous for you."

He shook his head. "I thought I could never repay what you did for me. Maybe now I can. I am a very good pilot."

"I trust you." She laughed. "When can we do this?"

"Melinda, I don't think you should go," Jack started.

"He's right," Sam joined him. "There's nothing you can do—"

But Melinda cut them both off. "Ottavio, I want to come with you. Is that all right?"

"Whatever you want."

"I want to go," she said adamantly.

He nodded. "I need to make plans. I will let you know soon."

He shook hands with all of them, and Melinda walked him to the door.

The minute her sister was out of hearing, Sam turned to Jack. "Are you thinking what I'm thinking?"

"I'm afraid so," he said, sighing. "We both know there's no way I'm going to let her go alone. Now, I'm just going to have to explain it to Daisy!"

At first, when Dr. Horvath informed Sarah Symington Taylor that she had multiple personality disorder, she did not believe him. But gradually, as he relayed to her things the others had told him, filled her in on the blank spaces that had constituted her life for so long, it began to make sense to her. Her immediate reaction was fear. It terrified her to think of herself as some sort of psychotic freak. Again the doctor reassured her. Each of her personalities had handled an element of her life that might have been unbearable otherwise. Far from turning her into a monster, they had helped her to function in a world that had been rendered too cruel for a vulnerable child. But now that she was grown and safe, now that her life had taken a positive turn, she didn't need them anymore. Instead of protecting her from suffering, they were preventing her from feeling. And what the doctor thought they should do was let Sarah meet each of them, get to know which aspects of their personas would be helpful to her, and then integrate them into her own body.

Through hypnosis, Horvath put Sarah in a trance, and then calling on each of the personalities in turn, he suggested they introduce themselves to Sarah and tell her what they each knew. For a long time, Sarah lay on the leather recliner, her eyes closed but moving rapidly, her body alternately stiffening and relaxing, her lips moving in silent communion with herself. He did not interrupt. She had a good deal to tell herself. When, finally, she stopped moving, he understood that she was done, and making sure that it was Sarah in control, he brought her out of her hypnotic state.

"It's unbelievable," she said, both aghast and amused. "It was like there were all these other people living inside me. Not just, you know, aspects of my personality. But real people. They were talking to me like we were friends or something."

"Well," he said with a smile, "they have been your friends. Some better than others."

"I really liked Susan," she went on, as if she were talking about an individual she had met at a party. "She seemed very smart, very nice. She's the one who told me all the things that had happened."

"Me, too. Susan's been your facilitator, the one who kept all the knowledge and decided when the others had to take over."

"Shana was sweet. But so sad. And of course, Sunny I guess I could live without."

"Even Sunny has her place," Horvath pointed out.

"There's a physical aspect to her that, directed in the right way, could make things easier for you."

"And I've got to tell you, it is absolutely weird having a man live inside my body." She laughed at herself. "It sounds so strange, but that's what it feels like. Like they're all residents in an apartment building whose address just happens to be me. It's funny—and it's terrifying," she added.

Horvath nodded. He knew that in the security of his office, the novelty of what she had discovered about herself would be a relief. But she was only starting to navigate the stormy sea that had been her life, and there would be plenty of rough passages before the crossing was done.

Ian was the first outsider to meet all of Sarah's people. Without waiting to be invited, Sunny bumped everyone else out of the spotlight and took over the body. Horvath had warned Ian of what he was going to see, but nothing prepared him for his initial confrontation with Sunny.

"Baby," she began, "I've been wanting to talk to you."

Ian looked at Horvath, unsure of how to respond. The doctor had told him to react to each of the personalities as though he was meeting another person, but it was disconcerting to see his wife appear in a wholly different character, like an actress in a play.

"Don't you want to be introduced, Sunny?" Horvath asked, letting Ian know indirectly whom he was dealing with.

"What for? I know who he is." She got up off the chair and started to slink toward Ian. Even though Ian tried to remain neutral, Horvath could see him shrink from her approach.

Sunny saw it, too. "Afraid of me, baby?" she laughed. "You ought to be. I was tempted more than once to send Stuart out after you when you started poking that thing in her without a condom." She pointed in the general direction of his lap, and for a minute, thinking she might make a grab at him, Ian's hands went to protect himself.

"Haven't you ever heard of safe sex?" She was still railing at him.

Ian looked at Horvath again. He didn't know what to say. This was Sarah, and yet, it most definitely was not. He tried to do what the doctor had told him, to act as if she was another person.

"Actually," he said hesitantly, "Sarah and I were trying to have a baby."

"Jesus, not only are you boring, you're fucking stupid."

Horvath saw Ian clench and put a restraining hand on his arm. There was a fine line between treating each personality distinctly and reacting as though this were a person in control.

Ian forced himself to remain calm. He reminded himself that this was not his wife talking. But it was hard not to think that at least some part of Sarah believed what this new person was saying and this was just a psychic gimmick that allowed her to say what was really on her mind.

Sunny was going on. "Why the hell would you want to bring a kid into this world? She's already got one who just sits around blubbering all the time."

Horvath decided that perhaps Sunny was a little strong for Ian to take at the start. "Why don't you let Ian meet her," he suggested.

Ian watched in amazement as Sarah's eyes rolled back in her head, and the brazen body that had been Sunny's suddenly crumpled to accommodate the whimpering Shana. Not daring to meet his eyes, she climbed back onto the chair and, drawing her legs into a fetal position, sniffled quietly to herself.

"My God," said Ian, no warnings in the world having prepared him for this, "she looks like a little girl."

"She is," said Horvath. "She is four years old and always will be. She was created to share the pain, so she doesn't speak." He could see the confusion on Ian's face. He hadn't intended to introduce him to his wife's personalities in quite this way, but he had underestimated their ability to take over. It was time, he decided, to give Ian some explanations. "Shana, I want you to go away now," he addressed the child gently. "You go back to your room and let Susan come out."

It took only a moment, and Ian, watching, understood now what was happening.

"I'm Susan," she offered congenially as soon as she appeared. "I've wanted to meet you for a long time, but I'm sure you can understand why I was a little hesitant."

Ian smiled at her intentional understatement, and Horvath drew a sigh of relief. As usual, Susan was going to make his work a lot easier.

"No matter what Sunny says"—Susan was looking

warmly into Ian's eyes—"I want you to know that we greatly appreciate what you've done for Sarah. I really believe that without you, we would have lost her."

Ian accepted the compliment graciously.

"I would have done more if I had known . . . if I could . . . I love you . . . her." He switched uncomfortably, still not sure what he should be saying.

"It's okay," said Susan, understanding. "We think of ourselves as separate people, but your love for Sarah is something we all treasure."

"Susan," intervened Dr. Horvath, "since you're the one who knows everything, and it's easiest for you to articulate, would you mind telling Ian the whole story from the beginning of what happened to you and how you came to be?"

She sighed. "I expected you were going to ask me." She turned to Ian. "It's not very nice. Are you sure you want to hear it?"

"I think I have to," said Ian. "I owe it to the woman I love."

Susan nodded, and Horvath could see her lip trembling just a little. It was the first time he had seen Susan display any real emotion, the first time she had allowed herself to be touched. It was a good sign.

For the next two hours, Susan remained in control. As she had with Dr. Horvath, she told the story of her abuse at the hands of her father in a flat voice, maintaining her dissociation by referring to Forrest as "that man" or "her father" and speaking of herself in the third person. Ian said little, but his face registered the horror of what he was hearing, and several times, his eyes filled with tears.

When she had finished her story, Susan said, "I'm

sorry. I'm really tired now. If you'll excuse me . . ." And before they could respond, her body went rigid, and then Sarah emerged.

"Ian?" she called softly to her husband, wondering what affect the recitation had had on him. Instantly, he went to her and took her in his arms. For a long time, they just held each other.

"Dr. Horvath?" Sarah finally said, breaking away from her husband for the moment. "I heard everything. Before Susan came out, they had a little discussion in my head and decided I should be allowed to listen. I know it sounds strange, but it felt like I was an observer in my own body. I knew my mouth was moving, but it didn't feel like I was the one talking. But I know what happened to me now."

"How does it make you feel?" Dr. Horvath asked carefully.

"Sad. Broken. And angry. Really, really angry. I wish he were alive so I could kill him."

They understood. It was an emotion they shared.

"And what about everybody else?" Sarah choked on her own emotion. "I don't understand how that could have happened to me. Why didn't anyone protect me from him?"

"It's a legitimate question, Sarah," Horvath conceded. "They might not have known. They might have been too frightened of Forrest themselves."

"That's no excuse," she said angrily. "I want to talk to my mother, to my brother. If they knew . . ." She stopped, rage contorting her face.

"You can confront them," Horvath said. "But they may not give you what you want."

"I don't care. I want them to know what happened

to me. I was just a little girl, and they should have found a way to help me. I want them to know that, to admit that."

Horvath nodded. It was not unusual for abused patients to need some acknowledgment and apology for what had happened to them. But it could backfire. He had seen mothers turn on their own daughters, either accusing them of lying or of instigating the sexual conduct. But if Sarah was to get any sort of closure, he knew it would have to be done.

"I'll get in touch with your mother and your brother," he volunteered. "Let's see what they have to say."

She began to cry, and Ian closed his arms around her again, softly stroking her hair.

"I was such a good girl," Sarah sobbed. "I did whatever he told me to. All he ever did was hurt me, and my whole life, I did what he wanted."

"Except marry me," Ian reminded her. "We did that on our own. And that's the one thing that will get us through this."

12

They were all nervous. Sarah and Ian, because they could not be sure of what was going to happen. Drew, because had he not promised to be at this meeting, he would have taken Moira and gone to Washington where he knew Sam was getting involved in some dangerous plans with Jack Bader and her sister. Mathilde, because she had cut short a visit with friends in Cap d'Antibes to return to America, which always depressed her. And Dr. Horvath, because in spite of having made all the arrangements, he wasn't absolutely certain that it was the right thing to do. Still, Sarah was his patient, and she had insisted this was what she wanted. If he had any hopes of fusing her personalities into one whole person, she would have to give herself over to him, and this was a way of proving she could trust him.

Sitting behind his desk, looking at the family spread across his small office, he did not get a good feeling. Sarah and Ian sat on the couch holding hands. Sarah was white-faced and clearly frightened. Drew had taken a chair halfway between Sarah and Dr. Horvath and looked from one to the other with mild concern, waiting for the proceedings to begin. But Mathilde D'Uberville Symington, who knew only that this confrontation had been arranged because of her daughter's pain, had chosen to place herself farthest from the group in a chair near the door, where she glanced surreptitiously at her watch every few minutes, as if wondering how long before she could make a polite escape.

"I want to thank you all for coming here," the doctor began.

"Sarah said eet was eemportant," Mathilde said impatiently, letting the doctor know that she was here because she was fulfilling her parental obligation, should he have any doubt.

"Yes," he concurred without argument. "It is." He looked at Sarah, clutching Ian. He could see little half-moons forming on Ian's flesh where his wife's nails were digging in. Ian didn't even flinch. "Would you like me to explain, Sarah?" he asked.

She nodded.

He decided to do it quickly and simply. "Sarah is suffering from multiple personality disorder, which means that at moments of stress, she becomes different people."

"Wait a minute," said Drew, incredulous. "Are you saying Sarah is a split personality. Like Sybil or something?"

"Yes."

"Who ees thees Seebul?" asked Mathilde, uncomprehending.

"I become different people, *Maman,"* Sarah broke in. "When I can't handle a situation, I turn into someone who can."

"Zees ees good, no?"

"No. Not the way I do it. I have these different people living inside me. They talk to each other and tell me things."

Mathilde waved her hand dismissively. *"Mais, c'est rien.* Zees ees nothing. You always had zee imagination." She pronounced it in the French way.

Sarah was already getting aggravated. "It's not imagination, *Maman.* These people take over my body and do things that I would never do. I can't control it."

Horvath could see the gravity of his sister's problem was registering on Drew, and now Drew intervened.

"It's like a disease, *Maman.* And it's very serious. So why don't we let the doctor finish what he was saying."

Mathilde shrugged as though letting two obstinate children have their way.

Horvath nodded his gratitude to Drew and went on. "Although not everything is known about this disorder, once the condition has been discovered, it can sometimes be corrected by fusing the various personalities into the core individual. But in order to do that, a certain amount of resolution of the initial problems that caused the breakup of the personality must exist. That's what this is all about. Sarah wants you to know why this has happened."

He paused for breath and was sorry to see that the effect had been to increase the tension in the room while they waited for him to continue. He had no choice but to go on. "Sarah believes that from the time she was four years old, she was sexually abused by her father."

"Argh, quel stupidité," burst out Mathilde, reverting to French. *"C'est ridicule!"*

She stood up, ready to turn her back and walk out the door. Sarah trembled and looked as though she might burst into tears, and Ian's face clouded with anger at his mother-in-law's instinctive reaction. Horvath waited a moment to let the family dynamics play themselves out, and as he had hoped, Drew took over.

"Sit down, *Maman.*"

"Mais c'est fou," she protested, outraged. She glared at Horvath. "You deed thees. Thees heepnosis you gave her. Eet made her crazy."

"I'm not crazy!" screamed Sarah, her rage releasing her from her fear. "It happened."

"When?" said Drew quietly. "Where?"

Horvath could see that though it appeared that Drew had indeed been in the dark, he knew his father well enough to know it was possible.

"In the stable," Sarah said shaking. "When we were supposed to be riding. Sometimes, he'd do it to me, then lock me in there."

"My God," Drew's voice was hoarse with shock. "I remember. You used to cry when it was time for your riding lesson. But *Maman* would always make you go anyway."

There had been no recrimination in his voice, and

none had been intended, but Horvath knew instantly that it had been the wrong thing to say. That was why, as necessary as they might be, he never liked these confrontations. There was no control over what was said, and there was no predicting what the reaction would be. He saw Mathilde stiffen and buttress her defenses as surely as if he'd watched a steel door clang shut over her heart.

"Eet ees a deesgusting lie!" she said, her words cloaked with venom. "Thees ees not something that happens in my home. Never. *Jamais!"* she added for emphasis.

It was not the first time he had seen denial in the spouse of an abuser. There was the reputation of the family to protect. Even more important, there was the inference to be countered that by not objecting to the abuse and protecting her child, Mathilde herself was a silent accomplice.

Outraged, it was impossible for Sarah to react with clinical detachment. Suddenly, to the horror of those who knew what was happening and the dismay of those who didn't, her body stiffened and her eyes rolled back into her head. When she focused again, both Ian and Horvath knew that Sarah was gone and Sunny had come to take her place.

"Qu'est-ce qui arrivé?" Mathilde looked baffled, aware that something had happened, but not sure what.

"Don't babble at me, bitch," mocked Sunny. "I don't understand a word of your frog language."

"Oh, my God," said Drew, "This is . . ." He didn't even know what to call it.

"Believe me now, bro?" Sunny laughed.

"I always believed you, Sarah," he mumbled.

She shook her head. "Still don't get it, do you. Tell him who I am, jerk," she addressed Ian. His pain was evident.

"This is Sunny," he explained. "She's one of Sarah's alters."

"Oh, don't we have the lingo down pat," mocked Sunny.

Horvath tried to intervene. "Sunny, the purpose of this meeting was for Sarah to be able to confront her family. You're not helping her by doing this."

"Spare me, Doc. This is all bullshit. The bitch is going to deny it even though it's perfectly clear that she would rather have had old Forrest fucking me instead of her. Even if I was only four years old."

"She says she didn't know," tried Horvath.

"No," corrected Sunny sternly. "She says it didn't happen. There's a difference."

"Don't you think it's possible she didn't know?"

"Yeah, I think it's probable. She didn't want to know. All she wanted to do was talk French and keep away from her pig of a husband."

Horvath sighed. She was destructive, this Sunny, but she wasn't stupid. She had nailed his theory, a little more expressively than he would have put it, but accurate nonetheless.

"We didn't know, Sarah" interceded Drew, feeling obliged to defend his mother, even though he could understand his sister's rage. "Really, if I had—"

She didn't let him finish. "Get it through your head. I'm not Sarah. She's a wimp. A victim. That ain't me. I'm Sunny. I not only get mad, I get even."

A light went on for Drew. "You're the one who took Moira."

"Big deal. You should be more worried about what I can do to you than what I did to her."

Horvath knew she was waving a red flag. "What are you talking about, Sunny?" he asked.

She laughed. "See, Doc, you don't know everything. Susie Q isn't as reliable as you thought."

"Who's Susie Q?" Drew asked.

"Susan is another one of Sarah's personalities," explained Ian, his face growing paler. "She's the one who kind of keeps things in check."

"Used to," corrected Sunny.

"Where is she?" asked Horvath, hoping to get her to come forward.

"Languishing," moaned Sunny. "Just like she was when I planted that little bomb at DMC. Or when I sent out those letters to the stockholders. I thought that was a particularly fabulous ploy."

"Sarah!" cried Mathilde, recovering from her shock enough to register her disapproval.

"She's not going to get it, is she, Doc?"

Horvath shrugged helplessly. He had been nervous about the confrontation from the start. He saw now that his original instincts had been correct.

Drew was shaking his head. "Why, Sa . . . Sunny? Why would you do something like that? It's your company, too."

"I can see you're trying, big boy," Sunny taunted him. "But it's not *my* company. It's *her* company. It's a Symington legacy. And as far as I'm concerned, everything that that fuck, Forrest, ever touched should be destroyed."

"Que tu es méchante!" Mathilde spat at her only daughter, finally recovering her voice. "He ees dead. Eet ees over. What you are doing here ees evil."

For a minute, Sunny looked as though she'd been struck in the face, and Horvath hoped that perhaps Sarah had returned. But in the blink of an eye, her chest was thrust forward in a gesture that was purely Sunny.

"Evil?" She laughed. "You think this is evil? I'll show you what evil is. Fuck you. Fuck all of you."

And before any of them could stop her, she had run out of the office and down the hall.

In the breath it took for all of them to realize what had happened, Ian jumped up and ran after her. He caught up with her at the elevator, reaching out to grab her by the arm and stop her from entering. Horvath saw it coming, but it was too fast to warn anyone. Her eyes blinked twice, and then she drew back and delivered a right upper cut that connected with Ian's jaw and sent him reeling backward into Drew's arms while the elevator doors closed after her. Sunny had become Stuart.

They took the stairs, but by the time they reached ground level, she was gone. Horvath agreed to stay in his office in case she called or returned, while Drew and Ian took separate cars and cruised the streets looking for her. Only Mathilde remained rigidly detached, as though she, disbeliever though she was, could accept the reality that escaped the rest of them—that this violent, angry creature was no longer her daughter, but someone dangerous and destructive, who, if they pursued her, could ruin them all.

* * *

Jack had asked Daisy not to come to the plane, but she had insisted.

"How are you going to get there? You can't very well take a cab. And it wouldn't be too politic to leave your car parked for three days near some military airport."

"Sam can pick me up on her way to get Ottavio."

"I see," said Daisy. "It's okay for her to go, but not me."

"Don't," said Jack, sorry he was hurting her. "It's just that she's already involved."

"Excuse me," said Daisy, far from mollified. "You're taking off in a Piper Cub with your old girlfriend to fly to an abandoned air strip on an island where you could be imprisoned or even killed, and you don't think I'm involved?"

He didn't blame her for being angry. This could not be easy. He wanted to tell her this was the last time. That even though he had always run to Melinda whenever she was in trouble, dropped everything to go to her, this time was different. This time, it wasn't about being with her. There was no more need to win her over with his selflessness so that she, in turn, would feel obliged to accommodate him. This time, it was strictly a humanitarian effort. He was going to help a woman, as he would any woman, get back her baby. And this time would be the last time.

"Daisy, when this is over—" he began.

But she cut him off. "Let's not talk about it."

He could see she was afraid. She didn't want to hear about a future she might not have. It made him love her more. He took her hand.

"When this is over," he said more forcefully, "we are getting married."

She smiled. "I've heard that one before."

"I mean it. I've reserved a place."

"What?!"

"The Department of State Diplomatic Reception Rooms. What do you think?"

Daisy started to laugh. "That's where we first—"

"I haven't forgotten. I've had a particular fondness for the James Madison Dining Room ever since. I've asked the powers that be, and we can use it next week."

"A week!"

"It's only available on the seventeenth this month! That is, unless we want to wait until fall. I told them we didn't want to wait."

"That's not very much time to plan a wedding."

"Hey, not everybody gets permission to get married at the State Department. I think we can be a little accommodating. What do you say?"

She didn't respond while she studied the crudely drawn map Ottavio had provided. A moment later, she made a sharp left onto a road that Jack hadn't even noticed and drove into a military compound that looked like it hadn't been occupied since World War II.

"This is it," she exhaled sharply, suddenly aware that she'd been holding her breath.

Jack saw the others up ahead. They were huddled in the shadow of a small plane, eerily lit by the blue dots of light that marked the air strip. Daisy pulled within twenty feet of the plane and stopped. They sat in the car for a long moment, neither one of them speaking.

Finally, Daisy said only, "She's very pretty," and got out of the car. Jack followed, thinking how much bravery was required for those who were left behind.

He introduced her to Ottavio and Melinda, and even though she expressed solidarity and sympathy, he could see she was sizing up the woman she had come to view as her rival.

Sam and Daisy greeted each other warmly. They hadn't spent much time together, but they had traveled in the same circles in Washington, and because of their connection through Jack, they felt that they knew each other better than they really did.

"She's very pretty," Melinda whispered to Jack while Sam and Daisy exchanged hurried pleasantries.

"She's special," Jack affirmed.

"I wouldn't expect you to be with anyone who wasn't." Melinda smiled, including herself in the category.

Ottavio was anxious to leave while there was still a moon. "You take this," he said to Sam, pressing a folded piece of paper into her hand.

"What is it?"

"My flight plan," he grinned sheepishly. "Regulations. I have nowhere else to file it."

Sam hugged them each in turn. "Just come back safe."

Ottavio went around to the pilot's side and climbed into his seat. Jack helped Melinda step onto the wing and into the back. Then he turned to Daisy.

"Okay," she said, holding him close.

"What?" he asked, not getting the reference.

"The seventeenth. You haven't changed your mind have you?"

"Are you kidding? Invite whoever you want."

Reluctantly he let her go and climbed into the plane. "I love you," he said. But Ottavio had already turned on the ignition, and his words were lost in the whine of the engines. He blew her a silent kiss and pulled the door shut behind him. In seconds, they were airborne.

The flight to San Domenico was uneventful. The night was cloudless, and the entire route was blessed with the light of the moon. A strong tail wind gave them added speed, and in less than four hours they spotted the island floating in the gentle swell of the Caribbean Sea. As Ottavio began their descent, Melinda could see the lights of the walls fortifying the presidential palace. Without examining the authenticity of her beliefs, she started to pray.

Buzzing low over the jungle, Jack pressed his face against the pane, hoping to see something to indicate their intended landing place before anyone saw them. It swooped into sight with dizzying immediacy, all dark and tangled underbrush one moment and then suddenly, a clearing, flat and gray, almost directly beneath them. He saw no movement, no tiny figures huddled and waiting by the open field.

"Shit," he muttered, looking at his watch. "We're too early." The tail winds had helped too much. He raised his voice above the engines, "Do you think we should circle, Ottavio?"

Ottavio shook his head. "It's dangerous. Nobody pays attention to a plane flying by. But the sound staying in one place, someone will notice."

"But someone will also notice if we land. And then,

we won't have much time on the ground before someone comes to investigate."

"Let's just go down." Melinda was getting upset, afraid to even think what would be if Clara had not been able to get the baby out of the palace. "We should be there when she gets there. Then we can just take off."

It was her call. It was her baby.

On the ground, Jack got out to see if there was any sign of Clara and the baby, instructing the others to stay in their seats. But cramped in the back of the tiny plane, Melinda's panic distended until it threatened to choke off her air, and she scrambled out to join Jack on the makeshift tarmac.

They waited in silence for what seemed like an inexorably long time but may have been only five minutes.

"I won't leave without him, Jack," Melinda said quietly. They hadn't discussed that particular scenario, even though it had occurred to Jack that there was no guarantee that Clara would be able to bring the baby at the appointed hour. He considered the possibility of conking Melinda on the head, aware that if things went wrong, the only way he'd get her back on the plane was if she was unconscious.

He felt her grip his hand and heard the sound at the same time. A car was approaching. He pulled her into the shadow of the plane. There was no point in providing a well-lit target if it wasn't who they were expecting.

They heard the muffled cry of the baby before they saw him, and a moment later, Melinda had leaped from his side and run toward the sound. He wanted to shout at her to wait so he could be sure that it wasn't some sort of trap. But it was too late, and it wouldn't have mattered. Nothing would have kept her from racing to her baby no matter what the perils.

He was relieved to see that it was indeed Clara who held the infant in her arms, and he hurried to join them as the two weeping women embraced, sandwiching the child between them.

"Go," Clara said when she had carefully laid Nico in Melinda's arms. "There was trouble. Diego knows Nico is gone."

"What happened?" Melinda cried, but Jack was already pushing her to the plane.

"It doesn't matter now," he said. "Just get back into the plane."

She forced him to stop for a minute and turned to Clara. "Come with us."

"No," the older woman said. "I can't. San Domenico is like my baby. I die without it."

"What about Roca? Is he going to do anything to you?" Jack asked, preempting Melinda's question.

Clara laughed. "Yesterday, I pretended I was sick and asked permission to go home. Today, I did not go to the palace at all. I have witnesses to say I couldn't move from my bed. He made soldiers guard the baby. When Nico went to sleep, they started playing cards. That's when I got him. The sweet thing didn't even wake up. Diego will blame the soldiers."

"Smart woman." Jack smiled. "Now get out of here before someone sees you."

The women hugged one last time, whispering blessings in each other's ears between kisses on each other's cheeks.

"We've got to go," Jack interrupted.

He watched Clara disappear back into the jungle while he held Nico and Melinda climbed back into the plane. Then he handed the baby to her and got in after them.

Because Ottavio had started the engines running, they hadn't heard the jeeps driving onto the airstrip. Melinda thought the first burst of gunfire was the engine backfiring and was only mildly concerned. But peering at the ground as Ottavio lifted the nose of the plane into the air, Jack could see the soldiers, scurrying onto the runway, raising their weapons into position. There was no mistaking the staccato blasts that followed. Melinda screamed, and the baby began to cry. There was a boom followed by a sudden drop in altitude, and the plane lurched wildly to the side.

"We're hit," said Ottavio, trying to maintain a tone of calm as the sweat poured down his forehead. "I don't know how long I can keep the plane from going down."

13

They would probably never have found Sarah if Sam hadn't called Drew to tell him that her sister and Jack Bader had flown to San Domenico to try and retrieve her baby. Drew had offered words of comfort and let her speak to Moira to bolster her fundamental belief that whatever powers ruled the heavens, they wouldn't want to keep a mother and her child apart. But Sam knew him well enough to sense there was something else on his mind besides concern for her sister.

"You're right," he said when she gently challenged him. "But you've got enough troubles with your own sister not to have to be concerned about mine. Just deal with that. I'll tell you what's going on here when you get back."

"Sorry, it doesn't work that way," Sam responded.

"Believe me, I'm so anxious now, one more thing to worry about won't even make a dent. Share with me."

Trying to be as concise and unemotional as possible, he told her what had happened at Dr. Horvath's. But he couldn't filter out the horror as he recounted what Sarah had claimed was done to her by their father.

"And on top of everything," he concluded, "I remember being jealous of her because I thought my father liked her more than me. Every time he'd take her out without me, and she'd cry, I'd think what a spoiled brat she was, getting all the attention and still complaining. Can you imagine? If only I could have done something instead of . . ." He trailed off, knowing there was little he could have done but feeling guilty nonetheless.

"You were just a kid yourself. And you were all afraid of him."

"Well, he's dead now. And I'm grown up. And I still can't help. Sarah got upset when my mother refused to acknowledge what had happened and just ran off. We don't know where she is. Ian and I have been out combing the streets, and you can imagine what a basket case he is."

"Oh, God, Drew." Something was clicking in Sam's brain. "I think I know where she is."

"What?"

"Remember when I was driving myself to the airport to go down to Miami to meet Ottavio?"

"Yeah. I wanted you to get a driver because you sounded so tired. But I guess you did fine."

"Actually, you were right. I got lost in Oakdale, and I had to go into a sleazy bar to get directions to the highway. I saw Sarah there. She was drunk and making out with some creepy guy. She was acting really strange."

"It must have been Sunny," said Drew, putting it all together. "Where was the bar?"

"On the corner of Twelfth and Rush."

"Whoa. That's a really bad area."

"I know. I put her in a cab and made her go home. She was really pissed off. So much has been going on since then that it completely slipped my mind."

"Okay, thanks, honey. Are you staying in Washington?"

"Just another day. If everything goes according to plan, Melinda should be here with the baby by morning. I'll bring them back to Belvedere with me."

"Can't wait. We miss you."

"Me, too."

He hung up and went to find Ian, who was on another line, waiting to talk to the police. At first, they had agreed to spare Sarah the embarrassment and handle it themselves. But when they couldn't find her after several hours, their apprehension precluded the need for delicacy.

"I'm still on hold," Ian informed him impatiently as Drew approached.

"Hang up. I might have a lead." Drew relayed what Sam had told him, and Ian eagerly agreed they should check the bar before turning the matter over to the police. Drew offered to come with him, but Ian declined.

"It sounds strange, but I've met all her different people, and I think they kind of all know me. It might be easier to get through to her if I'm alone."

Drew started to protest but then he stopped. "I guess since I was there when it happened, she'll always see me as part of the problem. You never were. You got her out. You were her savior."

Ian made a self-deprecating face. "If I was, I didn't do a very good job, did I? Maybe if I hadn't encouraged her to come back to Belvedere—"

"Stop. We've all got things we can blame ourselves for. That isn't going to help Sarah. Just go find her."

The two men hugged, patting each other on the back in the way that men do to keep from showing how emotional they are. As the door closed behind his brother-in-law, Drew turned to see his mother watching from the stairway, where she'd made her grand entrance every evening of his youth, sweeping down in her designer gowns to preside over her externally elegant, deeply dysfunctional family. Now, in spite of the best plastic surgery money could buy, she looked old, beaten.

"Are you all right, *Maman?"* he asked solicitously.

She straightened her shoulders and put her head back on the jaunty angle that passed for coquettishness in a woman of her certain years.

"Pourquoi pas?" she asked as though denial could still grant reprieve from the dismal truths that were threatening to curtail the careful fiction she had made of her life.

By the time Ian arrived at the bar on Rush Street, Sunny had already managed to get through three-quarters of a bottle of Scotch. But she still had no trouble recognizing him as he walked through the door.

"Look," she announced to the cluster of hard-core drunks hanging over the bar, "it's the pill of a husband. Looking for your little sweetie? Sorry, she's gone."

"Hello, Sunny," said Ian, approaching her calmly as though this were just another casual encounter. He ordered a drink from the bartender, who looked him up and down. This wasn't the usual sort of guy that Sunny consorted with, and he'd seen her consorting with quite a few.

Ian was aware that she was watching him, and he made no move to confront or even acknowledge her beyond his earlier terse greeting. Out of the corner of his eye, he saw her sidle up to one of the other patrons and drape herself around him. It caused an inner shudder, but then came the realization that she was doing this for his benefit, trying to get a rise out of him, so that she could respond in her Sunnylike way. He showed no reaction.

A moment later, she was at his side. "You know, big boy," she said, positioning herself so that he couldn't help but be aware of the expanse of chest that was revealed by her unbuttoned blouse, "we've never made it together. I'm a lot more fun than that wimp you're married to. She doesn't do half the things I do. Want to find out?"

"Not from you," he answered, barely glancing her way.

"Fuck you," she said unceremoniously.

"Not likely," he responded before turning to the bartender for a refill. He wasn't really interested in drinking, but his instinct told him that Sunny would find him a lot more disarming if he didn't appear to be moralizing by his abstinence.

She ordered a drink for herself. "He'll pay," she told the bartender.

Ian shook his head. "No, I won't."

"What's with you?" He could see she was disconcerted.

"I don't like you," was all he said.

She was hurt. "Oh, really? I thought you just loved your little wifey-poo. It's the same goddamn body, you know."

"You're the one who keeps insisting you're not the same person. I love her. I don't like you."

Sunny wasn't used to this. Men always responded to her sexual come-ons. She was the attractive one, the one who got what she wanted. Of course, she had always been sure only to approach the kind of men who would react the way she wanted. Ian was different. And it distressed her to realize that in spite of all her derogatory remarks, she wanted him more than anything she'd ever wanted before. It wasn't like her, she thought, and instantly knew she had the answer. It was like Sarah. Something was happening, and she was becoming like Sarah.

"I've got to get out of here," she barked and tried to get up off her stool. In a flash, Ian reached out and grabbed her arm.

"You're not going anywhere."

"I thought you didn't want me."

"I don't. I want Sarah. And I'm not letting you go until you let her come back to me."

Something was hammering in Sunny's head. She

felt like something was pushing at her, pressing against her, trying to uproot her from the position she had claimed as her own. She didn't care. She would fight. She would not give up the spotlight.

"Don't you get it, you idiots?" she shouted at them, though she had no idea whether she spoke aloud or not. "It's better when I'm in charge. It's only going to hurt you if you push me out." She started to shove them back, flailing at them with her arms.

"Oh, Jesus!" yelled Ian as he tried to put his arms around her, get her under control. "Sunny? Sarah? What's happening to you?"

Her mouth was moving rapidly, but only strange gurgles were coming out. Her eyes had rolled back into her head, and he thought she might be having a convulsion.

"Oh, shit, what have I done!" Ian castigated himself. "How could I play amateur shrink with you. I'm sorry, baby, I'm sorry. Come back. Anybody. Sarah. Sunny. Susan. Anybody."

She lashed at him one more time, then suddenly went limp, falling onto the bar. A bottle overturned, finally getting the bartender's attention.

"Hey, what's going on? Is she sick or something?"

"Yes," said Ian, panicking. "Here, call this number. It's her doctor."

"Whose going to pay for the bottle? There was at least ten more drinks in there."

Ian slapped a fifty on the bar. "Here, now just call that goddamn number and tell the doctor I'm taking her home."

Then he gathered her unconscious body into his

arms and carried out the woman he cherished and all the others that she brought with her.

By the time he had driven through the gates and pulled up the circular drive to Belvedere, Horvath had already arrived. Ian was relieved.

"I was afraid the bartender might not call," he said. He carried Sarah's limp body into the study as Drew and Horvath hovered near, walking with him like a protective convoy.

"Tell me what happened," Horvath said as he took her pulse and lifted her eyelids.

Quickly, Ian told him, not trying to spare himself, disparaging the arrogance of his attempts to control a situation that was obviously beyond his understanding.

"You didn't do anything wrong," Horvath assured him. "She's not exactly unconscious. She's just put herself into a deep trance. I suspect what happened was that as her ego got stronger, the barriers that she had put up to dissociate one personality from another became semipermeable. It was easier for her to admit her disorder on the outside than it was to face it internally. She's got a raging battle going on inside her, and I don't think we can help her."

"How long is she going to stay like this?" Ian asked, frightened.

"I don't know," Horvath said. "I'll try to bring her out of it the way I do when we have our sessions, but I doubt that she'll respond. The thing about hypnosis is that ultimately you won't do anything you don't really want to do."

"Qu'est-ce qui ce passe?"

Drew turned to see his mother standing in the doorway, whitefaced as she saw her only daughter lying listless on the couch.

"Sarah's had some kind of episode, *Maman,*" Drew said by way of explanation, aware that it was woefully inadequate but not sure how else to explain it.

Mathilde hesitated. Drew was sure she had no idea what he was talking about and, for that matter, probably just regarded the whole situation as indiscreet and in bad taste. He expected her to turn and flee, but instead, she took a few steps into the room.

"C'est trop difficile pour elle."

"What, *Maman?* What's too hard for her?"

"Être."

Ian and Dr. Horvath looked to him for translation.

"To be," he said quietly, realizing she understood more than he had given her credit for. "It's too hard for her to be."

"That about sums it up," said Horvath.

Mathilde came closer and with a sweep of her elegant wrist indicated that she wanted them to make room for her. Even Ian, who felt nothing for his mother-in-law at the moment, relinquished his space on the couch.

"Thank you," she said simply as she took his seat beside her unconscious daughter, and he thought perhaps it was the first time that she had addressed him without the undertone of disdain she reserved for anyone who did not speak her native tongue.

Ignoring the three men who watched her, she took Sarah's hand and brought it to her cheek. Sarah's finger twitched as a teardrop escaped Mathilde's eye and rolled onto her palm.

"Eet was 'ard for me, too," Mathilde said as if they had been having a conversation and were simply carrying on. "I did not want to see either. So I drank. And you suffered. I know now eet ees better to be there. Worse things happen when you are not. Eef eet ees bad, say eet ees bad. Don't hide. *Comme moi.* All my life I am hiding. And thees ees the result. *Je suis desolée.* I am sorry."

Drew caught his breath as his mother lay her head down on his sister's chest and began to cry. He had never seen her anything less than utterly contained before. It took them all a minute to realize that Sarah's hand had begun to stroke her mother's hair.

Excitedly, Ian moved to be near his wife, but Dr. Horvath held him back. Gently, he lifted Mathilde from her spot and asked her to stay with the others for a moment.

"Sarah? Are you there?" he asked quietly. "Can you open your eyes?"

They waited tensely. Her eyes fluttered open, but before they could respond, she said, "It's not Sarah. It's Susan."

"That's okay," said Dr. Horvath, reassuring his patient, not wanting her to leave them again. "What's happened, Susan?"

"I don't know exactly. Sunny was in the spotlight, and then Sarah, who's supposed to be asleep when Sunny's out, woke up and started trying to push Sunny off. It was pretty scary, Dr. Horvath. That's not the way we work, and I just couldn't get control."

"Do you understand why?"

"I guess Sarah is getting stronger. She doesn't want the rest of us running her life."

"That's right. Where's Sarah now?"

"I don't know."

"Where's Sunny?"

"That's just it. I don't know that either. There was this body on the floor in the spotlight. I had to push it away to come out. But I can't exactly tell who it is."

Horvath took a deep breath. The others looked at him. They could tell he was excited about something, but he wasn't sharing it with them. His total focus was on his patient. "Is it possible, Susan," he prodded, "that the body is both Sunny and Sarah? That they've merged into one?"

"Why would they do that?"

"Because Sarah saw that Sunny was ruining her life, and she wasn't going to let that happen anymore."

"Sunny had her place," said Susan defensively.

"I don't deny that," Horvath said quickly, "but maybe she wasn't needed anymore. We talked about that."

"I know. I guess I just didn't expect it to happen so spontaneously."

He laughed. "Neither did I. Where are the others?"

She gave a derisive snort. "Stuart is punching a wall and giving us all the biggest damn headache we've ever had. And Shana is curled up in a corner, whimpering as usual. We're all feeling kind of bad. And we've never really all felt the same before."

"I think maybe you're all feeling the same because you're ready to be integrated. Do you want me to try and help?"

"Sure, anything."

"Okay. Close your eyes. I want you to get Shana

and put one arm around her. Then go get Stuart and put your other arm around him. Bring them both back to the spotlight with you. And now just bring your arms together in a circle as though you're hugging them. But squeeze them harder and harder into you until they're just absorbed by you and you're hugging yourself."

She started to moan, and Mathilde's eyes filled with tears again. "Eet hurts her, Doctor."

"It's okay, *Maman,"* Drew said, taking her hand and pulling her back. "Maybe this will help her."

Mathilde bit her lip and nodded. Then she turned to Ian and reached out her free hand. He took it without hesitation, and the three of them stood there, pressed together, watching the integration of someone they loved.

Finally, Susan opened her eyes. "I did it," she said, sounding weak but triumphant. "They're gone."

"How do you feel?" Horvath beamed at her.

"Well, the banging in my head has stopped." She laughed. "That's good."

"What about Sarah? Is she still lying on the ground?"

"Yes."

"Go to her."

"Okay," Susan said, but they could hear the trepidation in her voice.

"I want you to fall on her."

"What?"

"You heard me. Just let yourself float down on top of her. It won't hurt. She'll cushion your landing. It'll be like jumping into a vat of feathers."

"I . . . I don't know if I can do that."

"Try it. Just stand with your feet at her feet and let yourself go forward. Will you do that, Susan?"

"I won't be me anymore if it works, will I?"

"No, but you'll be Sarah. All of you will be. You won't have to work so hard keeping track of the others. You'll be together."

"Okay, then, I guess this is it." She was quiet for a moment, and they wondered if she had done it. Then she spoke again. "Thank you, Dr. Horvath. It's been a pleasure knowing you."

"The pleasure has been mine, Susan. You're a wonderful person, and I know you're going to add so much to Sarah's life."

"And thank you to the others, too," she added. "We were considering not coming out at all. None of us. We thought maybe we'd just leave the spotlight empty. But you all seemed to care so much, I couldn't allow it."

"That was very wise, Susan. Now will you do what I asked?" He didn't mean to rush her, but he knew that she was stalling for time, and he didn't want her to have to think too much.

"Okay," she said again. "Here goes."

They watched as her body went rigid and then slack. For a moment, there was no movement, and then, surprisingly, she bounced. It made them all smile.

"I think that's it," said Horvath. "Sarah," he commanded, "when I count to five, you're going to be wide awake and feeling wonderful. One . . . two . . . three . . . four . . . five."

She opened her eyes and smiled at them.

"Hi," she said a little shyly.

"Do you know what happened?" Horvath asked her.

"Do I ever." She sighed, sounding happy but exhausted.

"How do you feel?"

"Strange. Full and empty at the same time." She noticed that they were all standing a little away from her, watching her as if they were afraid she might explode and wanted to stay clear of flying debris. She understood they were waiting for a sign. She got up and went to her mother. Slowly, she leaned over and kissed her on the cheek.

Mathilde began to weep softly. "I am sorry, *ma petite chou-chou.*" It had been years since Sarah had been called that.

"So am I," echoed Drew, his eyes filling as well.

"We were all his victims." Sarah sighed, accepting their apologies. "And it still makes me angry. But I forgive you both. And more important, I forgive myself. That's what has made me free."

She turned to Ian, and he closed his arms around her, holding her so tightly she could barely breathe. But Sarah wasn't complaining.

Using a sextant, which he had only thought to bring at the last minute, and the stars, Ottavio figured they were probably on one of the Caicos Islands. Or it could have been the Turks Islands. Even though he had a map and assumed his calculations were fairly accurate, there was no way of knowing for sure.

He had avoided an outright crash into the side of the mountain, managing instead to execute a bumpy landing on a barren plateau near the top of what appeared to be an extinct volcano. Forcing his foot to remain on the brake as they skidded over the stony terrain, he had ended up with a broken leg. It was only the grace of God that had kept the others from being injured. As for the plane, it lay in pieces on the ground, salvageable only as scrap.

"Well," he said to Melinda, trying to sound less concerned than he was, "we're definitely not in San Domenico. So whoever finds us is going to be friendly."

She was sitting with her back against a large rock, Nico at her breast, quietly nursing. At least the baby had no idea what trouble they were in. "It's hard to believe anybody will find us," she said, looking at the desolation around them. "It doesn't look like people come here much."

"It only takes one." Ottavio tried to sound encouraging.

Jack returned from a foray around the immediate area. They both looked at him expectantly.

"There's not much," he admitted. "The ground's been too burned out. It seems to be mostly volcanic ash and rock. Not much grows here."

"I have two flares in a safety kit in the plane. Also maybe a liter of water. No food."

"I have two oranges and a banana in my bag," offered Melinda. "Oh, better yet," she remembered, "I have a bottle of vitamins. They're designed for nursing mothers, but I'm sure they won't do you any harm."

She dropped her head and planted a soft kiss on the

top of Nico's head. He had wailed vociferously during the shaky landing, more because he sensed his mother's panic than for any discomfort of his own. Now, he snuggled contentedly at her breast, secure with his own source of food and shelter, oblivious to any of the dangers they faced ahead. Melinda was glad that she had insisted on using a breast pump every day that she was away from Nico so that her milk would not dry up. It had been an act of faith for her baby at the time, now it turned out to be his guarantee of survival.

"Let's save the flares for when we see a plane or some sign that someone's in the vicinity. Otherwise, they'll just be wasted," Jack said. He didn't add that from what he'd seen, he doubted that anyone would be in the vicinity any time soon. "We also might have to ration the water and the food. I'll be able to tell more when it gets a little lighter."

The night was cold, and they huddled together under a tarp that had been used to cover the plane on the ground. Clara had come with a bag full of supplies for the baby, so there were plenty of blankets and diapers to keep him warm and dry. Using metal from the wreckage of the plane and strips of torn clothing, Jack fashioned a makeshift splint for Ottavio's leg, and exhausted by the ordeal, they all managed to sleep fitfully until the sun rose.

In the morning, they realized that they had reason to be grateful for the cold. Even though it was well into spring, pockets of snow still lingered in the cool crevices of the dark and solid rock. As the day warmed, they gathered the snow in the scoop of metal that had once been the nose of the plane and left it to melt. At least they knew they would not run out of water.

Jack was relieved to see that Melinda's vitamin bottle was almost full. There would be enough for the three of them for longer than he could anticipate surviving in this wilderness. But both he and Ottavio insisted that Melinda should keep the fruit for herself.

"It's not enough to make much of a dent in your appetite, so save it and use it as a treat when you feel you just can't stand it anymore," suggested Jack.

"Do you think it's going to be that long before anyone finds us?" Melinda asked.

"No, of course not," Jack said jovially. "But just in case," he added with a nonchalant shrug. It was the shrug that convinced her he was lying.

"I'm sorry," she said to both of them. "Because of me, you might . . ." She couldn't say the words. If Jack and Ottavio perished, so would she. And then, what would happen to her baby.

"Hey," said Jack forcefully. "Do you hear the fat lady singing?"

"There is music?" asked Ottavio confused.

Melinda started to laugh. It was more hysterical than amused, but Jack was grateful for Ottavio's limited knowledge of English idiom and started to laugh as well. By the time they had explained the reference, the tension had eased.

"Now that it's light, I'm going to look around again," Jack said.

Melinda stood, trying to stretch without disturbing the sleeping baby.

Ottavio reached out his arms. "Give Nico to me.

You go walk with Jack. You need it. I can't move anyway."

"Are you sure you can manage?" Melinda asked politely, but he could see she was dying to go.

"What is there to manage? He's asleep."

Melinda knew from Clara that Nico's routine had not changed. After his morning feeding, he would sleep for a good two hours. And after the calamitous night before, she wouldn't be surprised if it was even longer.

She looked at Jack. "Is it okay?"

"Sure, why not?" he said noncommittally, reluctant to reveal, even to himself, how much he still wanted her with him.

For almost an hour, they walked in silence, searching for signs of life, human or otherwise. Every few hundred feet, Jack stopped to shape a little marker of scrub or stones to ensure they would be able to find their way back, because the landscape itself, though sometimes dramatic, was repetitive. They found no distinct paths, and every route they attempted to take that might lead down the mountain to civilization ended abruptly in a precipice or was hampered with so many other impediments as to be impossible to traverse.

"I have to stop," said Melinda finally, feeling breathless and dizzy as she parked herself on a flat boulder.

"It's the altitude," Jack explained. "You'll get used to it." He sat down beside her. By now the sun was high overhead, and its heat seemed particularly penetrating in the thin air. He took off his sweater, rolled it into a ball, and placed it under her head. She accepted gratefully and closed her eyes, breathing deeply but still getting the sensation that she could not fill her lungs.

"Jack," she said quietly, "tell me the truth. Do you think it's possible we could die here."

"Anything is possible," he answered, knowing he probably should have lied.

"I'm still not sorry, you know," she mused. "I mean, I am for you and Ottavio. It's unforgivable what I put you through. But I couldn't have just left Nico in San Domenico. I was already dead without him."

"What a thing it must be to love that way." There was a hint of envy in his voice.

"I guess it's what happens when you have a child. I'm not sure it's possible between consenting adults."

"It wasn't with us," he pointed out, knowing there could be no argument. As much as they had loved each other, when things became difficult, they had both run for cover.

"Nor with Diego either—obviously," she added. "What about you and Daisy? Would you walk through fire for her?"

"She's everything a man could want," Jack responded, avoiding her question all together.

"She looks that way," Melinda said without rancor or irony.

"Until Daisy, it was always you, Melinda, you know that. Daisy's the only one who made me think that it would be possible to have a complete life without you."

"Until Diego, it was you."

"But Diego was a mistake."

"Yes. Is Daisy?"

"No," said Jack, vehement in his defense of the woman who had mended his heart. Then, looking at the woman who had broken it, he modified his stand. "I don't think so. I hope not. We're going to get married. Unless . . ." He didn't finish the morbid thought.

"Unless," echoed Melinda and turned away. She did not want him to see that she was not entirely sorry. She wanted to live. But if she were going to die, her one compensation would be that after all their missed opportunities and shattered dreams, she finally got to stay with Jack forever.

When Melinda's altitude sickness had passed, they headed back to the wreckage without having accomplished much. The baby was awake and was happily gurgling at Ottavio, who bounced him on his one good knee. Needing to boost their morale, they toasted each other with melted snow and solemnly swallowed their vitamins. Then they shared an orange, which Melinda threatened to throw over the side of the mountain if they refused to eat it with her. The baby ate and played and laughed and ate again. The sun set and the air grew cold. The baby cried and would not sleep, and Jack and Melinda took turns walking him until he finally closed his eyes. Again, the three of them huddled together under the tarp, colder, hungrier, and more frightened than they'd been the night before.

By morning, with their empty bellies growling, they felt viscerally what they had all been refusing to admit aloud: they were in deep trouble. Melinda fed Nico, washed him in snow water heated by the sun, cradled him gently while he fell back into satisfied sleep, all while tears coursed endlessly down her cheeks. Neither Jack nor Ottavio tried to offer comfort. Both knew consolation was futile.

Again, when the baby slept, Ottavio suggested that Jack and Melinda search for possible paths down the mountain. It seemed to be their only hope. They agreed, expecting little result, but they accepted the challenge as one last act of faith.

Heading off toward the east this time instead of the west, their explorations brought them no closer to deliverance than the day before. There were no paths, no trails, no outposts; only volcanic protrusions frozen into sheer walls after years of molten activity. The landscape had a distinct, harsh beauty of its own, but its starkness added to their feelings of impending doom.

When the sun had reached its highest point, they took refuge in the cool shade of an overhanging promontory.

"Guess what?" said Melinda, leaning against the rock.

Looking at her beatific smile, considering their circumstances, Jack had absolutely no idea what she was about to tell him.

"I have chocolate."

"What?! You don't, really, do you?"

It was as if she had announced the second coming, and her pronouncement had to be met with equal measures of awe and disbelief.

"I do. It was only half a bar, but I've been saving it for when we started to feel really low. I think I'm about there. How about you?"

"I'm low. Definitely."

"I left a piece for Ottavio back at the plane. This," she said, brandishing the instantly recognizable wrapper of a Hershey bar, "is for us."

He watched her unwrap it with great ceremony. The heat had melted it just a little, and when they each took their segments, small stains of melted chocolate were left behind on the silver paper lining. They placed the soft, brown chunks on their tongues and shut their mouths around the sweetness, closing their eyes in ecstasy. In reverent silence, they allowed the chocolate to dissolve in their mouths, and when all that was left was the lingering sweet taste, they laughed and licked their fingers, then took turns licking the silver paper.

"Thank you," he said with mock solemnity, although he meant every word. "You have given me some of my best moments."

"I know you're making a joke," she said, calling him on it, "but it is true, isn't it? We've always been the best when we are together."

"Too smart, too late," he said, sighing.

"The reasons we gave up seem so silly now, so small. Do you remember? You wanted to stay in Oakdale, and I wanted to go to Hollywood, and neither one of us ended up being where we thought we'd be."

"But we ended up together. It just happened to be on the top of a mountain with no way down."

"If I had known," she offered generously, "I would have just stayed with you in Oakdale."

"If I had known," he matched her, "I would have come to Hollywood."

And knowing now what they could not have predicted then, they slowly drew together. There were hints of chocolate on their lips when they kissed, but it could not match the sweetness in their souls as they found themselves again entwined, far away from everything they had ever wanted or expected but home at last in each other's arms.

He led her out of the shadows to a flat rock, smoothed by the flow of lava centuries before. Slowly, he undressed her and then himself. The sun blanketed them with its heated rays. He remembered her body the way Proust remembered his madeleines or Citizen Kane, his rosebud. She was the pivotal point in his life, the epiphany before which nothing was known, and after which, nothing could be the same. And when their bodies joined, it was clear that no matter what happened, whether they survived or perished, apart or together, they were locked to a common destiny, if not on earth, then somewhere in the realm of the undying spirit of love.

Afterward, they lay side by side, backs against the heated stone, basking in the shafts of sunlight that etched orange patterns on the lids of their closed eyes.

In the half sleep of contentment, both reluctant to rouse themselves to the dread of their reality, neither one of them took notice of the whir that began to fill the air. At first, it sounded like the wind that rose at night and chilled them with its desolate draughts. But it was day, and the breeze was softly sibilant. Melinda was the first to notice its persistence. This was not a sound made in nature.

"Jack." She nudged him. "What's that?"

"What?" he asked halfheartedly, maintaining a low level of consciousness.

"That sound. Listen."

He sat up then and heard it, too.

"My God, it sounds like a helicopter." He was already jumping up, throwing her her clothes, pulling on his own. "We've got to get back to the plane and send up a flare before they're gone."

Scrambling frantically over the boulders, slipping on the ancient volcanic debris, they watched the blip on the horizon turn into the distant but definite form of a helicopter.

"Shit," swore Jack, pulling himself, then Melinda over a precipice. "We're not going to make it. The damn thing is going to pass right over us and have no idea we're here."

"Look," shouted Melinda, pointing.

A red flare had snaked its way into the sky, leaving a smoking plume in its wake. They hugged each other and started to laugh.

"Thank God for Ottavio," Jack said, as they hurried back to the plane, panting, though no longer panicked.

They found Ottavio breathless and soaked in sweat beside the remains of the cockpit, where he had dragged himself at the first sound of the helicopter. It had been an arduous fifty feet, as he had had to pull himself on his backside with one arm while balancing the baby on his lap with the other. Nico had found it all a charming game and was in joyous spirits, greeting his mother with a clap and a gurgle.

"Did you see it?" shouted Ottavio excitedly. "It's

still up there. Look. I think they're circling. They saw the flare."

They watched as the helicopter, still too distant to be able to distinguish figures, hovered over the volcanic island. Knowing it would do no good but too excited to wait with quiet patience, they shouted and waved their arms. Suddenly, the chopper seemed to turn and veer off in another direction.

"They're leaving," screamed Melinda.

"They can't figure out where the flare came from," said Jack. "We're probably hidden in the shadows."

The sun had already begun its descent, and they were no longer spotlit by its rays.

"Send up the other flare," he instructed Ottavio. But Ottavio had made the same observation and was already lighting its fuse.

Jack started to pull at the nose cone of the plane. "Give Ottavio the baby and come help me," he called to Melinda.

"What are you doing?" she questioned, seeing little need for their water receptacle at a time like this. But in a minute, she understood, as Jack found a stretch of remaining sunlight and began to maneuver the metal remnant so that it caught the setting sun. She hurried to help him flip it over so that the cone was pointing up, and then inch by inch, they maneuvered it until fiery rays glinted from its silvery sides and into the sky above them.

The helicopter reversed direction, circled, hovered, and then, to their sheer and utter relief, began its descent almost directly above them.

Finding the same basilitic plateau where Ottavio had performed their own emergency landing, the helicopter was able to touch down only feet away. Nico began to cry with the crescendo of wind and noise, and Melinda took him as far away as she could. Sheltered on the far side of a craggy outcrop, she did not see a woman, silky white hair flying around her face, leap out of the cabin before the rotors had stopped. She did not see Jack look for her and wonder why she was not at his side. All she saw when the engines had stopped and she could emerge with her child from their protective shield was Jack and Daisy locked in a tight embrace that seemed to exclude everyone else from their circle of salvation.

"I had to find you," announced Daisy, wiping away unaccustomed tears. "We're getting married tomorrow. You're not backing out, are you?" she teased, trying unsuccessfully to cover her genuine emotion.

"No," said Jack, acutely aware that Melinda was listening and that, once again fate, with inescapably bad timing, had divided them. "I couldn't do that."

14

Daisy had arranged for them all to be billeted on the eighth-floor club level of the Ritz-Carlton, a few blocks from the State Department Reception Rooms, where the wedding was to be held. It wasn't just the convenience she had considered. With its Sister Parrish–designed rooms in shades of yellow and blue, she had thought to make them forget the hardship of their voyage and luxuriate in the warmth and elegance of restored civilization. There was nothing to revive the spirit like bathing in a deep tub filled with aromatic bath salts, wrapping oneself in a plush terry robe, and sinking into the comfort of an overstuffed antique floral chintz sofa.

Understanding that Jack would need time to unwind before being confronted by the clutter of his own apartment, she had suggested he stay in the hotel as well. With the bonds of their shared experienced not yet truly severed, he had been just as happy to receive the same treatment as Melinda and Ottavio. Drew and Moira had arrived to be with Sam, bringing Mrs. Halsey along to help care for the two children. Sam had asked Ian and Sarah to fly in the day of the wedding with Harvey and Diane Myles to give her sister a chance to recuperate before being swallowed by the genuine, but emotionally taxing, concern of her extended family.

In the chaos and exhaustion of the rescue, there had been little communication among them. Tired but anxious to exchange details of their individual adventures, Melinda, Ottavio, and Jack met Sam, Drew, and Daisy in the beautiful eighth-floor lounge, overlooking the neighboring embassies, with the promise of a short dinner and a long night's rest before the day of the wedding.

"I still can't believe that you found us, stuck on the top of that mountain in the middle of nowhere," Jack congratulated Daisy.

"It was the flight plan that Ottavio gave Sam that got us started. And of course, that Navy pilot that Dad got for me. That man could find a flea on a horse. I just went along for the ride," Daisy demurred.

"Right," mocked Sam. "Like she didn't start bugging everybody from about ten seconds after you were due and didn't show up. I have to admit, I'm the one who kept saying maybe you'd had some sort of legitimate delay and we should give you more time. I'm glad she wouldn't listen to me."

"Well, I had this wedding date." Daisy laughed,

settling herself on the sofa beside Jack and twining a proprietary arm through his.

Melinda sat with her back propped against the rigid outline of a straight back chair she had selected for its ability to keep her from collapsing with fatigue. The weariness of her body was nothing compared to the disintegration of her heart. Rescued and assured of life, she felt more dead than she had in the bleakness of the volcano. Still, she smiled at Daisy and her family and thanked them graciously, never even intimating that they had undone one of the great resolutions of her life. Only once, when she felt Jack's eyes on her and allowed herself to meet his gaze, did they both acknowledge, in a look alone, that in being saved they had both been lost.

"I wish I could go on," said Melinda, though, in fact, she had registered very little of what had been said by or to her. "But I'm just too beat. You guys can fill me in tomorrow. I think I've had it for today."

"Of course," Sam responded immediately. "All of you must be wiped out. It's very selfish of me to want to hear every little detail immediately. I haven't been chasing around extinct volcanoes."

"I think it would be a good idea for us all to get some rest before the wedding tomorrow," Drew echoed his wife, signaling for the check, which he signed without a second glance.

They rose slowly and bid each other their goodnights, kissed and hugged, and thanked God for bringing them back together.

"Halsey has Moira and Nico in a room adjoining ours," Sam informed her sister. "Why don't you leave him with her, and you can get some uninterrupted sleep."

"Thanks," Melinda said, "but I'd just as soon keep him with me. I'll come get him." She started out with them to collect her child. Tonight, more than ever, she wanted a future to hold on to.

"Oh, wait, I almost forgot," Daisy said, rushing after them. "I know it's last minute, and you may think it's kind of stupid, but I'd be honored if you two would be my bridesmaids."

Caught off guard, Melinda could only say, "That's so sweet, Daisy, but . . ." She wanted to make some sort of protest, but she couldn't think of the right one.

"If you're worried about a dress," said Daisy, laughing, "I did happen to spot two very nifty Donna Karan sheaths at Neiman Marcus that I put on reserve. If you agree, the seamstress said she'd come to the hotel and fit you tomorrow morning. I know it's presumptuous of me, but I didn't have much time to plan."

"Of course," said Sam, speaking for both of them, while Melinda exchanged a sidelong glance with Jack, who shifted uncomfortably from one foot to the other. "We'd love to."

When the sisters had gone, Daisy turned the full dazzle of her brilliant smile on Jack. "Do you want me to stay in the hotel with you?" she asked.

His heart ached. Whether for her or for himself, he could not tell.

"I don't know, sweetheart. I'm completely dead. And you've probably got a thousand things you want to do before the wedding. And you know what they say, the groom shouldn't see the bride the day of the wedding."

"You're right," she said, relieved because she did, in fact, have too busy a schedule to spend a leisurely night with her husband-to-be. But she was just a little wounded that he had not pressed her to remain with him in spite of time or custom.

They kissed good night, and suddenly, with her lips lingering against his, she sensed that something had changed.

"Are you okay?" she asked.

"Of course. Just exhausted. I'll be fine by tomorrow. I promise."

"You don't want to change your mind, do you? Because if you do, you can. I don't give a shit about what anybody says."

He could see that she was telling the truth and understood that if Melinda had never been a part of his life, this woman could be everything to him. But she had risked much to find him and bring him back to her. He would not betray her.

"No, I don't want to change my mind." He forced himself to sound jovial. "I just want to get some sleep."

"Okay, you had your chance," she said, reassured, and with one last kiss, she left him at his door.

He watched the elevator doors close behind her, then, after a moment's hesitation, turned away from his own door and went to the one across the hall. He tapped lightly, almost hoping that she'd be sleeping already, and the knock would go unnoticed. But in seconds, Melinda had opened the door.

"Nico's just falling asleep," she said quietly, expressing no surprise at finding him at her threshold. "I don't want to disturb him."

"That's fine. We can talk here. Just for a minute."

"What is there to say?" she asked.

"Do you understand why I'm doing this?"

"Yes."

"Do you think I'm wrong?"

"No."

"Do you know that I love you and I always will?"

"Yes."

"But you've turned my life upside down too many times before, and I can't let it happen again."

"No."

"And there's Daisy. She's a wonderful person."

"Yes."

"And I can't just walk out on her. It wouldn't be fair."

"No."

"Are you going to say anything besides yes and no?"

"I love you, too, Jack," she said softly.

Without meaning to, they found themselves with their arms wrapped around each other, love clinging to them like scent to a dying rose. Weeping, he buried his face in the thicket of her chestnut hair, while her tears pooled in the hollow of his throat. Submitting to the sacrifice, they allowed themselves to succumb to the suffering it created. Their anguish encased them like a cloak, enveloping them both, and for that moment blocked out all other sound and sensation. They did not hear the subtle ping that announced the elevator's arrival or the muffled whoosh of its opening doors. They did not see the platinum-haired woman step out and stop in surprise to see them clasped together. They did not notice her quickly step back into the elevator before the doors had closed and descend without having delivered the message that she had forgotten to relay before.

In the lobby of the Ritz-Carlton, Daisy Howard took a deep breath and walked over to the desk.

"Did you find him, Miss Howard?" the night clerk asked.

"Actually, it occurred to me that the reason he might not have answered his phone is that he's fast asleep. If I write him a note, will you deliver it in the morning with his coffee?"

"Sure, no problem."

She took the pen and paper proffered and wrote quickly without taking time to choose her words. Then after folding the note, she placed it in an envelope, sealed it, and wrote Jack's name on the front.

"Don't forget," she admonished, handing it to the night clerk. "It's important."

"Maybe we should skip the wedding," Ian said to his wife as she gently woke him and told him it was time to get up.

"That wouldn't be very nice," said Sarah. "We've already accepted the invitation."

"We could still decline."

"We also promised to take your parents, remember? Your whole family is going to be there. And your sisters are going to be bridesmaids."

He groaned. He knew she was right. Even though he'd never been that close to Jack Bader and he didn't know the bride-to-be at all, Jack had been a good friend to the Myles family. And since Ian had been accepted by them as one of their own, he owed it to them to act like it.

"All right," he acquiesced, as she knew he would. "We can go. But not yet."

He pulled her back down into the bed and folded her in his arms. She smiled at him, a pure, untroubled grin of affection, and he marveled at how normal it all seemed. She still had moments of unease, still felt the grip of harrowing memories. But she faced them squarely now, allowing herself to feel the pain and then to gain the comfort instead of abdicating all emotion to an alter ego. Sometimes, when she was frightened, she seemed like a child, and sometimes, when she was aroused, she acted like a vamp. But always, it was her own reaction, just Sarah Symington Taylor responding, like any ordinary person, to whatever was going on around her.

They made love with quiet tenderness, without demands or expectations, and delighted in the tranquility of the act. But even though he felt a sympathetic vibration in both body and soul, Ian could not stop himself from asking.

"Sarah," he started carefully as she lay in the crook of his arm, too content to move, "do you ever miss . . . I mean, is it . . . I don't know . . . boring . . . to be just you with me?"

She propped herself up on her elbow and looked at him. Embarrassed, he studied the pattern on the sheets.

"I said something to you when I was Sunny, didn't I?"

"Oh, I didn't pay any attention to that," he insisted,

but it was true. Sunny had been angry and raw, but life for her had been an adventure that went beyond anything he could provide.

She took his face in her hands and made him look at her. "Look, I needed those other people to survive at one time. And I'm still not sure whether they did more harm or good. But if you stay with me and you love me, I won't ever need or want anything else again."

She kissed him softly and the featherlightness of her touch was enough to make him want to start again. But eyeing the clock over his shoulder, she pulled away.

"I lied," she said brusquely. "I need to take a shower and I want you to get up," and then grabbing the topsheet with her, leaving him exposed, she ran, laughing into the bathroom.

Jack had left a wake-up call for ten o'clock. But when room service discreetly knocked on his door and rolled in his breakfast cart, he was anything but ready.

He had no success keeping his eyes open while the waiter laid out the china and napkins, the silver coffee service and oversize cup, the fresh fruit, croissants, jams and jellies, an assortment of daily papers, the perfect rose in a silver bud vase, and, propped against it, a sealed white hotel stationery envelope.

"Your breakfast is ready, sir," the waiter announced.

"Do me a favor," Jack said groggily. "Add five bucks to the bill and sign it for me."

"Yes, sir. Thank you, sir. Will there be anything else?"

"Not a thing, thanks."

He waited for the door to close.

He had every intention of getting up, of downing the hot fresh coffee and allowing himself the leisure of a few hours reflection before he was due to set out for the State Department Diplomatic Reception Rooms where his wedding was to be held. But his eyelids felt weighted, and he closed them for just a moment to ease the pressure.

His peace was jarred by the ringing of the phone, and he groped for the receiver without opening his eyes. "What?" he said, still not fully awake.

"Your car is waiting, sir," he was informed.

"You've got the wrong room," he barked, annoyed at having been disturbed for a mistake.

"Uh . . . Mr. Bader?"

"That's me."

"Well, there's a car here from the State Department. The driver says he's taking you to your wedding."

"Jesus, that idiot. He's not supposed to come until three o'clock in the afternoon."

"It *is* three, Mr. Bader."

"What?!"

He looked at the clock on the night table, thoughtfully provided by the hotel. It did, indeed, say three. He checked the watch on his wrist. It said three as well. For a moment, he was certain that someone was playing a none-too-funny practical joke on him. That they expected him to rush to the building in Foggy

Bottom only to find he was the only one there. Ha-ha. But then, almost instantaneously, it occurred to him that even if someone had been able to sneak into the room and change the clock at his bedside, how could they have adjusted the watch on his wrist without his knowing. And then, with a sinking feeling of dread, he was forced to concede that this might not be a joke at all.

"You're sure it's three o'clock?" he asked, fearing confirmation.

"Absolutely, sir. Do you want to talk to your driver?"

"No, just tell him I'll be down in ten minutes."

He hung up the phone and jumped out of bed. He almost slipped on the marble floor as he raced to the shower, grabbing the razor and shampoo, also thoughtfully provided, on the way. He was clean in record time and dressed in the shirt and slacks that Daisy had brought for him from his apartment. Dashing toward the door, he stopped to take a bite of a now-stale croissant and pour himself a glop of cold coffee. Nearly choking on the bitter taste, he reached for a napkin and knocked the envelope from its waiting position. He stooped to pick it up and, assuming it was a message of some sort from the hotel, slipped it into his pocket as he ran out the door.

Down one flight from the reception rooms where the wedding was to be held, the colonnaded Treaty Room had been converted to a dressing room for the bride's party, and by three-fifteen, the women had begun to gather.

"Are you hating this?" Sam whispered to her sister

as they waited for the Neiman Marcus seamstress to arrive with the dresses she had taken for alteration that morning.

"Yes," admitted Melinda. "I don't blame anyone but myself, but I think I really fucked up my life."

"Don't say that. You have Nico. You wouldn't want to change that."

Melinda thought of the tiny baby boy who had been left with his cousin in the charge of Mrs. Halsey back at the hotel.

"You're right. But I just wish that Jack and I . . ." She broke off as Daisy entered the room, calm and smiling.

"You look far too serene for a bride-to-be," Sam teased, covering her sister's discomfiture.

"Well, except for the fact that the groom's not here yet, what's there to worry about?" she joked.

"He'll show up," encouraged Melinda, feeling guilty for resenting this woman who had been nothing but kind to her. "Jack is a man of his word."

"I know." Daisy smiled and startled Melinda by taking her hand in a gesture surprisingly sympathetic.

A moment later, he was peeking in the door, an apology on his lips. "Believe it or not, I closed my eyes for five minutes and slept an extra five hours."

"I'm sure you needed it," Daisy said, not in the least perturbed, while Melinda busied herself with a thread on her shirt, not trusting herself to look at him.

"I'd better go get ready," Jack said, just as anxious to avoid Melinda as she was him.

"Wait a minute," said Daisy. "Did you get my note?"

"What note?"

Jack and Melinda sneaked a look at each other. They couldn't help it.

"I left it with the night clerk at the hotel. They were supposed to deliver it with breakfast."

"Oh, that! I thought it was a message from the hotel or something. I've got it right here." He reached into his pocket and pulled it out.

"Read it," ordered Daisy.

Jack opened the envelope. Melinda realized she was holding her breath.

"Happy Wedding Day," Jack read. "I bought you a new tuxedo. It's the same size as all the other suits in your closet so it should fit. It will be waiting for you in the ceremonial office, which they're letting us use as the men's dressing room. Hope you don't mind."

He stopped reading and kissed the top of her head, conscious of Melinda's averted eyes.

"Of course I don't mind," he said. "Anything you want is all right with me."

He was bending over backward because he knew that the one thing that Daisy really wanted, the only thing she absolutely required, he could not give her and would not tell her.

The dresses arrived, ankle-length sheaths of pastel peau de soie for the bridesmaids. For the bride, it was the same basic shape but with an overskirt of tulle, in a champagne color, simple but elegant, like something that Audrey Hepburn might have worn while playing a princess in a movie.

Sam took the pale melon dress for which she had been fitted, and Melinda reached for the pale lemon. She studied it for a moment, thinking there was something strange about it, and after a second of reflection, she realized what it was.

"Oh, no, Daisy," Melinda called to her, feigning deep consternation to hide her relief. "There's been a mistake. The seamstress must have gotten my measurements wrong, because there's just no way I could fit into this dress."

"That's impossible," said Sam. "She fitted the dress right on you."

"I know, but she must have gotten it mixed up or something. Look at it. There's no way in the world I'm going to get into this."

Sam peered at the dress and realized her sister was right. Melinda had always been somewhat voluptuous, even more so since Nico had been born. It served to emphasize her tiny waist, which would have given an almost hourglass shape to a body-fitting dress like the ones they were to wear. But this dress was narrow all the way down, with no evidence of the allowance for the bosom and the nip at the waist that had been pinned on her that morning.

"Actually, it's not a mistake," said Daisy quietly. "That dress is for me."

"What do you mean?" asked Sam, while Melinda just stared.

"I had the seamstress fit the yellow dress to my measurements. That's why it's so slim."

"I don't understand," said Melinda. "Then why did she measure me?"

"So she could fit *that* dress for you." Daisy pointed at the champagne tulle. "See? It's your size."

"But that's the bride's dress," declared Melinda.

"That's right," responded Daisy serenely.

"Are you crazy?" Melinda was utterly perplexed.

"No, just a realist. Jack loves you. You love him. You're the one he should marry."

Sam started to choke, but she forced herself to keep her mouth closed. This was no job for the Myles Militia. This was something Melinda would have to handle on her own.

"I . . . But . . . ," Melinda stuttered, unable to deny the truth, knowing that she should. "He loves you, too," was all she could finally manage.

"I know that," said Daisy. "But not the way he loves you. And to tell you the truth, I think I deserve better."

"Oh, God, Daisy, I'm sorry," Melinda lamented, genuinely abashed at the turn of events. "It was over between us. At least we thought it was. We never meant . . ."

"I know that, too," Daisy assured her. "I don't blame you, and I don't hate you. And I still love Jack enough to want him to be happy. And he's never going to be really happy unless he's married to you."

"I can't believe this. I don't know what to say."

"Just say okay, so you two can get on with your lives, and then I can get on with mine. You've really wasted too much of everybody's time already," she quipped good-naturedly.

"What does Jack have to say about this?"

"He doesn't know."

Sam couldn't keep silent any longer. "Don't you think this is something he should be in on? It's not fair to do this without him."

"Yes, it is," argued Daisy. "We all know him. We all

know what a man of honor he is. He'd deny everything to keep his word to me. Then I'd have to fight with him about it, and really, I'm not up to that. I need a bit of a break." She turned to Melinda. "Is there any question in your mind that Jack would want to marry you if he could?"

Melinda didn't even have to think. "No," she answered honestly.

"Then why don't we stop jabbering and put on the damn dresses!"

Because Ian and Sarah were late picking up Harvey and Diane, they missed their flight. They were able to get one an hour later, but with air traffic at Dulles and a cab driver who wasn't sure where he was going, it brought them to the State building at a quarter after five, fifteen minutes after the ceremony was to begin. Taking the elevator to the lavish sixth-floor suite, they hurried past the gallery, through the John Quincy Adams State Drawing Room and the Thomas Jefferson State Reception Room, unable to linger long enough to appreciate the splendor. At last, they came to the Benjamin Franklin State Dining Room, which had been set up with two quadrants of gilded chairs on either side of a carpeted aisle. Close to two hundred people were already in their places, and the couples had to split up to find seating just as a string quartet took up a Purcell overture for the processional.

Wearing his new tuxedo, Jack entered from the side, taking his place in front of a flowering trellis next to the state supreme court justice who was going to perform the ceremony. Moments later, Sam began her march down the aisle, her dress the color of a pale sunset, radiantly complimenting her tawny hair. Passing her parents, she caught their eye and winked. They beamed proudly as their lovely daughter reached the front of the room and took her place beside her adoring husband. Their heads swiveled to the back of the room again, anticipating the appearance of their second child. Instead, they saw a stranger, an elegant beauty with flaxen hair that echoed the muted daffodil of her dress.

"Who's that?" Harvey asked Diane.

"I don't know," answered his wife. "Must be a friend of the bride or something. We don't know her side."

Jack smiled as he watched Daisy make her way down the aisle. Always a minimalist, it was just like her to dress like a bridesmaid instead of a bride. For a moment, he forgot that Melinda should have entered first, and when he remembered, he assumed she had balked at participating. He could not blame her.

And then, he saw her. Looking exactly like a bride, clouds of gossamer fabric wafting around her, Melinda advanced toward him. Convinced he must be dreaming, Jack tried to force himself into a different state of consciousness, afraid that somehow he must be sleeping through his wedding to Daisy. But still, she came toward him. He gave up and let the bliss he felt at her approach transport him. If this were sleep, let it last forever.

And then, she was beside him, taking his hand, and he knew that she was real. And that at last she was his.

THE SUMMER OF LOVE TRILOGY

by Leah Laiman

FOR RICHER, FOR POORER

FOR BETTER, FOR WORSE

TO LOVE AND TO CHERISH

POCKET BOOKS
PROUDLY ANNOUNCES

The Third Title in Our
Another Summer of Love Trilogy

BRIDE AND GROOM

LEAH LAIMAN

Coming from
Pocket Books
mid-August 1995

The following is a preview of
Bride and Groom . . .

The play was supposed to be a comedy, but so far, the only laughs seemed to come when the actors flubbed their lines. Melinda Myles reminded herself that they were only in the second week of rehearsal; it was too soon to expect things to come together. But she had to admit that she was nervous. She didn't want her first foray onto the legitimate stage to be a complete and utter flop.

The production, written and directed by a young playwright named Gilbert Gruen, was called "The Truth About Hortense." Melinda, aware that she had been cast because of her star power at the box office rather than her talent, had the title role. In fact, the play had originally been scheduled for the 180-seat Old Vat Room of the Arena Stage, but once her participation had been announced, demand for tickets had been so high that they decided to move the production to the larger 500-seat Kreeger Theater.

At least, working with the experienced ensemble players of the Arena Stage proved to be a treat. She had expected a certain amount of hostility at the beginning because she might be considered a Hollywood interloper, but instead, she found them all familiar with her film work and quite respectful of her acting skills, even though her experience was exclusively in film and she'd never worked on the stage before. Still, she had a strong sense of her own limitations, and a great fear of overstepping her range.

"Listen, Gil . . ." She approached the writer-director when rehearsal had ended and the cast members had gone their separate ways, laughing and promising to do better the next day. "I know I've got a contract, but if you don't think I'm getting this, I won't sue or anything if you want to let me go. I'm not Faye Dunaway."

"Thank God," Gilbert joked, before turning serious. "Aren't you enjoying this?"

"Are you kidding? I don't know when I've had so much fun. The other guys are so great, and they're being really kind to me. But so much of the humor falls to Hortense, and I'm just not sure I can carry it. It's such a fabulous play. I'd hate to ruin it."

Gilbert smiled. It had been a long time since he'd heard an actor, let alone an Academy Award–winning leading lady, assume any responsibility for something that wasn't working. The usual tendency was to blame the writing, the directing, the audience, the political atmosphere, anything except one's own performance. It was refreshing to meet someone so talented and so unassuming that she was more concerned with the work than her own ego—especially, since as far as he could ascertain, she was doing a great job.

"Let me put it this way," he said. "If you even think about leaving my show, I will sue you."

She laughed. "You like courting disaster, don't you."

"What are you talking about? You're great for this part. Hortense is beautiful, a little insecure, smart, not always sure she's doing the right thing. It's type casting."

"But I'm not funny."

"Wait," he said with confidence. "It always starts like this. There's too much to think about at the beginning to concentrate on the laughs. Once everyone knows their lines and the action is blocked, you'll see. Everyone will relax and it will all just fall into place."

"Promise?"

"I promise." He hugged her for reassurance, then let her go. "What are you still doing here, anyway?" he joked, realizing the rest of the ensemble had long since de-camped. "Do you need a lift somewhere?"

Like everyone else who ever read a gossip column, he knew that Washington was still relatively new to Melinda. For two years, she had been married to Diego Roca, the President of San Domenico, a small island nation in the Caribbean. She met Roca when they fought side by side to overthrow the dictatorship that had preceded him. They had a child together, but when Melinda realized her husband was turning into the same kind of tyrant he had deposed, she had stolen their son away in a daring maneuver and returned to the States. The rescue had been arranged by Jack Bader, an old flame of Melinda's, who had become her current husband. And, Gilbert was aware, it was because of Jack's burgeoning career in the State Department that Melinda had chosen to forego the money and acclaim of Hollywood in favor of doing what Gilbert liked to think of as a small but important play in Washington.

"I'm waiting for Jack to pick me up. He's late as usual," Melinda explained. She noticed Gilbert glance at his watch, a worried frown furrowing his brow. "Is there a problem?"

"Since rehearsal was late today, I sent the janitor home, said I'd lock up."

"Oh, I'm sorry. I'm holding you back. I can just wait outside."

"No, no," he said hastily. "The windchill factor is something like ten. I can't have my star freeze her butt off. I wouldn't even mind waiting with you, except I'm supposed to meet someone."

"Well, can I lock up for you?" she volunteered. "I'm pretty trustworthy."

"That would be okay." He looked hopeful. "Except that means you'd have to be the first one here tomorrow."

"Just tell me when," she said, holding out her hand for the keys.

He hesitated for a moment, then looked at his watch again. He had recently begun an affair with the young, beautiful wife of an older cabinet minister, a major contributor to the Arena's yearly budget. She was meeting him at his apartment. If he kept her waiting, he could lose both her affections and her patronage.

"Well, if you're sure. You don't have to do anything except lock the door behind you when you go. I'll turn off all the lights except for the stage light that stays on all the time. Rehearsal's at ten, so if you could be here at, let's say, a quarter to?"

"No problem," she said, accepting the keys in her hand and a kiss on her cheek.

She sat on the edge of the stage, her feet dangling over the proscenium, watching him hurry up the aisle and disappear into the shadows of the auditorium. She heard a series of clicks, and suddenly the darkness had spread, except for a small circle of light that reached out to her from the single bare bulb on its stand. His footsteps receded, and then the door slammed shut, introducing a surreal quiet.

She stayed where she was for a moment, losing herself in the serenity of the empty theater. Then she remembered the monologue with which she was supposed to bring down the Act 1 curtain, and shuddered. She turned to the page in her script. She read it silently, smiling to herself. On paper, it was funny and charming, but in her mouth, the words seemed somehow lifeless. She got up and started to say the lines, quietly at first, but then, remembering she was alone and no one would hear her anyway, louder and more confidently. Realizing she had long since memorized her part, and that only fear kept the script in her hand, she threw it into the wings. It was, in fact, a delicious speech, and she had always felt it cried out for a healthy dose of overacting. In rehearsals, embarrassed by her own inclination toward melodrama, she had underplayed it. But now, with no one watching, she let loose with every histrionic bone in her body, banishing all subtlety and declaiming her comic emotions to the rafters. It was working, she could feel it. She knew exactly where the laughs would come, and once or twice she even imagined she heard them. Ending with a flourish and a pratfall, she envisioned herself bringing the house down in a barrage of laughter and applause. And then, she realized, with sudden sickening clarity, that the laughter and applause were no fantasy. There really was someone out there in the dark, laughing and clapping at the sight of the movie star making a fool of herself.

"Jack?" she called, peering out over the stage, praying it was him and no one else. She was relieved to see her husband come forward into the light, grinning from ear to ear.

"I've never seen you like that," he said, as he ignored the steps and hoisted himself onto the stage beside her.

"And if I had known you were there, you wouldn't have seen it this time either. Why didn't you tell me you'd arrived?"

"You were busy."

"I was just trying something out. I'm having trouble with the part. Obviously."

"Why do you say that? You were great. Really, really fantastic."

"Do you meant it?" She was taken aback, but pleased. "You're not just saying that because I'm your wife and you don't want to ruin the evening?"

"Didn't you hear me laughing? You were hilarious. And totally believable."

"You know what? I don't care if you are just saying it. It's exactly what I want to hear."

"So the evening's a go?" he asked slyly.

She punched him. "You meanie. You *were* just saying it."

He laughed and caught her in his arms. "No, I wasn't. I'm just teasing. It's still hard for me to believe that anybody can be as gorgeous and as talented as you are and not know it. How did I get so lucky?"

"I'm the lucky one," she said quietly.

They looked at each other, both aware of how long it had taken them to reach this moment. When they had first met, Melinda had been a naive secretary in Oakdale, having an affair with her boss, Forrest Symington. Jack had been a pony-tailed assembly line worker, concealing his education and his law degree while he helped Melinda's sister organize workers' demonstrations against the very man that Melinda professed to love. She had gone to Hollywood to become a movie star, then had an ill-fated marriage to Diego Roca. Jack had cut his hair, had become a high-powered lawyer in Washington, and was prepared to marry a smart and beautiful socialite named Daisy Howard when

Melinda came back into his life. At the time, they had both thought it was too late for them, but Daisy, with her intuitive wisdom, had known better, and courageously stepped aside to let Melinda take her place at the altar.

Now, at last, Jack and Melinda were together, and neither one of them could believe their good fortune. She was still beautiful, with lush chestnut hair and a flawless ivory complexion. But life's lessons had matured her, and now, instead of the hungry ambition that had once brightened her hazel eyes, she was lit from within by a vital awareness of what really mattered: her hometown husband and the little boy, nearing his second birthday, whom he had accepted as his own son.

She touched his face as if to assure herself that he was real, then brushed a stray lock off his forehead. She let her fingers linger in the sun-streaked silkiness of his golden hair, a legacy of his California youth that she knew frequently made female undersecretaries at the State Department try to assume more-than-diplomatic relations. Regular workouts in tae kwon do had kept him from losing any of his vigor, and in spite of the time he now spent behind a desk, his body was still toned and muscular. He caught her hand and brought it to his lips.

"Where is everybody?" he asked, and she knew the question was not an idle one.

"Gone," she said quietly, jingling the keys. "I have to lock up."

"So we're all alone?"

"Completely."

Jack grinned, and he didn't have to tell Melinda what he was thinking. He had never been interested in a life in the theater, but the stage seemed, suddenly, a very enticing place to be.

"Well, Ms. Myles," he said, assuming the tone of a patron of the arts, "I believe this calls for a command performance."

"And just what did you have in mind?" Melinda teased, as beguiled as he was by the endless prospects.

"I don't know exactly. I'm casting for a very important part."

"Really? What is it?"

"Sexiest woman in the world. Care to audition?"

"I'm a star, Mr. Bader," she drawled. "I don't usually have to audition. I'm play or pay."

"Well how do I know if you're right for the part?"

"Check my résumé."

"Just what I had in mind," he said, slipping his hand under her sweater. Her breasts, full but able to support themselves, were soft and warm. He could feel her heart beat quicken, and as his fingers grazed her nipples he heard a sharp intake of breath. "You definitely have the right credentials," he whispered in her ear, breathing in her scent. "But how well do you take direction?"

"Try me," she said, her voice husky.

Deftly, he moved his hand under her short skirt, circumventing the tights she had worn to protect against the cold. Barely moving, she accommodated him, letting him feel the moist heat and the pliant flesh that told him she was ready to play the part.

"I see you're very responsive," he said, between tiny kisses that brushed her lips. "I like that in my leading lady." With a sweep, he lifted her in his arms, and placed her on the edge of the table where only hours earlier she had sat with the entire cast reciting her lines. She flicked her shoes to the floor, and with a single movement, he slid her tights down her shapely legs and tossed them out of the way. Pushing up her skirt, he buried his head in the nirvana between her thighs.

Edging toward completion, she stopped him, forcing herself to pull away. "You know," she said, not having forgotten the game they were playing, "an actor of my caliber gets to pick who she works with. How do I know you're the right director for me?"

"I'll tell you the truth," he said, "My past experience wouldn't qualify me. You're the only one I could do my best work with. I'll show you what I mean." With the speed that comes with desire, he slid out of his pants.

"I see," she said, taking him in her hands and bringing him to her. "This is going to be one powerful performance."

Standing between her knees, not rushing, he guided himself into her. Slowly, almost languidly, he teased her with his body, bringing her closer, then letting her go. Finally, she could stand it no longer, and wrapping her legs around him, she locked him to her, clinging to him as their play reached its climax. And though the only applause was in her heart, looking over the footlights into the silent theater, she knew that here, in her husband's arms, she had at last found a role she would be content to play for the rest of her life.